LUDOVIC BRUCKSTEIN

The Fate of Yaakov Maggid

Translated
from the Romanian by
Alistair Ian Blyth

Ludovic Bruckstein
The Fate of Yaakov Maggid

Translated from the Romanian by Alistair Ian Blyth

First published in 2023 by
Istros Books
London, United Kingdom www.istrosbooks.com

Copyright © Estate of Ludovic Bruckstein, 2023

This collection of stories from The Fate of Yaakov
Maggid and the Semi-Historical Tales also first appeared
in Romanian as Destinul lui Iaacov Maghid and Trei
Istorii, Panopticum, Tel Aviv, 1975

The right of Ludovic Bruckstein, to be identified as the
author of this work has been asserted in accordance
with the Copyright, Designs and Patents Act, 1988

Translation © Alistair Ian Blyth

Typesetting: pikavejica.com

Illustrations: Alfred M. Bruckstein

Printed by CMP (UK) Limited, Poole, Dorset

ISBN: 978-1-912545-36-0

The publishers would like to express their thanks
for the financial support that made the publication
of this book possible:
The Prodan Romanian Cultural Foundation
Arts Council England

PRODAN ROMANIAN
CULTURAL FOUNDATION

Supported using public funding by

**ARTS COUNCIL
ENGLAND**

CONTENTS

Part Two
The Earthly Tribunal
Semi-Historical Tales

Glossary

Introduction

Alistair Ian Blyth

By 1 April 1972, when the story 'The Fate of Yaakov Maggid' was published in *Revista Cultului Mosaic* [Review of the Religion of Moses], Ludovic Bruckstein had been sacked as director of the Sighet Art College and ostracised from the writing community as a 'traitor' to the Romanian communist state, all for the unpardonable sin, in the eyes of the régime, of having applied for an exit visa to emigrate to Israel the year before. Bruckstein and his family were finally able to emigrate later that year, after which he was erased from the literary memory of his native Romania, an erasure that continues to this day, more than three decades since the fall of the communist régime. In Israel, Bruckstein was able to publish his work once more, through the Panopticum press that he set up in Tel Aviv to serve Romanian-speaking immigrants, named after a collection of short stories that he published before his official ostracism (*Panopticum. Schițe și povestiri*, Editura pentru Literatură, Bucharest, 1969). And in 1975, Panopticum was to publish a collection titled *The Fate of Yaakov Maggid*, which, in addition to the title story, also included 'The Guarantee', another Hassidic tale set in Bruckstein's native Maramuresch and what is now western Ukraine during the time of the Austro-Hungarian Empire, along with a number of the Holocaust stories translated into English in *With an Unopened Umbrella in the Pouring Rain* (Istros Books, 2021).

In the context of Bruckstein's time as a social and literary outcast in communist Romania, caught in a limbo between two worlds, it was certainly a bold act of defiance on the part of the Jewish community to publish in their official magazine, Bruckstein's story of a haunted *maggid* seemingly doomed endlessly to wander from shtetl to shtetl, from synagogue to synagogue, telling parables that impart deep spiritual wisdom to the common folk, but ever consumed by the nagging doubt that his might be a voice crying in the wilderness. In his obituary of Ludovic Bruckstein, published in *Viața Noastră* [Our Life] on 12 August 1988, Jewish-Romanian literary critic Eugen Luca (1923–1997) was to write that like the protagonist of his story, Bruckstein himself accepted 'the condition of the *maggid*', the vocation of storyteller within the East-European Jewish tradition of Hassidism that was particularly strong among the Jews of Maramuresch. The *maggid*, says Luca, is a storyteller not for the sake of fame or fortune, but in fulfilment of a *mitzva*, a solemn, divinely ordained obligation towards his fellow man. In Bruckstein's tales, there is also a strong sense that the *maggid* is a homeless wanderer between this world and the next, perhaps even a heavenly messenger in disguise, like the angel in the *Book of Tobit*. In Hebrew, the word also carries the meaning of *daemon*, a denizen of the interval between the celestial and the mundane planes, such as the *maggid* that conveyed messages regarding the divine mysteries to Rabbi Joseph Karo (1488–1575) during a series of nocturnal visitations stretching over five decades, recorded in *Maggid Mesharim* [Preacher of Righteousness] (Lublin, 1646).

The Hassidic *maggidim* can be distinguished from the earlier, widespread tradition of the *maggid* as wandering preacher, in that rather than admonishing their listeners for their sins and holding out the prospect of divine retribution—the Tocheichah, or the list of terrifying punishments laid out in the fifth book of Moses—they emphasised the indwelling divine holiness to be found in the simplicity of everyday communal life, the joy of prayer and celebration of the Sabbath and Pesach. In particular, they told hagiographic tales of the life of the movement's founder, Israel ben Eliezer (1698–1760), a *tzaddik*, or holy man, who was to gain the title of Baal Shem Tov, abbreviated as 'Der BeShT', or 'Master of the Good Name'.

Born in Okopy in what was then Poland, now part of the Ternopil Oblast of western Ukraine, Israel ben Eliezer made the mysticism and spiritual discoveries of the Kabbalah accessible to the common people, giving rise to a popular movement that spread throughout the region, including southward to the Romanian-speaking Maramuresch, then part of the Austro-Hungarian Empire, where many of Bruckstein's Hassidic tales are set. Within early Hassidism, from the death of the Baal Shem Tov to around 1810, there was a spiritual emphasis on the personality of the *tzaddik* rather than on Halacha, or Jewish law, on *pilpul*—exacting exegesis of the Talmud—or on the arcana of the Kabbalah. Although little is known of the life of the Baal Shem Tov, the legends and parables surrounding him grew in the telling, often taking on local colouring. For example, there are legends that the Baal Shem Tov used to visit Maramuresch, and here the tale in which the *tzaddik* meets the leader of a band of outlaws, typically the Ukrainian Oleksa Dovbush, is adapted to the local mythology of the Romanian *haidouk* Pintea the Brave (1670–1703). In 1968, Bruckstein wrote a play in Yiddish, *In himl vi oyf der erd* [In Heaven as on Earth], produced by the Jewish State Theatre in Bucharest, which was set in Maramuresch and centred on one such encounter between the Baal Shem Tov and Pintea the Brave, as well as incorporating the standard characters of the storytelling tradition of the Hassidic *maggidim*, such as Ze'ev Volf Kitzes, Hirsch Soyfer, and the *balegule*, or rugged, unlettered carter, with whom the rabbi exchanges clothes in a common narrative trope and who evinces a wisdom equal to that of the rabbi whose outward identity he has taken. *In Heaven as on Earth* was published in the author's own Romanian version by Panopticum in 1981, along with the Hassidic tales included in Part One of the present volume.

In the secular setting of the theatre and the short story form, Bruckstein was in fact drawing on a long family tradition of Hassidism, an ancestry stretching back to the early followers of the Baal Shem Tov. 'The Guarantee', a story included in the present collection, is typically Hassidic—the movement is centred on the branching 'dynasties' of rebbes descended from the first followers of the Baal Shem Tov—in that it is a genealogy of the Brucksteins, narrating as it does the story of a *tzaddik*, Mordechai Leifer (1824–1894), the Rabbi of Nadvorna, who bequeathed his *tallit* to Moishe ben Israel-Nathan Alter, the grandfather of Ludovic Bruckstein. 'The Guarantee' also reveals that it was Israel-Nathan Alter, for reasons known only to himself, who took the name Bruckstein when a law requiring all citizens to have a surname was imposed in the Austro-Hungarian Empire.

The surnames law that forced Western-style surnames on the Jews was mild, however, in comparison with the kind of *gezerah* (Hebrew) or *gzar* (Yiddish), meaning '(evil) decree', that often features in the Hassidic tales told by the *maggidim* and which is typically circumvented by the *tzaddik* protagonist, often by means of a miracle. In the Russian Empire, for example, any law, regulation or decree that specifically named the Jews was automatically a *gezerah* in that it inevitably brought anti-Semitic persecution in one or another degree. The tales included in Part Two of the present volume, 'The Earthly

Tribunal: Semi-Historical Tales', three of which ('Rabeinu Yaakov of Orléans', 'The Book of Mordechai', 'Rabbi, Tsar and Faith') were first published by Panopticum in 1977, all centre on a *gezerah*, on officially sanctioned persecution of the Jews, and are set in the England of Richard I, the Egypt of Suleyman the Magnificent, and the Russia of Nicholas the First. 'Rabbi, Tsar and Faith' is typically Hassidic in its tale of the Rabbi of Rizhin, who disguises himself as the tsar and goes to the Kremlin in order to avert a pogrom, fooling the tsar's ministers into signing an act rescinding the order. Even the scientific-minded Dr Iserovitch, a descendant of the Rizhiner Rebbe, who recounts the episode, is forced to conclude that the story must be true: there is simply no other reasonable explanation, given that the appointed pogrom did not take place.

In 'The Good Oil', a story included in the present volume, another scientist descended from rabbis, Professor Johann-Josef Moellin, is likewise forced to recognise the existence of the miraculous, in the form of the otherwise inexplicable cures effected by Rabbi Moishe-Leib Sassower using ordinary sunflower oil. And this, ultimately, is what Ludovic Bruckstein invites his readers to do in short stories that draw deeply from the wellsprings of his ancestral Hassidism and the lost cultural milieu of Unterlander Jewry: to recognise and reacquaint themselves with the miraculous that exists in the pious simplicity of humble everyday life.

PART ONE

The Fate of Yaakov Maggid

The Fate of Yaakov Maggid

On a lane which was dusty in hot weather and muddy when it rained, not far from the level crossing that marked the edge of town, there stood a prayer house named Tiferet Israel, which is to say, 'Splendour of Israel'.

To tell the truth, the outward appearance of this little synagogue was in sharp contrast with its name. It was a house that was humble to say the least, lacking an upper storey and a porch, and therein it was no different from any of the other cottages along that out-of-the-way lane. It had a small garden in front, enclosed by a fence of rather shabby planks, and in that garden, there were a few fruit trees: four or five wild plum trees, a rather stunted apple tree, and a tall, handsome walnut tree, with a magnificent, shady canopy.

The house had three rooms, each with a door that gave onto the garden. The synagogue proper was in the middle: a long room against whose east wall was placed the ark, painted bright white, wherein were kept the Torah scrolls, behind a red velvet curtain embroidered with the words 'Ze haparo-het' in gold thread: this curtain belongs to the Tiferet Israel congregation. In the centre of the room stood the pulpit, or rather a table whose top sloped slightly and which was no higher—physically speaking, of course—than the pews for the congregation around it, made of unpainted boards cracked and stained by time. And in a corner at the back, there was a long table, at which lessons were held in the evenings. These lessons sometimes developed into debates that went on late into the night. It was at this table that the third meal of the Sabbath was also eaten, a repast of walnuts, herring and *koyletchn*, of spiritual words and murmured hymns, all washed down at temperately measured intervals with a little glass of rough plum brandy.

To the right of the long room of the synagogue was a small antechamber, where a bucket of water and a mug for handwashing were kept in a corner by the door, and by the wall at the back there was a long, narrow table, with old wooden benches of coarsely planed wood. On the Day of Atonement, the soul candles for which there was no room in the synagogue were placed on that table. On the other side of the wall, in the house of prayer, while the barefooted congregants, wracked by fasting, prayed now in loud lament, now in silence, while they thrice fell to their knees and beat their chests with their fists, begging forgiveness for every sin real or imagined, there in that antechamber hundreds of little flames would flicker as silently as memories, bending, twisting. As evening fell, they would die, drained of strength, sputtering out, like the souls of the departed ...

The third room of that house, the one on the left, where the women prayed, was separated from the synagogue by a wall of brick at the top of which were some narrow windows, or *Oberlichter*, screened with little net curtains.

What was the reason for the name of this little house of prayer? Who could know? Maybe it was because of the prayers and hymns, both joyous and sad, that rose therein so many times a day? Maybe it was because of the rich, inspiring voices of the cantors whom the community hired on holy days, without a thought to the cost? Maybe it was because of the learned preachers and maggidim, the wayfaring storytellers who from time to time came to speak to the community, after which the congregants would invite them to their homes, where they would find waiting for them a meal and a mattress on which to rest their far-travelled bones? Or maybe it was because of the numerous children, who lived on the seven lanes of that town and who received instruction at the synagogue?

For it ought to be said that that humble building was home to two schools on weekdays, during the hours when no prayers were being said and no candles were lit: there was a *cheyder* in the room to the right, where Moishe-rebbe taught the smallest children the letters of the alphabet, the composition of short set letters to their parents, and a little Chumash and Rashi, that is, the five Books of Moses succinctly commentated by Rashi, after which his pupils moved up to the other school, in the room on the left where the women prayed on the Sabbath. Here they studied the *Talmud*, the *Gemarah* and *Tosafot*, under another teacher, named Tcharder-rebbe.

Seldom did you find two men so unalike as those two teachers.

Reb Moishe Laies, the teacher of the smallest children, whom everybody called Moishe-rebbe for short, was a short, stocky man with a puffy face from which sprouted a round, untidy black beard. He always held a rod, with which he would rap the long table where his pupils sat, frightening the flies more than he did the children. His method was rote learning. He would recite a few lines from the book and then shout: '*Khazern! Khazern!*' (Repeat! Repeat!) And in a chorus the children would repeat in a singsong voice, '*Komets-alef: o! Beys: bo!*' or '*Bereshit bara Elohim et hashamayim ve'et ha'arets!*' (In the beginning, God created the heavens and the earth.) At first, the children would have fun, they would repeat the words with verve and in lively rhythm, while the teacher listened in satisfaction, chewing one end of the rod with his strong teeth. After which, as if rocked to sleep by that choir, Moishe-rebbe would doze off, with the end of the rod still in his mouth, and sensing the teacher was asleep, the children would drop their voices one tone lower and the repetition would begin to languish, before fading away completely. But then the silence would cause Moishe-rebbe to wake with a start, and in a rage he would whack the table with his rod, and cry: 'Repeat! Repeat!' and the chorus would start up again. And so it went, every day, dozens of times a day.

Moishe-rebbe wore a round, greasy hat, a coat made of frieze, worn at the elbows, and a shirt of thick cloth that may once have been white, without a necktie and buttoned at the neck with a loop of thread. He was always half-asleep, always weary; his eyelids were red and lacked lashes, and it was as if an irresistible force kept pulling them down over his small, dark, squinting eyes.

Moishe-rebbe had a family somewhere in Maramuresch, in a village called Oberrohnen, or maybe it was Lower, Upper or Middle Wischau. The fact was that nobody really knew where he kept his wife and children, nobody knew how many children he had, and he himself seldom went home, to avoid the expense of riding in a cart. He took his meals with the parents of his pupils, which meant he could send home almost every penny he earned. But even then, the money still wasn't enough. He lived out his life in the small room that served as the *cheyder*. All day long he sat at the head of that narrow table, with the children packed like herrings along the two benches. At night he slept on those same two benches, joining them together and laying on top a straw mattress, a threadbare black blanket, and a torturous pillow, which during the day he kept in the dark little niche for the ladder to the synagogue attic, which was crammed with dog-eared prayer books and old loose leaves that had fallen out of the holy books.

Tcharder-rebbe was a different kind of man altogether. In official documents his name was Josef Herschkowitz, but everybody called him Tcharder-rebbe, since he hailed from the village of Iapa, from a spot called Tcharda, or Keblitz, where his family lived: his wife and three daughters. Every morning, he walked the three kilometres or so to the Tiferet Israel Synagogue and, in the evening, he walked back home. He was tall and thin and had a bony face with rather prominent cheekbones beneath lively green eyes. His hair, which he wore short, was reddish-blond and he had a small, square beard that was as curly as that of an Assyrian king on an old bas-relief. His attire was clean and schoolteacher-like: in fine weather, a white or coloured shirt, but always with a necktie to match; a well-brushed coat; long trousers pressed to form a crisp seam; and in rainy autumnal weather or during winter, baggy trousers and highly polished boots.

His method of teaching was completely different than Moishe-rebbe's. He didn't make his pupils learn by rote; he was always impatient to teach them something new. He liked to explain things to them, to discuss with them, to seek new meanings. In short, he enjoyed teaching others, but perhaps more than that, he himself enjoying learning from others. In fact, he liked to learn anything from anybody at all: He was not ashamed even to learn from his pupils. In his *cheyder* for the older boys, where he taught the *Gemarah* and *Tosafot*, he had pupils who attended the town lycée in the morning and his lessons in the afternoon, and with them he liked to discuss matters of history and geography. He was particularly interested in faraway, exotic lands, but he was equally interested in chemistry, physics, zoology, philosophy, and astronomy. He had a hard life at home, with three daughters to bring up who were rapidly approaching marriageable age, which was no joking matter, but his passion for knowledge made him reckless with his money. Literally taking the bread out of his own mouth, he had bought himself an old Meyers Lexicon, with some of the volumes missing, and in spare moments he would devour whatever entry he happened to lay eyes on, since he was interested in absolutely everything.

But Moishe wasn't interested in the movements of the stars across the heavens, or the creatures that dwelled on earth, or the worms that dwelled beneath the earth, or the giant baobabs described in lexicons, or serrated fern leaves, or anything at all. He taught books full of meaning without delving into their meaning. He read to the children and translated each word literally: '*Vaidaber*—and so spoke Moses. *Moses*—Moses. *El*—to. *Bnei*—the children. *Israel*—of Israel …' without trying to read between the lines, or behind the lines, or below or above them. He was like a sleepy, shaggy bear, constantly in a state of hibernation. He took life at face value, without wondering about it any more deeply. He lived, or rather vegetated, without asking himself any of the big questions, or the small ones; he didn't look for answers. He knew he had to teach the children the letters of the alphabet and how to write. He knew he had to eat and sleep. He knew he had to send money back home to the village, in order to feed his wife and children. He didn't look for obvious or possible connections between things and events; in short, he was a man who was resigned to life, without realising that he was. The teacher from Tcharda, on the other hand, was irrepressible, curious; he was a seeker, who, since his daily bread was by no means guaranteed, fretted and was restless, and who looked for some larger meaning to life and the world and the whole universe …

To the Tiferet Israel Synagogue there sometimes came well-known maggidim, itinerant preachers and storytellers. They would come from faraway, unknown places, and Tcharder-rebbe would hover around them, agitated and restless, trying to strike up a conversation. He would try to learn something new about the places whence they'd come, about where they would go next, about the times in which they were living, or else he would try to find out from them some new interpretation of a passage from the old books.

One of those orators in particular stirred up the souls of the synagogue's little congregation. If was as if he held the heart of each of them in his hand and examined it on every side, revealing to them how good they were or, God forfend, how bad they could be ... Reb Yaakov Maggid, for such was the orator's name, was very tall and very thin. He had a long pale face, which a sparse black beard made look even longer. He had a long, thin nose and large, dark, glittering eyes, framed by translucent blueish rings. He wore a long caftan, a white shirt, buttoned at the neck, without a tie, and a round hat of black velvet. When he began to speak, in his slow, colourless, monotonous voice, nobody could foresee the thunder and lightning that were about to strike or the sun that would finally break through the dark clouds.

He had taken as his text a single verse from the Psalms of David. He explained the meaning of the words, then split the words into syllables, the syllables into letters, divining yet further meanings, profound, unheard-of meanings ... "'Zeh dor dorshav": This is the generation of them that seeks Him, that seeks Thy face ...'* he began, softly. And the hearts of the men were filled with warmth and pride, with goodness and a simple, inexplicable joy. Each felt that the dark, glittering, benevolent eyes of the maggid were turned on him

* Psalm 24:6.

alone, that he was speaking of him in particular … But after a while, anger welled up in the orator's voice. All of a sudden, his voice seemed to cut like the sharp knife of the *hakham*; it cut the word in two: "'Ze dor dor-shav! Dor shav! Dor shav!" A generation of liars, hypocrites, boasters!' he thundered. And his voice hung suspended in mid-air for an instant, leaving behind it a heavy, oppressive silence. The men bowed their heads in shame … Then, it was as if the anger ebbed from his throat and his voice reverted to its former gentleness, its former loving-kindness and permissive warmth; it spoke once more of those who seek the word of justice, humility and truth.

He was like a juggler, who tossed in the air then caught not skittles but blazing torches. And after he spoke for an hour or two hours or countless hours, the congregants left the synagogue and went home in silence, deep in thought. They felt better about themselves, they were reconciled to that grey everyday life of theirs, somehow proud in their humility, strong in their weakness, rich in their stark poverty.

This happened one Sabbath morning, and the same afternoon, Yaakov Maggid was sitting in a corner at the back of the house of prayer, deep in the study of a book. The synagogue was empty; there was perfect silence, broken by not so much as the buzzing of a fly, even though it was a hot summer and insects abounded. But it was as if not even the flies dared to disturb that magician of the word, who had so bewitched his audience.

Nor did Tcharder-rebbe dare to disturb him, although on other occasions and with other storytellers he had timidly, respectfully gone to them; had uttered a 'shalom aleychem', welcoming the wandering maggid in question, and had struck up a conversation. But with Reb Yaakov Maggid he did not dare to do so except in a roundabout way and not by himself. He went first to the little *cheyder* of Reb Moishe, whom he found at the long table, his head resting on his arm, sleeping the deep, snoring sleep of a hot summer afternoon. His shirt was unbuttoned at the neck and he was perspiring, a hot, steaming sweat.

Tcharder-rebbe woke him. Moishe lifted his groggy head, his tangled beard; he opened his eyelids, with their thick red rims, bare of eyelashes:

'What is it? What happened?' he asked, in confusion.

'How can you sleep like this, Moishe, when such a guest we have staying here with us? Come along, man, let us go to him and hear the good things he has to say!'

Moishe followed him, still half-asleep, mumbling, 'Hmm, yes, yes, the good things he has to say.'

They entered the synagogue. The stranger did not seem at all surprised to see them. He invited them to take a seat on the pew, next to him. The two teachers sat down and Tcharder-rebbe was amazed to find that all his timidity and anxiety dissolved in an instant. From close up, the maggid was a man like any other; the dark eyes rimmed with bluish bags were like those of any other weary wanderer, the sparse black beard was like those of many other men, and on his right cheek Tcharder noticed a wart as big as a hazelnut. Indeed, the man he now saw possessed nothing of the spell of him who had preached that Sabbath morning. What was more, Reb Yaakov Maggid even evinced shy reluctance when Tcharder suggested that they read together from the book he had in front of him, the *Pirkei Avot*, or *Chapters of the Fathers*:

'Rabbi Tzadok said: "Make not thy learning a crown to adorn and magnify thyself therewith, nor a tool to delve therewith …"'

'I don't understand this part,' interrupted the teacher from Tcharda, 'I've often wondered about it but have never found an answer ... What does Rabbi Tzadok mean by that? "Make not thy learning a tool to delve therewith?" Does he mean you shouldn't make a living out of it, that you shouldn't earn your daily bread with it? How can that be? You learn, but you don't teach others? Should there be learning, but no teachers from whom others might learn? Both Reb Moishe and myself have to make a living somehow. And so too your honourable self ...'

The teacher from Tcharda broke off in embarrassment. Had he not gone too far by placing the maggid on the same level with themselves? But Yaakov Maggid calmly said:

'Yes, there seems to be something unclear here ... some contradiction ...'

And after a few moments' silence, the stranger asked:

'Have you ever thought of making your fortune, Reb Josef?'

Tcharder-rebbe burst out laughing:

'Working as a teacher?'

The maggid went on in all seriousness:

'Have you ever had another occupation?'

'Actually, at first, I was a trader. But it didn't work out. When I dealt in apples, there was no harvest that year, when I dealt in herring, the herrings in the barrels they delivered to me were the puniest and the saltiest ... more salt than herring ... I was hard put to get rid of them at a loss ...'

They both laughed. Then the stranger turned to Moishe-rebbe:

'And what about you, Reb Moishe: what was your occupation before this?'

'I've always been a melamed, a teacher of small children. My father was a melamed and my grandfather was a melamed. Actually, they were tailors, patchers and menders by trade ... And I learned that trade from them. But you know how it is, the rich man doesn't send his clothes to be patched, and the poor man patches his clothes himself ... So, the fact of the matter is that I've always been a melamed to small children.'

In the synagogue a long silence fell. The stranger sat pondering, his eyes fixed on the letters of the book, which he didn't seem to see.

Finally, Tcharder-rebbe ventured to break the silence:

'I still have no answer to my question ... to the words of Rabbi Tzadok ...'

'Hmm, yes, it's hard to give an answer,' confessed Yaakov Maggid, in resignation. 'Not every question can be answered ... Maybe it has to do with what should take precedence: should we teach others in order to make a living or should we make a living in order to teach? But as you can see, this too is a question, not an answer ... I would do better to tell you a story!'

The stranger paused, smoothed his black beard with one hand, and began:

'It is said that two hundred or so years ago, when the great, the modest, the wise Rabbi Israel Baal Shem Tov, the Master of the Good Name, felt that his journey through this transient world of ours was nearing its end, he set out to divide his legacy among his disciples. What legacy? He had no land, he had no forests or meadows, he had no flocks of sheep or herds of cattle, he had no houses or sacks of gold coins. What then did he divide among them? He divided the large flock of his followers, of paupers who thirsted for the light and needed to be tended, a flock scattered throughout the mountains and valleys of the Maramuresch Carpathians, hither and yon, over the mountain crests, in the villages and hamlets strung out along the valleys of the Tisza, Iza, Mara and Wischau, from Borscha to Kossow, and from Wischau all the way into the distance ... Thus it was that he appointed a certain Reb Dov Ber to be rabbi of Mezritch, another named Reb Moishe he made the rabbi of Kitev, a third, Reb Nachman, the rabbi of Kossow, Reb Kopl he sent to be rabbi of Borscha in Maramuresch, and so on. Among his disciples, the Baal Shem Tov had one, Yaakov by name, who was very dear to him. He was poor and humble, he sat always at the far end of the Baal Shem Tov's table, he walked last in the procession of his disciples, and he had accompanied him on all his travels. Although he was very dear to him, to his sorrow, the Baal Shem Tov was unable to give him a place of his own, a flock to tend. Reb Yaakov was not very skilled in *halachah* and *pilpul*, at religious law and scriptural exegesis; he didn't do very well at giving advice. On the other hand, he did know how to tell a good story. The Baal Shem Tov fretted for a long time, a very long time, then one day, on the very eve of his departure from this world of light and shadow, he called him to his side and said, "Reb Yaakov, you have followed me on every journey, you have seen many things, you have heard many things, you will be a maggid, you will go from place to place and tell stories about all you have seen and all you have heard, and you will become a rich man.' Yaakov was greatly troubled. To wander from place to place, not to have a home, a pillow on which to lay your head ... This was not an easy life ... And he was both puzzled and troubled. How could he become rich? Where was his wealth to come from? From living the life of a wandering storyteller? He didn't understand and he didn't dare ask the Baal Shem Tov any question, lest the rabbi think that for a single instant he doubted his words: If the Rabbi Israel Baal Shem Tov had said so, then he knew what he was saying. And after they kept vigil as he made his final journey, after they wept for him seven days and seven nights, the disciples of the Baal Shem Tov each came into their inheritance. The flocks to be shepherded, the communities of Mezeritch and Kossow, of Borscha and Wischnitz, of Barditschew and Wischau, received pastors skilled in laws and disputation, wise rabbis to whom the people came from far and wide seeking advice and solace. And Yaakov took up the staff of the wanderer and went from village to village, from hamlet to hamlet, to tell the people stories from the life of the wise and humble Baal Shem Tov. He told of how sometimes the Baal Shem Tov would vanish on the eve of the Sabbath or high holidays while the people waited for him in the synagogue. The prayer had yet to begin but still he did not come. He was late because he had departed for somewhere on high, where not even the mind of man could follow him, having gone thither to ask for a *parnose*, daily bread for some needy pauper, or health for some invalid, or a husband for some hardworking woman who had been left waiting, overlooked, or to seek the repeal of some *gezerah*, of some bad law. For him there was no case too small or too large; there were only people in need who had to be helped. And the Baal Shem Tov used to pray whenever it was required and where the mind of no ordinary man could follow, he would pray and he would plead, he would even threaten not to budge, not to return to the synagogue and the prayer on the eve of the Sabbath, he would threaten not to let the high holiday begin until the congregation received good tidings. And so Yaakov told the story of many such journeys, known and unknown, which he had witnessed. He told of how many a time, in the evening, after *maariv*, evening prayers, the rabbi would suddenly tell Alexe the carter to make haste and harness the horse to the cart. The cart would then fill with disciples and the Baal Shem Tov would climb up on the box next to Alexe, who would grasp the reins and crack his whip. But the Baal Shem Tov would tell him to let go of the reins and let the horse walk where it willed. And the horse would walk and walk, it would take out-of-the-way paths that few had ever trodden, much to the amazement of Alexe the carter, until finally it came to a stop at some inn or house, and that would be the very place where help, a good word, a cure for sickness was needed. Yaakov the maggid would tell the story beautifully. He knew hundreds of such episodes and the people would listen to him in enchantment, filled with hope. Yes, yes, misfortunes cannot last forever. In the end, somebody would always suddenly open their door and bring the people solace in their sufferings. Yaakov's words bore the people through the deeps, through the unsuspected abysses of the mind, before lifting them up on high, to heights equally unexpected. And so he found his reward for all this in the curiosity that sparkled in the eyes of his listeners, in their open hearts. He always found a place at a humble board, and a mattress and pillow on which to rest his weary bones and lay his head. Thus it was that Yaakov lived from one day to the next, roaming the villages, telling his stories. He was young when he set out, and now he was beginning to turn grey, but he seemed at peace with his fate as a wandering storyteller. But somewhere in the depths of his soul there lingered a hope, a presentiment that he did not dare to admit even to himself, and which he did not have the strength to banish. And why should he banish it? The great Baal Shem Tov himself had once said: 'You will become a rich man!' How was he to understand those words? How were they to be understood other than how they were spoken? And Yaakov sensed that he would not live out his life always in that same way, that something would turn up, that something would happen to him.'

The maggid paused for a few moments. In the Tiferet Israel synagogue, a deep silence had settled. Tcharder-rebbe gazed at the maggid tensely, his green eyes full of anticipation, not daring to move. Moishe-rebbe rested his heavy bulbous head on his two rotund, column-like arms, and he squinted, his dark eyes peeping from between blinking, weary eyelids. After a while, the stranger continued:

'And indeed, Yaakov Maggid's presentiment was borne out. One day, a Friday morning it was, he set off from Săcel to Oberwischau. He expected to arrive in Wischau in the afternoon, in time to go to the mikveh, thrice to immerse himself in the water of the pool, and then to go to the synagogue and greet the Sabbath in a befitting manner. It was a beautiful clear winter day, the snow that clothed the earth glittered like diamonds in the sunlight. Yaakov was filled with a great joy. He himself didn't know why: perhaps it was because the caress of the sun was so tender, perhaps it was because the snow crunched so familiarly beneath his feet, perhaps it was because the hills were so white and the branches of the fir trees so green beneath their white covering? Or perhaps it was simply because he was alive and could gaze on all these wonders? Who could have said? He walked like this for half an hour when all of a sudden it grew dark and inky black clouds gathered in the sky, a strong wind began to blow, lifting veils of snow and blotting out hill and vale. Yaakov found it harder and harder to move forward. The strong wind was blowing curtains of powdery snow in his face barely allowing him to see. The country road had been blotted out and was indistinguishable from the hill on the one side and the valley on the other. Yaakov came to a halt on the snowy hillside, and it was as if he were suspended between heaven and earth. All of a sudden, in the darkness that had descended, he espied a light. It came from a cottage nearby. He was filled with wonder. He had taken this path from Săcel to Oberwischau and back again countless times and never had he seen any house in that place. He set off in the direction of the light. Strangely, whereas before he was barely able to walk forward, battling the wind and the swirling snow, with each step costing him a super-human effort, now he moved with ease, as if pushed along from behind by the wind. In a few steps he had reached the log cabin. He grasped the handle; the door was open. He quickly entered and closed the door behind him. Inside, a bright fire was burning on a large hearth, and on a bench next to the fire, a man sat warming his hands. The man looked familiar but Yaakov couldn't remember where he had seen him before. He was a wayfarer like himself, with a grey beard, wearing a threadbare black caftan and a black hat with a broad round brim. A traveller's pouch hung from one shoulder and next to where he sat a staff leaned against the bench. And it seemed that he too was familiar to the seated man, for he was not at all surprised at his sudden appearance. He addressed Yaakov in an ordinary tone of voice, as if he had been expecting him:

"'Sit down and warm yourself!"

'Yaakov sat down next to him on the bench and spreading his fingers he held his hands to the fire. They sat like that in silence for a long time, until finally Yaakov ventured to ask:

"'Whence comes this Jew?"

"'From far away, from very far away," answered the man straight away, with a soft laugh. He had been expecting the question. "I come from the south, from the land of the Italians, where there is a large city, a very large city, called Milan. Wandering through the villages on the other side of the mountains, one day I heard that in that great city to the south there lived a rich and generous man, who received wayfarers and regaled them at his rich table with great joy and honour. Above all he rejoiced to entertain those who knew stories of the Baal Shem Tov. And for each story about the great and wise Rabbi Israel, that rich man paid one gold piece. I then remembered that I too knew a story about the Baal Shem Tov and I went to him."

'The man paused. On seeing the look of puzzlement on Yaakov's face, he began to rummage in his pouch, and from among the crusts of stale bread and the onions, he took out a coin and showed it to him. It was indeed a heavy gold piece and shone brightly, a coin such as Yaakov had never seen before. Yaakov Maggid looked at it for a long time, fascinated by its lustre. The man had known only a single story about the Baal Shem Tov, he thought, but I know hundreds, not even I myself know how many. "And you will become rich … you will be rich … rich … rich …" Yaakov's mind began to work feverishly and he did not even notice when the wanderer vanished, and the wind and the swirling snow abated. The sun was high in the clear sky once more and he was on the same country road, walking quickly, the snow creaking underneath the soles of his boots. In Wischau, that Saturday, he did not tell the people any stories, and in the evening, after the three stars appeared in the sky, he made haste to travel on to Dragomireşti, then to Crăciuneşti. He also passed through the town of Sighet, before heading west. He walked without pause through villages and towns, sleeping on the porches of synagogues, taking meals wherever he could find them. He reached Pressburg, then he headed for Vienna, southward, until he reached the land of the Italians and the large city of Milan. Once he was there, it was not hard to find the house of the famed rich man. It was a large house, a true palace. Yaakov barely dared to enter the yard, to tread the white slabs of marble, but when the rich man heard that it was Reb Yaakov Maggid, the disciple of the great Baal Shem Tov, who had arrived, he came out to greet him with open arms; he ordered that a feast and kingly guest room be made ready for him. It was a Friday when Yaakov Maggid arrived and the whole house was in festive mood, in anticipation of listening to him. But not only the host and his numerous family were there: the master of the house had invited a hundred friends to the feast that Sabbath eve, all of them leading citizens of the town, that they might listen to stories about the Baal Shem Tov. Indeed, after they returned from the synagogue, which was larger and more beautiful than any that Yaakov had ever seen in his life, and after he ate at the rich man's table dishes and fruits such as he had never eaten in his life, the master of the house invited him to begin his stories. A deep silence of anticipation fell. Men dressed in rich clothes, women in expensive silks, adorned with priceless jewels, they all waited with their eyes fixed on him ... Yaakov cleared his throat, he cleared it again, he knitted his eyebrows, he wrinkled his brow, and then he turned pale. He was unable to utter a word. Not a single story came into his mind, not one of the wonderful tales of the Baal Shem Tov. It was as if they had flown away, leaving a vast emptiness inside his head. He strained to remember even one of the stories he had told so many times before. He knew that if he could begin just one story, then the others would follow, but he could not. Not one story came into his mind, there was nothing there.

The silence dragged on, embarrassingly, till finally, the master of the house spoke in a slow, gentle voice: "You must still be tired after your journey, Reb Yaakov. You will tell us your stories tomorrow afternoon." The next day, the afternoon of the Sabbath, the host and his family and his hundred friends, all fine upstanding men, gathered to listen to Yaakov. And again, Yaakov did not open his mouth. He could not remember a single story. The master then said to him kindly: "Maybe after the third meal, after the *shaleshides*". And toward evening, after the third Sabbath meal, the master of the house and his family and his hundred friends, all fine, upstanding citizens of that city, sat down, eager to listen to Yaakov's stories, but not one of those wonderful stories came to Yaakov's mind. Then, after the day of the Sabbath had passed and the three stars had appeared in the sky, Yaakov, ashamed and humiliated, bid the master of the house farewell. The master of the house filled Yaakov's pouch with provisions for the long journey, but he did not give him any gold piece, any coin with a reeded edge, emblazoned with a crown, since he had told not one story of the Baal Shem Tov. Yaakov returned the way he had come, north through Vienna and Pressburg, then east, through Sighet, finally coming to the villages of Maramuresch, where once more he told the people those wonderful stories. In his mind, which was now clear, he held all the stories of the Baal Shem Tov, hundreds of wonderful stories, and the people listened to him with shining eyes and open hearts and they invited him to partake of their modest meals, and in their houses he found a mattress and a pillow on which to lay his head and rest his bones weary from wandering.'

Reaching this point in the story of Yaakov, the maggid of some two hundred years ago, the stranger fell silent.

A deep, mysterious silence reigned in the synagogue.

'What a sad story,' murmured Tchardar-rebbe after a while, in a voice overcome with emotion.

The storyteller gave a soft laugh. The teacher from Tcharda looked at him, intrigued. Why did he laugh? What was there to laugh about?

The strange maggid blinked his dark, baggy eyes, and a strange smile appeared on his lips. He then carried on the story in a voice that was changed, an everyday voice, a colourless voice that no longer vibrated:

'According to some, things happened completely differently. Yaakov, the disciple of the Baal Shem Tov, forgot nothing, absolutely nothing. On the contrary, he told stories one after the other to his rich host and his one hundred guests, all fine upstanding citizens of that large city, he told his stories without pause, on Friday after the evening meal, and on the Sabbath after the noonday meal, and after the third meal of the Sabbath, he told them hundreds and hundreds of stories about the Baal Shem Tov, one more wonderful than the next, and after Havdalah, the prayer of parting from Queen Sabbath, after the three stars appeared in the sky, the host kept his word. The maggid received his gold pieces, hundreds and hundreds of gold coins, with reeded edges, heavy coins of glittering gold, as many as the stories he had told.'

The stranger paused, smoothed his sparse beard, then blinking his dark, baggy eyes meaningfully, he looked at the teacher from Tcharda and went on:

'The same as in all stories, here too everything can be explained, although nothing is explained. You see, that rich man from Milan was once a starving pauper, and he went to the Baal Shem Tov, who advised him to go south, for there he would make his fortune. And the man then swore a sacred oath that he would not forget the poor and those who wander this world, he swore to regale them with honour in his house, and to those that knew a story of the great and the wise Baal Shem Tov, his benefactor, he would give a heavy gold coin, with a reeded edge, emblazoned with a crown, one for every such story. Do you now see how this relates to the legacy that Rabbi Israel Baal Shem Tov handed down to his humble disciple, Yaakov Maggid? "You, Reb Yakov, will tell stories of what you have seen and heard and you will become a rich man..." Thus it was that Yaakov received hundreds and hundreds of gold pieces and became a rich man, he took up commerce, he bought vineyards and gardens, and houses and ships that crossed the seven seas and brought spices from the east, and caught up in his business affairs, in his worries about how to increase his wealth, he abandoned the stories. And because he forgot all those wonderful stories, and they remained forgotten forever, and finally, he too was forgotten by the people.'

Yaakov Maggid fell silent once more.

Finally, the teacher from Tcharda said with a sigh:

'This is an even sadder story ...'

In the Tiferet Israel house of prayer, a deep silence fell. All that could be heard was the heavy breathing of Moishe-Rebbe, the teacher of small children, who had fallen asleep with his bulbous head resting on his two log-like forearms.

The Angel
and the Bad Wife

The evening prayer was taking a long time in that small synagogue in Tolstoye, Tarnopol Gubernia. This was not unusual. It had happened more than once that Rabbi Israel ben Eliezer, known as the Baal Shem Tov, which is to say, the Master of the Good Name, would be there with his congregation, but at the same time he would be somewhere else, somewhere so far away that none could even venture to follow him. And during the *shemoneh-esrei* prayer—the prayer of the eighteen blessings—Rabbi Israel would stand with his pale brow pressed to the east wall of the prayer house, his eyes closed, without moving his lips, without moving his body, without a single hair of his bushy chestnut beard twitching. He would stand as motionless as a rock, and in deep silence the congregation would wait and wait for him to take the three steps back, in sign of deep respect toward 'Him Who Hears and Grants Prayers', in sign that he had silently recited the eighteen blessings in his mind. But still Rabbi Israel Baal Shem Tov did not take the three steps back.

The Jews now began to murmur the prayer to themselves, they silently recited it where they stood, as if the soles of their feet were glued to the floorboards, their bodies swaying like branches in the wind; in a whisper, they finished saying the blessings, some more quickly, some more slowly, they took the respectful three steps back, but still Rabbi Israel Baal Shem Tov tarried, as if lost. And for as long as Rabbi Israel delayed taking the three steps back, everything stood still. The people waited in silence, since the prayer, which had to burst forth all at once, to be unleashed, to be spoken and sung aloud, could not proceed.

Rabbi Israel stood motionless, as motionless as a rock, his eyes closed, his pale brow pressed to the east wall. But in fact, he was far away. When he reached the words of the prayer: 'Upon the just and the believing, upon the elders of Thy people Israel, upon the learned scribes left behind to serve Thee ... let Thy mercy descend upon them, O Lord ...' he had suddenly paused. And his mind began to ascend on high. It had been a long time since such an important commandment of the Lord had been obeyed: the commandment to serve a learned man, a scribe. And who knew how many poor scribes, how many good servants of God required to be served? Who knew how many were in need of succour? But most of all, he himself, Rabbi Israel ben Eliezer, needed to obey the commandment to serve, lest he succumb to the grave sin of pride. If you do not serve others, in time you come to believe that you are the only one who should be served, that you alone deserve to be served. He therefore had to serve those wiser, those more learned, those better than himself. 'But no, no! Lord God!' he prayed. 'One must serve those less wise, those less learned, those less good! For who can measure the magnitude of a soul? And who can compare one heart with another? And who can trace the lofty flight of a thought or plumb the depth of a feeling?' But where should he go? To whom should he go? Whose feet should he wash? Whose words should he drink insatiably and with all due humility?

Rabbi Israel ben Eliezer flew high, he ascended to the loftiest heights on the wings of his prayer. All of a sudden, he received the answer. Like a bolt of lightning, it illumined his mind: Rabbi Efraim ben Zwi of Brod. He is the one who needs you.

And the blood returned to Rabbi Israel Baal Shem Tov's cheeks. He raised his forehead from the east wall. He opened his eyes and his large beard began to twitch. And he took the three steps back.

That instant, the powerful voice of the cantor resounded: 'Lord, let my lips be opened and my mouth utter Thy Greatness!'

And the whole house of prayer rustled like a forest awoken by the wind.

That very evening, Alexey the carter came to Rabbi Israel to ask him whether he wanted to be driven anywhere. Yes, early in the morning he had to go to Brod, in the Lvov Gubernia. And Rabbi Israel paid him a silver rouble in advance.

But why in advance? And why a whole rouble? The journey from Tolstoye, in the Tarnopol Gubernia, to Brod, beyond Lvov, was quite long, and it crossed hills and vales. But even so, a silver rouble ... But Alexey took the silver, thanked him, and said no more about it. He knew Rabbi Strul, as they called him in that little town, he knew him quite well, and he knew that any question, any objection, would have been superfluous. If that was the sum Rabbi Strul had given him, then that was the price, no more, no less. Henceforth that would be the price for him too. But when his little son, his youngest, Ilya, was ill, when he could barely breathe and almost suffocated, Rabbi Strul gave him some herbs, which he called 'rabbi's wort', and told him to brew some hot tea from them. And when little Ilya got better, the rabbi refused to accept a single kopeck; he said that he knew best from whom to take and to whom to give. And besides, that herb grew as God willed, free of charge, on the banks of the Prislop; all you had to do was pick it and dry it in the sun, which the Lord Above also provided free of charge.

How could Rabbi Strul have known, thought Alexey in amazement, feeling the heavy silver rouble weighing in the pocket of his woollen coat, that that very evening he had to take his horse to the blacksmith to be shod for the winter? And that the time had come for him to buy cloth to make trousers for his eldest son, Vasili, who had given his trousers to his next youngest brother, who had given his to his next youngest brother, since Alexey had five sons, each younger than the next? And how had Rabbi Strul known that with that silver rouble in his pocket, he would drive his cart all the way to Brod and back with his cap cocked to one side, whistling as he went? Probably that was what Rabbi Strul wanted. Wasn't he the one who said that by the will of Him Above, you had to obey His commandments cheerfully, no matter how hard, no matter how onerous?

The next day, a Tuesday, was white: overnight snowfall had blanketed everything. Alexey took the sleigh from the shed, harnessed the freshly shod horse, and with Rabbi Israel Baal Shem Tov wrapped in a thick woollen blanket, they set off.

Arriving in the large town of Brod in the Lvov Gubernia, Rabbi Israel did not have to ask far. Everybody knew where Rabbi Efraim ben Zwi lived. The Baal Shem Tov entered his house, which was on the lane behind the synagogue, and was stunned. The house was a mess; on the dining room table there were dishes, crumbs and crusts. In the kitchen there were unwashed plates, and in the bedroom, Rabbi Efraim lay wrapped in a threadbare blanket, trembling like a reed. His thin, pale, almost translucent face, with its sky-blue eyes, seemed familiar to Rabbi Israel, but there was no time to waste thinking about where he had seen it before. In the house it was as cold as beneath a waterfall. And Rabbi Efraim was shivering with a fever.

Rabbi Israel, hale as he was, set about chopping wood and made a fire in the stove. He wondered to himself as to why Rabbi Efraim's wife was nowhere to be found about the house when her husband was ill in bed, wracked with a fever. But he asked no questions.

Once it was warm in the house, he helped Rabbi Efraim out of bed—he was emaciated, as light as a feather—dressed him, wrapped him in the thick woollen blanket and on Alexey's sleigh he took him to the mikveh, the communal bath house. There, he sat him on the steps of the steam bath, after which he bathed him in the hot water of the pool. Finally, he took him home on Alexey's sleigh, laid him in the freshly made bed, and made him a mug of hot camomile tea. He put more wood on the fire and made the room warm and comfortable.

After Rabbi Israel had done all this, Rabbi Efraim's wife, Haya-Perla, arrived back home. She was dressed up in all her finery, although it was the middle of the week, wearing an overcoat of blue cloth with a silver fox-fur collar, a wide-brimmed hat adorned with flowers and broad leaves, earrings and bracelets, and a pearl necklace. As soon as she entered the house, she opened her mouth and cried:

'What's with this unbearable heat? What do you think you're doing, husband? So much firewood you let go to waste? It would have lasted us half the winter. In this stifling heat it's no wonder that you idle the whole day in bed!'

Rabbi Efraim said nothing, and with his blue eyes that were as clear as the sky, he gazed in mute shame up at the time-blackened beams of the ceiling.

Rabbi Israel Baal Shem Tov remained silent, too, filled with sorrow. He had come from far away with the intention of giving succour, and look what had come of it.

At the synagogue, before the evening prayer, talking with the people of Brod, Rabbi Israel learned that Rabbi Efraim's wife, Haya-Perla, gadded about, that she did not look after the house or her husband, that she scolded him for studying and writing, since it wasted lamp oil at night, that rabbis and scholars and friends had no business coming to his house, since they disturbed her, and she was hardly going to wash up tea cups and clean the house after them. In that house were welcome only her friends and relatives, while on Friday evening, the rabbi did not dare to bring a wayfaring guest back from the synagogue to sit at his table. He tried to give to the needy on the sly, but she kept a tally of every kopeck and caused him no end of grief. On top of this, she went to charity tea dances, to which it wasn't appropriate for her to go, since there was more dancing than charity. He was ill, but she went to the baths, to treat her migraines and rheumatism: she took cold mineral water baths in summer and hot mineral water baths in winter. True, Haya-Perla the rabbi's wife tried to fulfil a few of the Merciful Lord's beautiful commandments: she visited the sick and went to funerals, but she only went if the sick and the deceased were rich and she could mingle with high society.

Rabbi Efraim ben Zwi was a true 'angel banished from heaven' and he suffered terribly because of her. He suffered in silence, so said the folk of Brod.

'An angel banished from heaven,' said the folk of Brod, and suddenly Rabbi Israel the Baal Shem Tov remembered where he had seen Rabbi Efraim before. And why he had been sent to him in particular, to minister to him in particular.

It had been many years previously, one evening in the little synagogue of Tolstoye in the Tarnopol Gubernia, during the *shemoneh-esrei* prayer—the prayer of the eighteen silent blessings—and Rabbi Israel ben Eliezer had been standing with his pale forehead pressed to the east wall of the house of prayer, his eyes closed, without moving his lips, without moving a muscle, without a hair of his bushy chestnut beard twitching. He had stood as motionless as a rock and the congregation had waited for him to take the three steps back, in sign that the whispered prayer was finished. But Rabbi Israel tarried, lost somewhere far, far away. And it so happened that on reaching the prayer of praise, 'with love Thou givest succour to the living, and the dead Thou dost mercifully resurrect, and Thou dost lift the fallen,' Rabbi Israel had suddenly paused. And he began to ascend, in great haste. Yes, he had to make haste to ascend on high. Three days previously, a congregant from the Tolstoye house of prayer, Simon Ben-Asher Koptchiner by name, had departed from among the living. For as long as he lived, people had not loved him and had spoken ill of him. And not without reason. Simon Ben-Asher Koptchiner was a rich man, a great leather and fur merchant, but he never welcomed wayfarers into his opulent house and never gave alms to the poor. Instead, he kept his wife in sumptuous dresses and expensive furs and gold jewellery and diamonds. That was what the folk of Tolstoye and the whole Gubernia of Tarnapol used to say when he was alive, and now Rabbi Israel Baal Shem Tov felt that he had to make haste, for perhaps there was need of his testimony. He had to make haste, lest an injustice be done up there, at the Judgement in Heaven.

And he arrived just in time. The judgement was underway:

'He didn't give alms to the poor!' cried Kategor, the heavenly prosecutor, in a rage.

'His wife didn't let him,' gently replied Sanegor, the heavenly counsel for the defence.

'He didn't invite a single needy man, a single wayfarer to sit at his opulent table on the Sabbath or feast days!'

'He was afraid of his wife's tongue.'

'Not a single scholar or scribe did he have in his house!'

'His wife didn't like them,' said the counsel for the defence, gently.

The heavenly accuser grew more and more outraged:

'He kept his wife in expensive clothes and furs and draped her in gaudy gold jewellery and precious stones!'

'It was the woman allotted to be his wife who craved all those vain baubles,' replied Sanegor in a soft voice.

'That Simon Ben-Asher never lingered very long when it came to the prayers in synagogue or the teaching of the Book!' shouted Kategor.

'His wife gave him no respite. She was always dragging him to parties and aristocratic balls,' said Sanegor, sorrowfully.

All of a sudden, a thin, innocent voice made itself heard:

'How so? A woman can overrule all the Commandments of the Torah, all the prescriptions of Law?'

Rabbi Israel Baal Shem Tov quickly turned to look at the place whence the voice had come. It was a member of the *pamalia*, the heavenly court, who had spoken. An innocent angel with a face as pale as a white cloud and translucent blue eyes.

Rabbi Israel yelled at the angel in a fury:

'What, you take the side of the prosecution? When the scales are so finely balanced? What do you know about what goes on down below? What do you know about what a bad woman means? What do you know, here in the tranquillity and serenity in which you float, about what it is to have a bad wife?'

The heavens were filled with amazement. If Rabbi Israel Baal Shem Tov could lose his temper like that and fly into a rage, then the matter had to be very serious indeed.

And that outburst on the part of Rabbi Israel Baal Shem Tov did not pass without consequence. The angel with the pale face and the translucent blue eyes was expelled from the tranquillity and serenity of the heavens, he was cast out, made to fall down to earth.

After long years of atonement, of illness and suffering, he who had borne with honour and humility the name Rabbi Efraim ben Zwi, left his earthly shell behind and returned to his place in the *pamalia*, in the heavenly court. And never again did he ask questions at the Last Judgement as to whether a woman could void all the prescriptions of Law, all the teachings of the Torah.

And his widow, Haya-Perla, lamented for the seven days of grief and sorrowed for the thirty days of mourning, and after the lapse of a year, she remarried. And she lived for many more years.

And her daughters and granddaughters had a long life on this earth.

And her great-granddaughters and her relatives live among us to this day.

Perhaps it was because through them might be punished the sins of men and angels alike?

The Inadvertent Sin

'The rabbi was reciting the prayers of forgiveness, one by one, in a soft, monotonous voice, and the synagogue congregation murmured after him:

'"*Ve-el chet shichatnu* ... For the sin which we have committed before Thee under duress or willingly.

'"And for the sin which we have committed before Thee by hard-heartedness.

'"For the sin which we have committed before Thee inadvertently ..."

'Reaching this point, the rabbi let out a cry of grief and repeated the words three times: "For the sin which we have committed before Thee inadvertently ... inadvertently ... inadvertently ... Lord of Forgiveness, forgive us! pardon us! atone for us!"

'And the rabbi thrice beat his chest with his fist and burst into bitter sobbing tears.

'And the whole congregation cried out the prayer of atonement after him, and they thrice beat their chests with their fists, and they wept bitterly, they sobbed ...'

Here, Yaakov Maggid, the wandering storyteller, broke off his story for a few moments. In the Tiferet Israel, which is to say, Splendour of Israel, house of prayer, that afternoon of the Shubat-Teshuvah, the Sabbath of Repentance, which falls between Rosh Hashanah and Yom Kippur, between the New Year and the Day of Atonement, the congregants were seated for the *shaleshides*, the third meal of the Sabbath, listening in silence to the stories of the maggid. None now ate of the ring loaves laid on the table before him, none now cracked walnuts, none now sipped slivovitz.

Yaakov Maggid smoothed the strands of his black beard and went on:

'So, that Day of Forgiveness, the rabbi wept and the people wept after him... And truly they had reason to weep and beat their chests, to beg forgiveness, to beg atonement from the Lord Above! For that year the whole community of that town, headed by their wise and learned rabbi, had committed a grave sin, an inadvertent sin, mistaking great goodness for evil, vast spiritual strength for weakness, rare nobility for intransigence... And all of them, young and old, had rashly, recklessly judged a Jew who had passed away to the world of the truly good and righteous. And they had adjudged him evil, when they ought to have adjudged him good.'

The Maggid paused once more. For a time, he sat deep in thought, as if seeking to remember something.

'It was long ago, very long ago, and I no longer remember the name of that little town in the mountains, where those harrowing events took place. Nor do I remember the name of the wise and learned rabbi, or the names of the other people of our story, I no longer remember them. It was a little town of a few hundred hearths, in the borderlands between Poland, Ukraine, and Romania. Over the course of time, it would seem the town had been part of each country in turn. The little town might have been called Sonczowa, in which case the name of the learned rabbi would have been Israel-Chaim Sonczower.

But the names are of no importance to our story. It all began the night of one Sabbath, early one Sunday morning, when suddenly the richest man of that little town, let us call him Reb Menachem-Mendel Hartmann, a cereals wholesaler and retailer, returned his soul to his Creator, without first having fallen sick, without having complained of feeling ill, without having been tended by those close to him, without hearing their sighs. Some said, "What a beautiful way to die!" Others said, "What an ugly life he led!"'

The people around the *shaleshides* table gave a start:

'What? An ugly life he led? How could they say such a thing of a man who had passed to the other world?' said a number of timid voices.

Yaakov Maggid made no reply. In the Tiferet Israel Synagogue the light was dim, the silence deep. None cracked walnuts, none ate of the ring loaves, none sipped the glass of slivovitz before him. Finally, the maggid opened his eyelids and his dark eyes flamed like glowing coals, as if to light up his thin bony face. His sparse black beard quivered as he resumed his tale:

'The rich man, Reb Menachem-Mendel Hartmann, died on the night of the Sabbath, early one Sunday morning. The same morning, his family went to the Chevra Kadisha, the Holy Funeral Association, and asked that he be laid to eternal rest in a place of honour, in the middle of the cemetery, alongside that little town's other wealthy men and leading lights. It was then that the storm erupted: "What? In the middle of the cemetery? In a place of honour? How can that be?" the people asked in indignation. "Simply because he was a rich man? So what if he was? How did the community benefit from his wealth? Whom did he ever help? Did he ever give alms? Did he ever spare a penny for a pauper? Look at the men far less wealthy than he, men who couldn't afford even the trash in his house, but still they gave alms and helped the needy. Look at Reb Schulem Rosenstein, for example, he donated a blue velvet curtain to the synagogue, for the ark that holds the Torah scrolls, embroidered with the words *Ze haparohet* in gold thread. That was the curtain donated by Reb Schulem Rosenstein ..." And so on and so forth ... "Or look at Reb Yehiel Abramovitz, who donated thirty psalters to the synagogue and the cover of each was stamped *Ze hasefer* ... Those were the books of the Thilim donated by Reb Yehiel Abramovitz, *neiro yair*, may his light shine ..." And so on and so forth ... "But there are men even less wealthy than that who are able to help, men who couldn't afford the trash even in the house of an Abramovitz or a Rosenstein, may their candles burn light, let alone the trash in the house of a Menachem-Mendel Hartmann, may he rest in peace, men such as Hersch Katzev the butcher, who every Friday gives a kilo of meat to all the needy people in town ... And there are a lot of needy people in the town, more than a hundred there are ... Or look at Leyzer-Beer Becker, the baker, who gives every needy man two braided ring loaves for the Sabbath meal ... But that red-headed, stubborn Jew, that man with a heart of stone, that rich man, that *nagid*, that *gevir-adir*, that Reb Menachem-Mendel Hartmann, may he rest in peace, what did he ever give the community? What did he ever give the poor? Nothing, nothing, and yet more nothing! And another portion of nothing to top it off!"

'The little town was in an uproar, indignant, seething with anger. The most vehement were naturally the poor, and among the angriest was Schmul Herschkovitz, the tailor, a short, stooped man, near-sighted from so much sewing, a sour, witty, sarcastic man. At one point, Schmul Herschkovitz made the observation:

'"In the middle of the cemetery, among the leading lights and the rich men? No, the place of Reb Menachem-Mendel

Hartmann is by the cemetery fence at the back, among the poor, because it was the poor he resembled most: the poor don't give to the poor, nor did he give to the poor."

'The wise and learned Rabbi Israel-Chaim Sonczower could find neither the strength nor the counterarguments to allay the public anger that had been unleashed. In truth, that Menachem-Mendel, may his memory be blessed, had been a pious man, he had attended synagogue, he had kept the Sabbath, he had obeyed all the commandments, but it was also true that when it came to giving, nobody had ever known him to give to the poor or to the community. And it was well known that it was not enough to obey the commandments that concerned relations between man and God, you also had to obey those that concerned relations between man and his fellow man. And even though he sensed in the people's words an unpleasant undertone besides their ring of truth, something that sounded like a thirst for revenge, the Rabbi of Sonczowa was forced to concede. Thus it was that something unheard of came to pass: Menachem-Mendel Hartmann, the town's richest man, was buried at the back of the cemetery, by the fence, among those who during their lives had been the poorest and most oppressed.'

The gloom within the Tiferet Israel Synagogue thickened. It was hard to make out the outlines of those seated for the third Sabbath meal.

The troubled voice of Yaakov Maggid had grown calmer when he took up the story once more:

'Reb Menachem-Mendel Hartmann, the town's richest man, the wholesaler and retailer of cereals, died on the night of the Sabbath, toward Sunday morning. All that Sunday and the following Monday morning there was uproar and commotion and quarrelling, until Menachem-Mendel Hartmann was buried that afternoon, by the fence at the back of the cemetery. Whereupon peace was restored to that little town as if by miracle. And there was peace all that Tuesday, as each went about his business as before ... And there was peace that Wednesday and that Thursday ... Three days of peace and mutual understanding ... But on the fourth day, that Friday morning, a fresh storm broke out. A storm bigger even than the first. And a wholly different kind of storm ... What had happened now? That Friday morning, the town's poor went to Hersch Katzev's butcher's shop for their kilo of meat as usual, but the butcher refused to give them anything. "What? Now you don't give us anything?" asked the poor in desperation. Hersch Katzev shrugged helplessly: "I can't any more! But I can't tell you why!" The poor folk, more than one hundred in number, then ran to the baker's shop to receive their two braided Sabbath ring loaves. Leyzer-Beer the baker shrugged helplessly ... "Why won't you give us anything?" "I can't say why! I can't!"

'What were the poor folk to do? To whom could they turn? Where could they seek justice? They went to the rabbi. Astonished and filled with a strange presentiment, Rabbi Israel-Chaim Sonczower immediately sent a messenger to bring the butcher and the baker:

'"Reb Hersh Katzer and Reb Leyzer-Beer, why don't you give these people what is due to them?"

'The two men remained silent. When he saw the doubt on their faces, the rabbi of Sonczowa shouted at them:

'"Yes, yes, it is due to them! For so many years they have received from you their kilo of meat and their *lechem mishneh*, their two Sabbath ring loaves, that it has become almost a *chazaqah*, a benefit established by custom, which cannot now be taken away without good reason. Why do you not give them their due?"

'"We cannot say, Rabbi!"

"'Why can't you say, when I, your rabbi, command you to do so?" shouted the rabbi of Sonczowa, sternly.

"'We cannot, Rabbi! We are bound by an oath. If you were to release us from it ..."

'The rabbi fell to thinking. He hesitated. To release a man from an oath was not a matter to be taken lightly. There had to be serious grounds. But outside his house more than a hundred poor folk were waiting. What grounds could be more serious?

'The rabbi recited the words to release them from their oath.

"'Now you may speak!"

"'Yes, Rabbi," began Hersch Katzev, and as he spoke, Leyzer-Beer the baker nodded along, in confirmation of his every word. "Many years ago, Reb Menachem-Mendel Hartmann, may his memory be blessed, called us to him in secret one night and told us: 'The Lord God has been merciful to me and my business has begun to do well. Every Friday I want the two of you to give every needy man in our community a kilo of meat and two braided Sabbath loaves, and I will pay for them. But I do not wish to boast and I do not wish to be thanked for what I give since it is only thanks to the Lord Above that I am able to give it. Swear that you will not breathe a word to anybody!' And we swore, Rabbi."

"'*Ve-al heit shehatanu* ... And for the sin we have committed before Thee, Lord ... *beyodin ubelo yodin* ... wittingly and un-wittingly ... and unwittingly ... and unwittingly ... May Thou, God of Forgiveness, forgive us! Pardon us! Atone for us!" The rabbi thrice beat his chest with his fist and wept bitterly, he sobbed. And the whole congregation cried out the prayers of atonement after him, and they thrice beat their chests with their fists and wept bitterly, they sobbed.

'And when the time came and the wise and learned Rabbi Israel-Chaim Sonczower left this world of shadow and light, in his will, signed by his own hand, he asked that he be buried, unworthy though he was, next to the great *tzadik* that was Menachem-Mendel Hartmann. And today, whoever chances to pass through that little town in the mountains, at the border of three countries, will be able to see at the back of the Jewish cemetery, next to the fence, among the sandstone and the corroded tin grave markers of the host of unknown paupers, the two grey marble gravestones of Reb Menachem-Mendel Hartmann and Rabbi Israel Chaim of Sonczowa, may their good deeds preserve us from evil and may their memory be blessed forever and ever more.

'The poor folk that had blackened the name of Menachem-Mendel Hartmann and adjudged him to be evil repented bitterly, and thenceforth they honoured and piously preserved his memory. Even Schmul Herschkovitz, the tailor, that man so sour and sarcastic, once noted:

'"I shouldn't wonder if Reb Menachem-Mendel didn't do the whole thing on purpose, so that he wouldn't have to lie with the rich men in the middle of the cemetery, but among us paupers. In any event, even after he passed from this life, he gave us a great boon. We now have the honour of having in our midst for all eternity two leading lights: the town's richest man and its rabbi."'

So ended the story told by Yaakov Maggid, the wandering storyteller, and the smile on his thin face was no longer visible, in the Tiferet Israel Synagogue, where all was now pitch black and silent. At the *shaleshides*, the third meal of the Sabbath, nobody ate of the ring loaves, nobody cracked walnuts, nobody touched the glass of slivovitz in front of him.

For Ten's Sake

He was sick of it. In which direction was he travelling? Westward. But he might as well have been going eastward, or southward, or northward. It would not have altered anything at all!

And what did he tell people? What did it matter? He could have said anything at all. If repeated endlessly, words begin to lose all weight. They even lose all meaning ... What more could he tell them? And how should he tell them? He might seek the choicest, the most piercing words. But it was pointless. The words still didn't sink in. They were to no avail, they didn't help anybody.

Reb Yaakov Maggid, the wandering storyteller, was seated in the cart of Menachem-Mendel, the carter from Borscha. The cart was drawn by two grey, resigned mares. They travelled along the bumpy country road that led to the market town of Sighet. Reb Yaakov Maggid's tall, thin, gangly body rocked to the rhythm of the bumping cart, his sparse black beard quivered, and his dark eyes glowed like coals. Although it was a warm morning in late autumn, and the sun rising above the hills was beginning to beat down on the backs of the people in the cart, Yaakov Maggid felt cold. He had a fever. From time to time he closed his eyes and then snatches of the other travellers' conversation would come to his ears. They were traders, commercial travellers, hawkers, ordinary men and women. They talked about the price of goods, about loans and credit books, profit and loss. In one corner of the cart, a commercial traveller was telling lewd jokes about easy women, in another corner a woman with a brown headscarf sighed and complained about her husband, who had disappeared, leaving behind five children. A ramshackle father and a mother like a weathered plank were on their way to Sighet, taking a daughter slightly past her prime, but still quite beautiful, wearing a purple dress with lace trimmings, for a 'viewing'. Reb Motl-*shadkhen*, the marriage broker, had arranged the 'viewing', which was for the benefit of a young man from the town. Neither the parents nor the daughter knew what the young man looked like, only that he plied a good trade. He was a chandler. And quoting the words of the wise, the *shadkhen* said: *Melokhe-melukhe*, a trade is a kingdom, if you have a good pair of hands and a good head, and a little luck besides.

A cart full of misfortunes. Every head was bowed, the sole of every foot splashed in life's mire. Not one gaze was lifted on high. '*Olam keminhago noheg*, the world goes on the same as ever,' Yaakov Maggid said to himself bitterly. Yes, yes, folk will do as folk do ... They deceive and are deceived. Some fiddle the scales, some refuse help to the orphan, some mock the widow. Some chase after a crust of bread and some chase after gain and covet their neighbour's goods, their neighbour's ass, their neighbour's wife. What was the point of his sermons? What was the point of his admonishments and his warnings about the evil deeds that men did, or of his words of praise for the good deeds that they did? What was the point of all his toil? He went from place to place, on foot or by cart, he ate at others' tables, he slept on strange straw mattresses, he spoke, he told stories and parables full of deeper meanings, but afterward folk went about their business as if they had heard nothing. His was a voice crying in the wilderness.

Emerging from the Wischau Valley, the road climbed the hill. The cart creaked from every joint. Menachem-Mendel the carter, with his shirt of thick homespun cloth unbuttoned to reveal his hairy black chest, which glistened with sweat, cracked the whip above the two straining grey mares, without touching them. The mares strained; the cart struggled uphill. Menachem-Mendel leapt out of the cart and took the horses by the bridle. Yaakov Maggid nimbly climbed down from the cart and began to push from behind. The commercial traveller, the one with the lewd stories about easy women, jumped down too, along with another two traders. Its wheels creaking and grinding, the cart gained the crest of the hill.

His was a voice crying in the wilderness, said Yaakov Maggid to himself, picking up the train of his thought once more, after he climbed back in the cart. No, no, folk came to the house of prayer, they listened to him, but they did not take his words to heart, they drew no connection between what he said and their own deeds; each deemed the maggid's words to be not about him but about the neighbour to his right or left, or somebody else entirely, anybody but him! And the next day he would carry on with his life the same as before, as if he had heard nothing.

What was the point of the maggid's toil, if the truth be told? Of all his tortured effort to find the right words? He would abandon travelling, sermons, stories, wise parables, tales of the Baal Shem Tov—the Rabbi of the Good Name— and of his disciples and their wonderful deeds, and he would take up some other occupation. Like any other normal man. He would go from house to house selling prayer books and tassels for prayer shawls perhaps. In fact, no, he would give up holy affairs and holy items; he would open a grocery and sell cooking oil and maize flour and blocks of salt and salt granules. Or a bodega where people would come to eat kosher food. And other than that, he wouldn't care about anything else. He would make sure he was an honest trader, his scales would be accurate, the needle wouldn't be bent left or right; he would give money to the poor, as much as he could afford, but he would no longer concern himself with other folk. What they did was their own business! Let each live his life in this world and the next as he saw fit. For in the end, what and who was he to preach to folk about the difference between good and bad? Who was he to bless and to admonish? Why should he worry about the community? A community of the deaf and blind.

Arriving in town, at the house of prayer named Tiferet Israel, which is to say, the Splendour of Israel, he immediately informed the warden and the usher, who were there to greet him, that he would not be giving a Sabbath sermon. The two were stunned. What? The maggid had come to their synagogue and he wasn't going to speak? Who could imagine such a thing?

Yes, Reb Yaakov Maggid was not going to speak! He would sit at the back of the synagogue, on the wooden bench, at a corner of the long table, he would say the prayer like any other congregant, but after the reading from the Torah scrolls, between the morning prayer and the *mussaf*, the additional Sabbath prayer, he would not mount the pulpit or say a single word.

So, Yaakov Maggid sat in a corner of the Splendour of Israel synagogue, on a wooden bench, with his elbows resting on the long table of age-blackened, time-weathered boards. He sat stiffly in his black caftan, which was too large for his thin body, his clean white shirt buttoned to the neck and his black round-brimmed felt hat shading his long, hollow-cheeked face and his sparse, straggly beard, not one hair of which twitched.

He sat like a statue and stared into space. And within him the emptiness persisted. He was not thinking of the evening prayer, or the prayer for the next day, or the third prayer at dusk, he was not thinking of his sermon or his stories, as there would be no sermon, there would be no stories, there would be nothing.

That hot Friday afternoon, before sunset, on the eve of the Sabbath, the news quickly spread throughout the lanes of the town: the Maggid, Rabbi Yaakov, had arrived, but he would not speak! Why not? In the name of the Lord Above, why not? Nobody knew. He would not give the Sabbath sermon after the reading from the Torah scrolls, and he would not tell his stories at the *shaleshides*, the third meal of the Sabbath's eve, his stories full of meaning, about the Baal Shem Tov and his descendants, and about their wonderful deeds. All over town the people were astonished, dismayed, and, at the bottom of their souls, they were afraid. They liked to listen to his sermons. When he had words of praise for their few good deeds, they felt they were floating in seventh heaven, and they felt the same even when he fulminated and thundered at their sins, their bad deeds, be they overt or concealed. For in the synagogue, wrapped in their prayer shawls, reciting the prayers, singing the psalms, and listening to his admonishments, each felt pure and blameless, at peace with the Lord Above, with his fellow man, and with himself. The sinner was always another. It was somebody else. Maybe even the person sitting to his left or right ... Or somebody who wasn't present ... Yes, yes, it was the one who wasn't present! Indeed, how many times had the righteous been upbraided and admonished, while those at whom the words were aimed were not present, as they didn't bother coming to the House of the Lord to listen.

Reb Yaakov Maggid had come to their house of prayer and he was not going to speak. The whole community was sad, downcast. And afraid. Might his silence foretell something? For when scolding and admonishment no longer avail …

It was a thought they were afraid to finish.

The warden, a little old man in a threadbare caftan and felt slippers, busied himself around the synagogue, making not a sound as he swept the corners, straightened the embroidered cloth that covered the pulpit, laid out the prayer books and psalters on the pews.

Yaakov Maggid, the wandering storyteller and preacher, was sitting on the bench next to the long table at the back of the synagogue, staring at the entrance. Not one strand of his sparse, untidy beard twitched. He looked tensely at the door, as if expecting it to open at any moment and for somebody to enter. And then the door did indeed open, softly, without a sound, without a squeak of the hinges, and a wayfarer made his appearance. A short, grey-haired man, who seemed to be shrouded from head to foot in the dust of the road; his eyebrows were grey, his beard grey, his eyes grey, his caftan grey, even his wide-brimmed hat was covered in a film of grey dust. His voice too was grey, when he uttered the traditional greeting: 'Shalom Aleichem! Peace be unto you!' The man sat down next to Yaakov Maggid and began to speak to him as if he had known him ever since both could remember. And indeed, the man's face seemed familiar to the maggid, but the dust that covered it prevented him from recognising it. The grey man began by saying he had passed through such-and-such a village. Yaakov Maggid did not catch the name of the place. A small village, somewhere in the mountains, nothing but a few dozen cottages dotted along a clear, narrow stream, with a larger building among them, which was the synagogue. There, at the end of that little village, lived a woodcutter by the name of Yechiel Bennet, or Panet, or Henech—Yaakov Maggid did not catch the name, uttered as it was in a toneless grey voice—a hardworking, honest man, who had laboured all his life with axe and cant hook, cutting and hauling logs from the forest. A tall, strong man, with a sunburnt face and chest, with a beard the colour of bronze, he felled the pine trees with a saw, he lopped off the branches with an axe, and he hauled the logs with a hook, toiling for his daily bread. And he lived at the end of that village with Brana his wife, his four children, and a goat to provide milk in the yard. One Friday afternoon, a stranger knocked at his door. A man in town clothes, with a soft felt hat, a round, neatly trimmed chestnut beard, and holding a leather briefcase. He was a timber merchant from the capital, who had come there to view and purchase some parcels of forest land. Yechiel and Brana gave him a joyful welcome. That evening, before Brana lit the Sabbath candles, the guest drew Yechiel aside: He had a sum of money on him and he did not wish to carry it about his person when he went to the synagogue on the Sabbath. He asked Yechiel to put the money in a safe place until the evening of the Sabbath, until after the lighting of the candles and the Havdalah, the prayer of parting with the Sabbath. And he would pay him well for both his lodging and for the safekeeping of his money. Yechiel agreed, and the man took off the girdle he had worn while travelling, a thick girdle stuffed with banknotes. Yechiel hid the girdle well, at the back of the cupboard. And he began to dress for the Sabbath: a white shirt, black trousers, brushed and ironed by Brana, a rather worn but clean black coat. After a while, a worm began to gnaw at his peace of mind. With so much money, he would be able to rid himself of his every care for the rest of his life ... He wouldn't have to toil so hard with his axe and grapple hook. And how much longer would he be able to toil like that anyway? What if a log rolled on top of him? What would become of his wife and children? He drove the thought from his mind ... But he would be able to open a grocer's shop ... Even a large timber yard in the town, with men to stack the timber, and an office with sales clerks and accountants ... He banished the thought once more, trying to turn his mind to other things ... His children would be able to grow up in a nice house. Like decent folk ... That timber merchant, with his soft felt hat, smelled like a rich man from afar, maybe he wouldn't even be missed ... He must have a hundred times that sum in his safe and in the bank. What if the next evening he gave him a look of amazement and told him he didn't know anything about it, that nobody had given him any money. It would leave him agape and no mistake. Yechiel clapped his hands over his ears. 'Have you caught a cold again?' asked Brana in alarm. Her husband looked at her in confusion. Then, Yechiel went out to the synagogue with the stranger. They returned. Yechiel's face grew darker and darker. The worm was gnawing away without surcease and he didn't know how to banish it. The man would obviously talk; he would have Yechiel arrested. But he didn't have a witness that he had given Yechiel anything! Yechiel tried to calm himself as he ate his supper. Obviously, the village gendarmes would come. 'No! No!' Yechiel said to himself before bed. That night, when the rest of the house was sleeping, he would toss around the clothes inside the cupboard, he would force a window, he would start shouting, 'Thieves! Thieves!' The stranger cries out! How to make him shut up! Shut up! Shut up! Why is the merchant yelling like that? Yechiel grabs his axe and strikes in a fury. The stranger falls to the floor with a thud ...

'What's the matter with you, Yechiel, why are you groaning? What's wrong?' He feels the warm hand of his wife Brana on his brow. Yehiel wakes up in his bed, bathed in a cold sweat.

The man with the grey face, the grey eyebrows, and the clothes thick with the grey dust of countless roads fell silent. After a pause, he carried on his story in a grey, toneless voice:

'That Sabbath morning, Yechiel, pale and anguished, went to the synagogue with his guest. The stranger's treasure, hidden in Yechiel's clothes cupboard, followed him there. In the synagogue, during the prayer, Yechiel found himself wondering: Why did the Lord Above send that wadded girdle to his house? Maybe to put him to the test? Or maybe the merchant was His emissary? His instrument? The temptation was great; it was hard to overcome. After the reading from the Torah scrolls and before the *mussaf*, the additional Sabbath prayer, it was you who spoke, Reb Yaakov Maggid. And you spoke of the evil of the inhabitants of Sodom and Gomorrah, who made a mockery of guests and weary travellers seeking a roof over their heads and a bed on which to rest their bones. You spoke of how they lodged rich guests in houses with cracked walls, and of how as they slept, the walls fell down around them, and the folk of Sodom and Gomorrah then took their money. And of how Abraham prayed for them and said: "Oh let not the Lord be angry, and I will speak yet but this once: Peradventure ten shall be found there." And the Lord said, "I will not destroy it for ten's sake." But ten good men were not to be found, and "then the Lord rained upon Sodom and Gomorrah fire and brimstone. And he overthrew those cities, and all the inhabitants of the cities, and that which grew in the ground." At home, over the Sabbath meal, Yechiel was now at peace. And in the synagogue at the *shaleshides*, the third meal of the Sabbath, he was of good cheer. He drank slivovitz, perhaps a little too much, and he cracked walnuts, and he sang, perhaps a little too loudly. And in the evening, after the lighting of the candles and the Havdalah, the prayer of parting from Queen Sabbath, his guest, the timber merchant from the capital, with the round chestnut beard and the soft felt hat, received from the strong hand of Yechiel his broad girdle wadded with banknotes. And since that day, the same as thitherto, Yechiel has lived in his house at peace, with his wife Brana and their four children, and with their goat for milk in the yard. And with his axe he lops the branches off the pine trees, and with his grapple hook, he hauls them down into the valley.'

At this point, the grey man, who looked as if he was covered from head to foot in the grey dust of every road, finished his story and fell silent.

'A man ... in a small village ...' Yaakov Maggid said to himself with a bitter smile. A man ... Perhaps his words had not made a difference even to him ... Maybe it had been the dream he had, his own conscience, which had stayed his hand ... But where had the dream come from? And how had he come to distinguish good from evil? How had he known that what had seemed so obviously a good thing for him was in fact evil? Was it not thanks to the Word uttered on the heights of Mount Sinai and repeated ever since in different voices from the heights of so many pulpits? Who can know how the Word pierces a man? Or when and where it pierces him? Or how and where and when it becomes a commandment? Or an impediment? Or an urge? Or a misgiving? Or how it combines with other words, spoken by others, in other times and in other places? What can we know? How are we to explain the simplest of things? Why does the bird chirp? And why does the lion roar? Why does the odourless, bitter-tasting leaf of the wild tree grow, and why are just so many leaves needed, not one more nor less? A man! One man, in a little village ... But maybe there are others? There have to be others! Maybe there are even five men in five little villages? Maybe there are even ten men in one little village? The eyes of the Maggid began to shine ... 'Abraham said ... Maybe ten good men will be found therein. And the Lord said: I will not destroy the city for ten good men.' And if there are ten men to listen, have I the right to be silent? If there are ten men who need a good word, guidance, a story, whether they know it or not, have I the right to be silent? Yes, how many are there who are in need of this without knowing it, like the child who does not know that he needs a good up-bringing and education? What if I, Yaakov Maggid, was sent to tell people something that others cannot say? Have I then the right to abandon everything and flee? To flee from myself? The wandering preacher all of a sudden burst into bitter laughter. Should I open my own grocer's shop and sell cooking oil, and maize flour, and salt both ground and by the block? Should I do a thing I am not made for? Is it not against nature, against God's Creation? What if the birds all of a sudden began to roar and the lions to chirp?

Yaakov Maggid's whole body began to tremble. His eyes blazed. His face grew more and more pallid, more and more haggard, and the strands of his sparse black beard began to twitch violently. He opened the book in front of him and began to read, in a fever.

The next day, the Sabbath, the morning prayer was recited in monotonous voices and there was an atmosphere of gloom in the synagogue named Tiferet Israel, which is to say, the Splendour of Israel. There was gloom because the congregation found it hard to reconcile themselves to the thought that Reb Yaakov Maggid, the disciple of the great Baal Shem Tov, the wonderful preacher and storyteller, was among them but would not speak between prayers that morning, and that he would not tell his stories that evening at the *shaleshides* in the synagogue. Some even saw it as a bad omen, an omen of wrath and punishment, without their knowing why.

The prayer was recited amid gloom and desolation. But after the reading of the *pericope* from the Torah scrolls, and before the commencement of the *mussaf*, the additional Sab-bath prayer, no little was the surprise and the joy of the congregation when they saw Reb Yaakov Maggid mount the pulpit with determined steps before beating the bookrest thrice with his palm and beginning:

'Did you hear this week's *pericope* from the Book of Genesis about how Abraham stood before the Lord, with his face turned to Sodom, and asked him, "Wilt Thou also destroy the righteous with the wicked?" After which, Abraham said, "Oh let not the Lord be angry, and I will speak yet but this once: Peradventure ten shall be found there." And the Lord said, "I will not destroy it for ten's sake."'

The Maggid suddenly raised his voice, speaking in anger and grief:

'But they were not to be found! Ten good men were not to be found!'

Yaakov Maggid broke off. A heavy silence fell within the synagogue. Then the preacher's voice thundered:

'Then the Lord rained upon Sodom and Gomorrah fire and brimstone. And he overthrew those cities, and all the inhabitants of the cities, and that which grew in the ground.'

The congregation sat stock still, their heads bowed, frightened and humiliated. Yaakov Maggid paused for a long moment, as if letting the dense silence rarefy. Then he continued in a voice softened by gentleness:

'This is why I say unto you: We do not know, we cannot know how many of the ten are missing. Perhaps one is missing. Only one! This is why each of us must strive to be that one who is missing. The one who can bring salvation.'

During his sermon, Yaakov Maggid searched the faces in the congregation for that of the grey man with the grey eyebrows and the grey hat and the grey caftan, as if caked by the dust of every road. With his eyes he searched every corner of the synagogue, but he could not see him. Maybe he had gone to a different synagogue, thought Yaakov Maggid. Or maybe he was there, but had shaken off the dust and now looked like any other face in the congregation?

The Silver Pocket Watch

Rabbi Nachman was sitting on the bench at his table of un-polished pine planks, absorbed in an old book, seeking new meanings for the ancient sacrifice of the Pesach lamb, for the bread baked in the sun from dough that has not had time to leaven—after centuries of bondage, emancipation had arrived too quickly—and for the bitter herb that even in good times must recall the hard times of bondage.

It was a hot spring day. The door and windows of the room were open wide. And there was silence. Deep silence. All of a sudden, happening to lift his eyes from the book, he saw a figure, dark against the bright sunbeams. Screwing up his eyes, he saw that it was a tall thin man with a matted white beard framing a pale face with prominent cheekbones; the man's forehead was high, bulging, his clear blue eyes were sunken in their sockets; a long bluish weatherworn caftan hung like an altar cloth from his thin body; and he held a long, knotty staff of oak.

The rabbi had not heard the man's footsteps as he ap-proached. He had heard nothing. And now the man now stood in the doorway, without saying a word. It was a wanderer, who probably had not dared interrupt him as he read. But on seeing the rabbi looking at him, the stranger spoke in a soft voice:

'I come from afar and I still have a long way to go, Rabbi Nachman. And on the eve of Pesach, I find myself without any money to buy unleavened bread, meat, wine, bitter herb ...'

So that was it: he was a beggar caught out late on the road. Late, indeed, thought Rabbi Nachman, since at that hour every other wanderer had taken shelter under a roof or was at home with his family, if he had a home and family, or in a synagogue, waiting to be invited to another's home to partake in the *Seyder*, the Pesach evening meal.

But here was a wayfarer, waiting in his doorway. What could he give that wandering beggar, when he didn't have two pennies to rub together? There was never money in the rabbi's house overnight, since what he received in the daytime, he shared among the poor before the evening prayer.

At a loss, Rabbi Nachman began rummaging in the drawer of his table, in his cupboard, under his bench, in the hope of finding a stray penny to give the wanderer as alms. But, of course, he didn't find a single penny. Only in the houses of the wealthy do you find pennies forgotten in drawers or which have rolled into corners. The rabbi fretted as to what he should do. He could hardly let this wayfarer leave his house empty-handed, on the eve of Pesach of all times.

All of a sudden, he remembered something. From his waistcoat pocket he took his watch and gave it to the wayfarer with the white beard. He might still have time to sell it and buy what he needed for the feast day.

The man thanked him and left without a sound, the same as he had arrived.

A few minutes later, the rabbi's wife entered the room.

'What time is it, Nachman? I think it's time to bake the *chametz*!'

'I don't have a watch any more, Batya,' replied the rabbi. 'A wandering beggar came here and I gave him it so that he could buy what he needed for Pesach. I couldn't let him leave empty-handed.'

For a long moment, the rabbi's wife was speechless with amazement. But when she found her voice again, she yelled in a fury:

'What are you talking about, husband? I saw no wayfarer enter or leave the house.'

'If you didn't see him, it doesn't mean he wasn't here,' said the rabbi gently.

'But how could you give away that watch, for goodness' sake? Have you forgotten it was a wedding present from my father, may he rest in peace? Do you know how expensive that watch was? My father, Moise the sandal maker, blessed be his memory, toiled till he was bent double, he scrimped and saved for years so that he could give his learned son-in-law Nachman that expensive solid silver pocket watch, handmade by a famous silversmith ...'

'You're right, woman,' stammered the rabbi, as if waking from a dream. 'I forgot it was such an expensive watch ... I'll run after him, maybe I'll catch him. He can't have gone far.'

And Rabbi Nachman put on his wide-brimmed black hat and his caftan, took his knotted walking stick, and hurried out of the house to catch the stranger.

Not half an hour passed before Rabbi Nachman returned, his face radiant.

'Well, did you find him?' asked Batya from the doorway.

'Yes, wife, he hadn't gone far.'

'And where is the watch?'

'What watch?' the rabbi asked in amazement.

'Didn't you run after him to get back the silver pocket watch, husband?'

'What are you thinking, Batya? That I could ask for it back when I'd already given it to him? I ran after him to tell him what you told me, that it's an expensive watch, made by a famous silversmith, so that he would know not to be swindled when he sold it.'

The rabbi's wife wanted to scream, to scold him, but her voice caught in her throat. All she could do was run to the kitchen and weep there, muffling her sobs, without anybody else seeing her. For it wasn't fitting that the rabbi's wife should be seen weeping on the eve of the feast of joy at the liberation from bondage.

And the evening of the *Seyder* arrived, the meal to celebrate Pesach. The candles burned merrily in the brass candlesticks. The table was laid with a white cloth, glasses, enamelled clay crockery; the cheap tin cutlery shone bright and clean. Rabbi Nachman, in his white caftan, sat at the head of the table, on a bench, resting on pillows like a king; to his right sat his wife Batya, wearing a headscarf of white lace, straight-backed, as dignified and solemn as a true queen of the evening; then their daughters, daughters-in-law, and granddaughters, each in order of age; to the rabbi's left sat their sons, sons-in-law, and grandsons, each in order of age, and among them, the few wayfaring guests whom the holiday had found in the village.

In a loud, singsong voice, the rabbi began with the verse that opened the Haggadah, from the old book that recounted the miracle of the Exodus from Mizraim: 'This is the poor bread,' he began, pointing at the unleavened bread on the table in front of him, 'this is the poor bread that our parents ate in the land of Mizraim! Let all those who hunger come and eat! Let all those who are needy eat their fill!' Reaching this point, Rabbi Nachman felt the urge to make a pause, not even he knew why, and lifting his eyes from the book, he saw on the threshold of the open door the tall thin figure of the wayfarer with the tangled white beard, the clear blue eyes sunken in their sockets, the long weather-beaten bluish caftan. He stood there in the doorway, framed by the silver beams of moonlight from outside. Nobody had heard his footsteps, but the stranger stood there, waiting.

'He has returned? But why?' wondered Rabbi Nachman. 'He had time enough to be far away by now, he could have reached the seventh village from here.' He said none of this aloud, for one doesn't ask a guest on one's threshold, 'Why have you come?' The rabbi made a sign for the stranger to be seated at the table. No matter how crowded the table, there was always room for a newly arrived wayfarer. The rabbi filled to the brim a glass of wine, which was then carefully passed from hand to hand from the rabbi's end of the table to the end where the newcomer had taken his seat. And they all sang, and they ate, and they drank of what the Lord Above had provided .

During the meal, Rabbi Nachman noticed that the stranger with the tangled white beard did not touch the glass of wine in front of him, even though it was more than a custom to do so, it was almost a *mitzva*, a commandment, to drink four glasses, or at least more than half of four glasses. It struck him as odd, but he said nothing.

Then, when they reached the fourth glass, Rabbi Nachman, according to the ancient custom, poured a large glass of wine, which he placed in the middle of the table: the glass for Eliyahu HaNavi, Elijah the prophet.

And the songs and the stories continued until late into the night. The children, the little grandsons and granddaughters, fell asleep, and Batya, the rabbi's wife, dozed off, and then the guests departed to their homes in the village.

At the table remained only the rabbi, murmuring psalms, and his dozing wife. Outside, dawn light began to glimmer.

All of a sudden, on the threshold of the wide-open door, the warden from the synagogue and a few members of the congregation appeared and said:

'Rabbi, it's time for the morning prayer!'

By reflex, Rabbi Nachman slipped his hand inside his waistcoat pocket and brought forth his watch. He looked at the hands:

'Yes, you're right! It's time for the morning prayer!'

And then he exchanged startled glances with his wife Batya. The watch! The solid silver pocket watch, handmade by a famous craftsman! How had it found its way back inside his pocket?

They looked at the place at the end of the table where the stranger had sat. It was empty. The cup of wine that had stood before him remained untouched.

But the large cup for the Prophet Eliyahu in the middle of the table was empty.

The Good Oil

To Rabbi Yaakov Israel Davidovits, with gratitude

Along a country road down from the Carpathian Mountains came a coach carrying sacks of mail and passengers to Vienna, the capital of the empire. It was sometimes called the 'salt road', since heavy carts drawn by strong oxen, loaded with blocks and sheets of salt from the imperial mines in Maramuresch, also travelled along it on their way to the capital. Salt was worth a fortune: When he wanted to send a priceless gift to another crowned head of Europe, the Emperor of Austria and King of Hungary, Bohemia, Moravia, Bosnia, Herzegovina, et cetera, et cetera, would send him a few sheets of salt, as white as marble, sawed from the mines of Bredenbad, Rohnen or Slatina.

On that particular hot day, one summer at the end of the eighteenth century, among the passengers of that mail coach, who were wilting from the heat and being jolted up and down by the wheel springs, was to be found Professor Johann-Josef Moellin, Dr Med. Univ., that is, Doctor Medicinae Universalis. The professor was on his way home to Vienna. 'I was given every explanation, but still it is inexplicable to me,' he said to himself, with a soft laugh. 'Yes, the rabbi explained everything to me, he spoke to me with an open heart, but even so, here I am returning home as ignorant as I was when I first arrived.'

From those sub-Carpathian climes; from Maramuresch, famed for the purity of its salt and for its forests of oak and fir, where royal hunting parties came to chase the native aurochs, bears and boars; from that wild and picturesque region a strange rumour had reached as far as Vienna, a rumour that grew more and more insistent, concerning the miraculous cures supposed to be performed by a rabbi named Moishe-Leib Sassower. It was said that the sick from villages and hamlets on both sides of the Carpathians came to that rabbi, that he caused the crippled to throw away their crutches, the blind to see again, and the deaf to hear again. To the depressed he restored the will to live, he made mute children bawl and quieted children who bawled too much. In a word, veritable miracles! On hearing this, certain scientists, professors of the ancient and prestigious Faculty of Medicine at the Imperial University of Vienna, waved their hands in scorn, or shrugged their shoulders in indifference, uttering, 'witchcraft' or 'the superstitions of primitive folk'. Some even used such words as 'trickery', 'charlatanism', and similar terms.

Professor Johann-Josef Moellin was descended from an old family of rabbis, scholars, and physicians from Mainz, which during the pogroms of the dark times had settled in Vienna. He respected his family traditions and attended synagogue twice a year, on Rosh Hashanah and Yom Kippur, that is, at New Year and on the Day of Atonement, taking his place among the congregation like any other devout Jew. In the synagogue, like any other devout Jew, he went to the pulpit to receive the blessing in front of the unfurled sacred scrolls when he heard his name called out, 'Yaamod'—Rise—'Reb Johannan-Josef ben Nathan.' Professor Johann-Josef Moellin would never have employed the word 'witchcraft' in connection with a rabbi, and God forbid that he employ any other deprecatory term. But still it would have been a long stretch for him to believe in wonders and miracles, even if they were performed by rabbis; it would have meant him taking a very long road ... a road he could not travel.

Professor Moellin did not believe in miracles, but he did believe in medicinal herbs and roots, and the natural healing powers that inhered therein. Powers that ought to be discovered and put to use. And as the author of *Heilkraft der Heilkräuter* (The Healing Power of Medicinal Herbs), a book greatly admired in scientific circles, and which had even become something of a reference work in the field, Professor Moellin therefore found scientific curiosity was awakened in his mind, and he asked himself: 'How does this Rabbi of Sassow heal people, if indeed he does heal them?' This curiosity of his went hand in hand with the scepticism of the scientist. 'What treatments does he employ? What medicaments does he prescribe? Perhaps he knows of healing herbs and roots either not yet known to science or else forgotten and neglected.' The professor was all too aware of how many gaps his famous work contained and of how small and insufficient was his seven-hundred-page tome in comparison with the vastness of the subject.

It was then that he decided to spend a part of his summer holiday conducting an investigation in the field. He therefore packed a case and boarded the mail coach from Vienna to Lemberg, and thence by cart to Sassow.

On arriving, he realised that it would be better not to reveal his true identity. In that region, or rather in that world wholly different to the one in which he himself lived, where men never cut their beards and wore caftans and round black hats, or homespun peasant garb and peaked felt hats or pointed sheepskin caps, in that ancestral world, a gentleman in German clothes, with a short, neatly trimmed beard, a university professor of medicine from Vienna, might disturb the normal course of life. His presence might arouse suspicion, reticence; folk would not be open, they would not speak freely and unselfcon-sciously in his presence. Therefore, he decided to spend his time there incognito. He took a room in the only inn in the village, which was kept by a Jew, and presented himself as a timber merchant from Vienna, there to view some parcels of forest land in those Carpathian climes.

In the evening, he spoke with Reb Peisah, the innkeeper, who was in fact part innkeeper, part ploughman, and Reizel, his wife, who kept house, milked the cows, and provided the guests with fresh milk. He spoke with folk from the village, Jews and Orthodox Christians alike, who came to drink a tot of slivovitz or two at the inn, and with the men, women and children who came from afar to see Rabbi Moishe-Leib Sassower. All of them strongly confirmed the rumour that had reached Vienna. Yes, the good and wise rabbi really did heal the sick. Yes, yes, he restored sight to the blind. And hearing to the deaf ... Yes, yes, yes, he caused the lame to throw away their crutches ... And so on, and so on ... The folk told him all this with a conviction, a sincerity, an enthusiasm so great that it was almost impossible not to grant credence to their words. Professor Moellin was intrigued. He was unable to sleep the whole night. And the next morning, he complained to the innkeeper of pains in his back and fetched himself to the yard of the Rabbi from Sassow.

Here, his astonishment reached its height. The sick—the professor was a renowned diagnostician and more often than not he could determine a man's ailment merely by looking at him from a distance—people who were genuinely sick, entered the rabbi's house and a short while later, they came out again, their faces radiant and full of hope. A man bent double with stomach cramps came back out as straight as a candle, soothed, holding a small bottle of oily yellow liquid, of which the rabbi had prescribed he take a teaspoon daily. A woman with a babe in arms suffering from a convulsive fever came back out with it peacefully sleeping, a smile on its face. And the mother held a small bottle of the same yellow medicament. A blind man led by a small boy went in to see the rabbi and an hour later he came out blinking, holding a bottle of the same yellow liquid, to anoint his eyes with it twice a day. 'How strange,' thought the professor. 'All the patients, regardless of their ailment, are given the same medicine.' He realised before investigating any further, he would have to get hold of a bottle of that miraculous panacea, which was good for every ailment. He tried to buy a bottle from a sick man, then from another, and another still he offered a handsome sum for at least part of his bottle's contents, but none of them would part with the medicine they had received from the rabbi, not even a single drop. Given this was the case, driven by scientific curiosity, in his desire to obtain a bottle of the mysterious liquid, whatever the price, the professor decided to have a word in secret with the gabbai, the rabbi's assistant. The name of the assistant was Reb Nachman and it was he who ushered the people in to see the rabbi. Seizing a suitable moment, the professor drew him aside and asked for a bottle of medicine, offering him the sum of twenty silver crowns. It was in fact an attempt at bribery, and the professor was mortified and embarrassed at what he was doing; never in his entire life had Professor Johann-Josef Moellin done such a thing. But for the sake of science, he said to himself, deeds more blameworthy had probably been done. He expected the gabbai to turn down his offer in indignation, to be furious, even to tell him to leave at once the crowded waiting room of the rabbi's house. But to his surprise, none of this came to pass. On the contrary, Reb Nachman, a tall, thin man, listened to him carefully and thought for a few moments, scratching his sparse, straggly red beard with bony fingers all the while. After which, as if nothing untoward had happened, he told him to come the next day; in the meantime, he would do everything he could.

The next day, also in secret, the gabbai handed the professor a bottle of the yellow liquid, as requested, and received the sum of twenty silver crowns in return.

Professor Moellin immediately sent the bottle to Vienna by the first mail coach, along with a letter to his colleague, Professor Heinz-Christian von Kienzle, the head of the University's medical laboratory. He feverishly awaited the results. What was in the bottle? What was the chemical composition of the yellow liquid?

A few days later, the bottle was sent back to him, along with a few ironical, or so it seemed to Professor Moellin, lines in Latin, penned by his colleague, Professor von Kienzle. The bottle contained *Oleum helianthi*. Sunflower oil. Nothing more, nothing less.

Professor Moellin was furious. He had thought to bribe Reb Nachman, but the rabbi's gabbai had bamboozled him. He had led him by the nose, like a child. There was nothing else for it: he would endeavour to buy a bottle or at least part of its contents directly from a patient, whatever the cost. He would have to try and try again until he succeeded.

He took aside the next patient that came out from the rabbi's house and, to his amazement, the man agreed to sell him his bottle of oil. He tried again with the next patient and the same thing happened: He was only too glad to sell him the little bottle of yellow medicine. The professor no longer knew what to believe: whereas before, none had wanted to speak to him, none would hear of selling him a bottle or so much as a drop, now they were all too eager to hand over a whole bottle, for a few kreutzers, or even free of charge: Strange! But too many strange things had happened during his holiday for him to stop to wonder about them. Professor Moellin therefore bought half a dozen bottles from various patients and sent them all to the laboratory in Vienna, post haste. A few days later, they were sent back to him. On each bottle was pasted a label in Latin: *Oleum helianthi* ... Sunflower oil ... sunflower oil ... sunflower oil ... He felt as if he were losing his mind, nothing less! And enclosed was also a note from Professor Heinz-Christian von Kienzle, who sent Professor Moellin his warmest greetings and best wishes of success; Professor Moellin could just picture his colleague's chubby, ironical face!

There was nothing else for it except to be admitted to the Rabbi of Sassow himself and speak to him in person. The next morning, he asked Reb Nachman the gabbai to be taken in to the rabbi. Rabbi Moishe-Leib Sassower stood up from his table to greet him. He was a tall, dignified man, with a broad-brimmed black felt hat and a long black silk caftan. He had a smiling face, large green eyes, and a square-cut chestnut beard.

'*Baruch haba*! Welcome, Reb Johannan-Josef ben Nathan Moo-lin!'

'What? You know me, Rabbi?' asked the professor in amazement, both flattered and somehow embarrassed that his disguise had been exposed.

'Your fame precedes you, Professor! And besides, how could we not know the great-grandson of Rabbi Jacob ben Moishe Moellin of Mainz, whom we honour with the shortened name Maharil, that is, Morenu ha-Rav Jacob ha-Levi, the author of the *Book of Our Observances*, the preserver of our ancient songs. I have been expecting you ever since the day you arrived in Sassow.'

Professor Moellin fell silent in shame. The rabbi went on:

'When my gabbai Reb Nachman asked me whether he should give you the bottle of oil that you asked of him in a rather roundabout way, I told him to do so. And when he asked me whether he should take the twenty silver crowns, I told him to do so. For we have here many poor people in need of alms. But the sum of money will be restored to you ... *Shallah* *lahmeka al-hammayim*: Cast thy bread upon the waters, for you shall find it after many days* ... so said our wise men, blessed be their memory! That day, Chaim-Leizer, the carter, came to me, with his wife Yente, who was sick. I was unable to help her, so I sent them to Vienna to see Professor Moellin ... To you I sent them. And I placed in Chaim-Leizer's hand the twenty silver crowns to pay you with. Take them! The money is yours by right, for the light that the Lord Above kindled in your mind!'

The Rabbi of Sassow fell silent for a while, then continued:

'In any event, Chaim-Leizer, our carter, knows the road well: with his ox cart he takes blocks and sheets of salt from the mines of Bredenbad, Slatina and Rohnen to Vienna. He also takes timber from these forests to Vienna. A hardworking man, a good carter, is Chaim-Leizer. Before the holidays, he places planks crosswise in his cart for the congregation to sit on and takes them to the houses of the rabbis. And his wife Yente, *eshet chayil*, a virtuous woman, minds the house, the five children. I could not find the cure for her pain, but maybe you will be able ...'

The Rabbi of Sassow fell silent once more. For a few moments he sat deep in thought, staring darkly in front of him. Finally, he came to himself and continued with a smile:

'Once you received the bottle of oil from the hand of Reb Nachman, my assistant, I knew that you would doubt ... After all, the task of you men of science is to doubt, to investigate, to seek life's meanings ... So, I told the people that if anybody should ask them for their bottle of oil, if anybody wished to buy it, then they should sell it without fear, since it would all be to the good.'

Here, Professor Johann-Josef Moellin regained his voice and blurted:

*   Ecclesiastes, 11:1.

'But in the name of God, good and wise Rabbi, I see that you know the oil is useless, so why do you give it to the sick?'

The rabbi smiled:

'Lest the people think that what I do is witchcraft, God forbid! Or that I am the one who cures ailments, that I am the one who restores their health! Let them not descend to *Avodah zarah*, to the worship of strange gods, the Lord Above forbid! Let them not worship gods fashioned by the hands of men, let them not make gods of other men of flesh and blood like they are …'

'No doubt about it, I was given every explanation, but still it is inexplicable to me …' Professor Johann-Josef Moellin said to himself that hot summer day, in the mail coach on his way back to Vienna from Sassow, via Lemberg. The rabbi explained everything to me, he spoke with an open heart, and here I am on my way home, just as ignorant as before.'

And the professor gave a soft laugh, lest he rouse the other passengers from their torpor.

The day after his arrival in Vienna, when the professor entered his office, in his waiting room he found a Jew with a tangled beard and a woman wrapped in a faded brown shawl.

'You must be Chaim-Leizer, the carter,' said the professor, 'and this must be Yente, your wife.'

'Yes, that's us,' said Chaim-Leizer, overjoyed.

And he gazed at the professor, as if at a miracle-working rabbi …

The Seyder Evenings
of Long Ago

The Seyder evenings of long ago, when I was a young man, or rather a lad, still linger in my memory.

Every year, for the Pesach holidays, the whole family, young and old, gathered in the small town of V. at the house of my grandfather, Reb Moishe. The days before the holidays might find family members anywhere at all, scattered in every direction by the winds of necessity, away on business, carrying suitcases both visible and invisible, the latter packed with worries and cares, but also the occasional joy. But wherever they might be, once a year they set off on the pilgrimage with their wives and children, drawn by the lively peace and radiant homeliness of the low old house with its small windows and thick, weathered beams, where dwelled the family elder: Grandfather.

During those days, a lively peace did indeed reign. It was as if the house floated, spinning in the air like a top. All day long, we went from room to room, we played, we debated and argued, we chattered endlessly. Sisters and daughters-in-law bickered in the kitchen as they cooked and then made peace with each other at the dinner table. We talked and boasted and told stories, each of us fetching on the winged words of our animated talk something of the atmosphere of the places where we lived the rest of the year: events major and minor, joys and sorrows, the springs and autumns of the little towns and villages where our lives flowed along, taking their imperceptible course. And as our stories coloured the grey months that had passed, the headily pleasant aroma of *khremslakh* frying in the pans flooded the house.

But during those boisterous days, in one room of the house alone silence always reigned. A deep, respectful silence. Here, everything was tidy; not one item was out of place. Amid that ancestral tranquillity, it was as if silence lay slumbering on the soft felt rugs. This was Grandfather's room, far from the kitchen, far from the hubbub, which came to an abrupt end at his thick timeworn door, as if sliced off by a saw.

Only with timidity and respectful fear did we dare cross the threshold of that room. Within, it was as if the beams of the ceiling were heavier and darker with the passage of years, as if the whitewashed walls were smokier in the corners. His beard as white as snow, Grandfather would be sitting in a high-backed chair, deep in a large book. Among the tall cupboards crammed with yet other books, he sat at a desk piled with papers, files, thick address books, and in one corner there was a press for duplicating letters, as was fitting for a leading merchant of that little town, the father of many children, a man with a host of grandchildren scattered throughout the world.

Today, so many years later, I no longer have any reason to pass over in silence the fact that the beauty and joy of those evenings in that little town of long ago were due not only to the feast that filled the goblets with old wine, as if pouring them with drops from the sea across which our legendary ancestors passed dry shod. There was another reason too:

Esterl was a little girl with eyes as green as fresh grass, hair plaited in two pigtails tied with red silk ribbons, and a flowery apron, which she always wore over her dress. She was my cousin, the daughter of an aunt who every year made the pilgrimage to see my grandfather, her father.

Many a time we sat on the bench under the old walnut tree in the garden, which like any other nocturnal, philosophical walnut tree, was witness to such stirrings of first love. We would sit in silence looking at the moon, waiting for the falling stars that trailed behind them our unspoken words.

And none of this would have been at all blameworthy had Grandmother not noticed it. But she saw us sitting idly there, on that enchanted bench, she made a cross face, called for Esterl in a stern voice, scolded her for staying out so late, and sent her to bed. To me she said not a word.

That night, I couldn't sleep for shame and indignation. I was indignant on Esterl's behalf, on behalf of her good name, and I was ashamed on account of Grandmother, lest she think me a *khamer-eyzl*, a lecher … a skirt-chaser … Good God!

But it was with a far more malicious eye than Grandmother's that another cousin, my uncle's son, fat Yankel, viewed my romance with Esterl. It was easy to understand why.

Yankel was eager to get ahead, to stand out, to show the whole family who had arrived there on pilgrimage what a well-bred boy he was, how well-behaved, how obedient, how diligent at school. And he was always boasting about himself to Grandfather and Grandmother when Esterl happened to be present.

Those airs he put on greatly bothered me, precisely because I knew he wasn't better-behaved than I, he wasn't more diligent at school than I, he didn't know more than I, and in fact after half a page of *Gemara* the letters would start dancing around in front of his eyes and he would say he had to give up.

Even today, tears come to my eyes when I remember those Seyder evenings of long ago.

At head of the long table, its cloth starched a lambent white, Grandfather sat resting on soft cushions. His face radiant, his beard seemingly bigger and whiter than ever, he wore his immaculately white *kittel*. To his left sat Grandmother, her face thin and as wrinkled as a raisin, small beneath her large white silk headscarf, and next to her, the daughters, daughters-in-law, granddaughters, each in order of age. To the right of Grandfather sat his first-born son, himself the possessor of a round grey beard, and next to him the other sons, then the sons-in-law and the grandsons, each in order of age. And after them, timid and respectful, the poor wayfarers took their places at the table, those whom the evening of the Seyder, the paschal supper, had found travelling through that little town. Their faces bore the wrinkles of long wandering and their sad eyes seemed fixed on the homes they had left behind. But even the faces of the wayfarers would soon light up ...

For everything then became merry and lively. Every eye lit up as festively as the candles in the sculpted silver candlesticks.

The smallest grandson, whose nose barely came as high as the table top, began to recite the Seyder, that is, the order of the meal, in a reedy voice made shriller by nervousness:

'Kadesh.'

Our glasses were filled and the *kidesh*, or blessing, was made.

'Urchatz.'

We washed our hands and the *al netilat yadayim* prayer was recited to us.

Grandfather and all the adults listened and did precisely as indicated.

At intervals, I cast a glance across the table at Esterl, at my little queen, the one I myself had crowned, and I wracked my mind with the question: What was she thinking when our eyes met across the boundary we were forbidden to cross?

All of a sudden, I felt a deep silence fall and every eye turned toward me ... toward me, who had strayed and not only crossed the boundary, but had done so, Good God! in full view of the whole family.

I turned red to the very tip of my nose.

But it was not what I thought. It was merely that as eldest of the grandsons my turn had come to recite the questions, and all those seated at the table, but especially my parents, who were secretly proud of my knowledge, were waiting for me to begin by saying, 'Ma nishtanah.'

When I came to my senses and was about to recite the first question, all of a sudden, from two chairs down the table, there came a loud, triumphant voice:

'Mah nishtanah, ha-laylah ha-zeh mi-kol ha-leylot?' (What has changed, on this night of all other nights?)

It was the voice of fat Yankel, my uncle's son. He had blurted out the question, in a loud voice, he had taken my question away from me, usurped my rights as the first-born grandson.

The next day, I was ashamed in front of them all, in front of my parents, whom I had obviously disappointed, but above all in front of Esterl. I was ashamed to set eyes on her. I avoided the places where I had the slightest suspicion she might be found.

But when the sun set and the shadows slipped inside the house, into the corners of the rooms, and into the garden beneath the trees, I was very sad and felt dreadfully alone. Something drew me to the old walnut tree in the garden, to sit on the old bench, to hide myself in its shadow.

I don't know how long I sat like that on the bench, caught in the spell of evenings past, when I felt warm hands covering my eyes, as if in a game of 'guess who?'

When I opened my eyes, Esterl had vanished into the dark, but long afterward her light footfalls lingered in my ears like a whispered song.

At that evening's Seyder, the second, I didn't even want to ask the four questions, in keeping with the custom. Fat Yankel asked them again, in a voice brimming with satisfaction, the voice of the victor in battle:

'*Mah nishtanah, ha-laylah ha-zeh mi-kol ha-leylot?*'

Of all other evenings and all other years?

I was happy. I was no longer angry that he had usurped me and taken my questions away from me. For every question had now found its answer.

A Monday of Fasting
and Prayer

In Ostrava, a little town in the land of Moravia, there once lived a very rich man. Herr Josef Mehrisch was his name. He owned watermills and windmills, and he sent wheat, maize, flour, and bran for cattle feed to all four corners of the empire, to Austria and Hungary, to Bohemia and Moravia, to Bosnia and Herzegovina.

This rich man, His Lordship Herr Mehrisch, lived in a beautiful big house in the middle of gardens and parkland with his wife, Sarah-Bella—in the village of Dolina, where she grew up in a family of wealthy tenant farmers, she had been known as Sura-Beile—and their only daughter, Elisheva, a beautiful girl, quite tall, svelte, with silky black hair, and dark eyes that glowed like coals.

And this gentleman, Josef Mehrisch, was wealthy and held in high esteem; he was Commerzial-Rat and Geheimrat—Trade Adviser and Privy Counsellor—to the Emperor in Vienna, and also the head of his community in the little town of Ostrava. And he was a good man, a generous man; he kept his own synagogue with a minyan of ten scholars, who each received from him his *lechem chok*, the food needful to him, as is written in the Proverbs of Solomon, which is to say, roof and board, a modest living, so that they might fully dedicate themselves to the study of the Holy Books and the preservation of the Law.

But what was the use of wealth and honours if his beautiful and only daughter, having reached the age of seventeen, when suitors ought to have been arriving, fell gravely ill and was confined to her bed? Her face had become pale and drawn, her radiant dark eyes sank ever deeper in their sockets and grew ever greyer, like coals that have died and are caked in ash.

And how many doctors examined her! The most eminent and renowned healers of the Empire came to her bedside. And how many cures they tried! But to no avail. With each passing day, the girl faded. Finally, all the eminent physicians raised their hands in hopeless defeat.

And when he saw that all the doctors and all the cures they prescribed were to no avail and that his daughter, the light of his eyes, was fading with each passing day, Josef Mehrisch convened his minyan of ten wise and learned rabbis in his synagogue and said to them:

'All my hope resides in you, great and wise rabbis, preservers of the Law and scholars of our Holy Books. I ask you to keep a day of fasting and prayer. Pray to the Lord Above, who alone can be of help, who alone can have mercy on me and Sura-Beile my wife and restore to us our daughter …'

And to each of the wise and pious rabbis he gave a solid gold piece as *tzedakah*, a charitable donation.

And the minyan of rabbis decided that the following day, which was a Monday, would be a day of fasting and prayer, and of imploration for the health of their great benefactor's daughter.

One of the ten scholars and wise rabbis was the learned Rabbi Itzhak of Drohobycz, who at that time lived in the little town of Ostrava in Moravia and kept the Law and studied the Holy Books in the synagogue of the great *naggid* Josef Mehrisch, and who had his *lechem chok*, that is, a roof over his head and a modest, honest living, from the generous hands of that man.

And like the other nine scholars, Rabbi Itzhak of Drohobycz took the heavy gold coin, put it in the pocket of his black caftan, and went home.

The Rabbi of Drohobycz shut himself up in his little room, stretched out on his cot, and the whole evening he spoke not a word, lit not a candle; he did not sit down at the table to study, but merely lay there on the cot, deep in thought. Esther-Rachel, his wife, knew him well, and when he was deep in thought like that, she did not enter his room, she did not call on him to do any chores around the house, she did not announce the arrival of any member of the congregation to see him, but went about her business in the kitchen and around the house, and finally went to bed. The Rabbi of Drohobycz lay there on the cot, and he thought and he thought. He wracked his mind until midnight, when he finally fell asleep. After which he slept peacefully until the next morning.

The morning of the next day, the Monday set aside for the fast, Rabbi Itzikl, as folk nicknamed him, went into the kitchen, placed the gold piece on the table, and said to his wife Esther-Rachel:

'Go to the market, wife, and buy the best you can find, fish and meat, and the nicest, sweetest fruit. Buy white flour, for ring loaves and cake. Buy slivovitz and the best wine. Prepare a meal the way only you know how, Esther-Rachel, and let us eat and be merry.'

Esther-Rachel, the wife of the Rabbi of Drohobycz, was so astounded that it almost left her breathless. She couldn't understand where the gold piece had come from. Nor could she understand why, if they had a gold piece, they should spend it all in one day. They received their *lechem chok* from His Lordship Herr Josef, on which they lived modestly, from one day to the next, and if Rabbi Itzhak had received a gold piece from someone, wouldn't it be better to save it for a rainy day? Or to exchange it for silver crowns and to spend them sparingly, when needed? But she asked no questions; she said nothing. She knew her husband and she well knew that he wouldn't tell her anything more than that. So, she went to the market and did exactly as her husband had bidden her.

And she prepared a truly festive meal, the way only she knew how.

And that day, the rabbi said a short prayer and sat down at the table, with Esther-Rachel to his right, and began by drinking a tot of strong slivovitz, in which his wife joined him. Then he ate stuffed carp and soup, and chicken, ring loaf, cake, and compôte. And they drank good wine. The rabbi sang and Esther-Rachel sang along with him. And the rabbi took out his large blue sash and waved it in the air as he danced around the table. And Esther-Rachel grasped the other end of the sash and danced along with him. Then Rabbi Itzikl jumped up on the table and danced from one end to the other, and his wife joined him, dancing her heart out.

And so it was that on that very Monday of fasting, Rabbi Itzikl of Drohobycz and his wife laughed and sang and made merry, like children.

That same day, the other nine great rabbis, the wise and pious scholars, kept the fast, wracking their bodies, they recited prayers and implorations, they read psalms and other holy texts.

As the evening of that day fell, the pale face of Elisheva, the daughter of Herr Josef Mehrisch and Sarah-Bella, was imbued with a translucent rosy flush. She ran a slight fever and began to sweat. That night, she writhed in bed, muttered unintelligible words, and toward Tuesday morning, she awoke with a smile on her face. She drank some sweet tea and ate a slice of cake. Her appetite had returned. On Wednesday, she sat up in bed. On Thursday she was able to rise from her bed and take a walk in the beautiful grounds around the house.

Her parents, Herr Josef Mehrisch and Herrin Sarah-Bella, were overjoyed.

And in thanks to the Lord Above for his daughter's recovery, Herr Mehrisch decided to dedicate the *shaleshides*, the third meal of the Sabbath, to His pious servants here on earth.

And to the meal in his synagogue, he invited the ten learned rabbis and the congregation that regularly came there to pray.

But strange rumours had begun to circulate in Ostrava, that little town in Moravia. It was said that one of the ten rabbis had eaten on the day set aside for the fast. Yes, yes. But which one? Rabbi Itzhak of Drohobycz.

Impossible! Unbelievable! Rabbi Itzikl? That could not be ...

But nonetheless ...

The rumours persisted. And naturally they reached the ears of His Lordship Herr Josef Mehrisch in his palatial home surrounded by gardens and parks.

When he received the invitation to the meal of thanks, the third of the Sabbath, one of the nine scholars, who had fasted both willingly and in accordance with the law, was unable to refrain from pointing out to the synagogue trustee, none other than Herr Josef Mehrisch, that Rabbi Itzhak ought not to be invited to the meal, since he had 'already eaten'.

His Lordship Herr Josef was stunned. How could he have done such a thing? None other than Rabbi Itzhak of Drohobycz? And why had he done it? Why? He was both intrigued and indignant. And he didn't know what to do. Should he ask Rabbi Itzhak straight out whether he had eaten on the day set aside for the fast? And why had he eaten? Didn't a rabbi such as himself know what he was supposed to do? Was he the one to call him to account?

But maybe the whole rumour was untrue and the whole affair was nothing but a bad dream?

The hour of the *shaleshsides* to be held in Herr Josef Mehrisch's synagogue arrived. The evening of that Sabbath, a white damask cloth was laid on the large table at the back. On it were placed bottles of strong plum slivovitz, plaited loaves, stuffed carp ordered from the ponds outside Vienna, prunes, and walnuts. But nobody sang *zemirot* or one of the wordless hymns to be hummed at meals. A shadow hung over the table where the guests had sat down to that feast. Herr Josef Mehrisch, Trade Adviser and Privy Counsellor to the Emperor and head of the community, who sat at the head of the table, wanted to ask the question, even to demand a reckoning, but he could not find the words.

But Rabbi Itzhak sensed the question that hung in the air and asked it himself, speaking for all to hear:

'Why on the Monday set aside for the fast did the Rabbi of Drohobycz eat, drink and make merry?'

A profound silence abruptly descended inside the synagogue. Nobody dared so much as to take a sip of slivovitz or to carry on nibbling a walnut.

After a pause, Rabbi Itzhak went on:

'When I arrived home on Sunday evening, I lay down on the cot in my little room and I pondered, I wracked my brains, and I wondered what I should do. I fast so often that the Lord Above is accustomed to it and pays no attention to my fasts any more, I said to myself. Rabbi Itzhak is to spend another day fasting. So what? I thought and I thought, wracking my brains. I twisted and turned on the hard cot. All of a sudden, a thought struck me: This time I wouldn't fast, I wouldn't punish my body and soul with hunger and prayers. Instead, I would eat! Yes, yes! And not some ordinary, everyday meal. Rather a meal such as had never been witnessed in the house of the Rabbi of Drohobycz. Why else was it that the good Herr Josef, who gives us *lechem chok*, who provides our everyday bread, felt the urge to open wide his purse and give us a heavy gold coin? And I ate, and I drank, and I danced, and with my wife Esther-Rachel, I made merry.'

Rabbi Itzhak paused. The silence was absolute. It was as if the people no longer had mouths with which to speak, noses with which to breathe, but were all ears cocked to hear all.

In the meantime, the shadows of evening had seeped into every corner of the synagogue.

The Rabbi of Drohobycz went on:

'Up above, the whole *pamalia*, His entire heavenly retinue, crowded around to gaze at a particular spot down here on earth, to see what was going on in the house of Rabbi Itzikl.

'And then the question came:

'"What are you crowding around to look at down there?"

'"Rabbi Itzikl of Drohobycz, on a day set aside for fasting, is eating and drinking and making merry. Look at him dancing the *mitzve tanz*, hanging on one end of the sash, his wife Esther-Rachel on the other."

'And in heaven there erupted uncontrollable laughter and great joy filled all the heavenly *pamalia*.

'"And how did he come to have such a copious meal and to be able to make so merry?" boomed the question, although the answer was already known. He who asked the question knows all the answers already, but wishes merely to hear them spoken.

'"He received a rich gift, a gold coin, from the *naggid* Reb Josef. For his only daughter, the beautiful Elisheva, is very ill and needs a speedy cure. Look at Rabbi Itzikl, now he's dancing on the table!"'

Rabbi Itzhak of Drohobycz fell silent for a few moments. Then he continued:

'And there was great merriment in Heaven above. For up in Heaven there is always merriment and joy when there is joy and goodwill in a house of decent folk down here on Earth.'

The Rabbi of Drohobycz fell silent once more and said not another word.

By now there was darkness in the synagogue of Herr Josef Mehrisch. And silence. All that could be heard was the dull cracking of walnut shells and the munching of kernels along with crusts of plaited ring loaf.

At one end of the table, somebody began to hum a wordless melody. And gradually, all the others joined in, humming along with him.

Naturally, to this day it is unknown whether Elisheva, the only daughter of Herr Josef Mehrisch recovered thanks to the nine who fasted or thanks to Rabbi Itzhak of Drohobycz, who ate, drank and made merry.

Probably it will remain a mystery for all eternity.

But what does it matter? The fact is that suitors began arriving to woo the beautiful Elisheva and with the blessing of the Lord Above, she soon married her heart's chosen one. And she lived happily ever after, surrounded by her children and grandchildren, until advanced old age.

The Ascent.
Three Tales

1. THE COURT DOWN BELOW

Twenty-one rabbis and scholars set sail for the Land of Israel, where they intended to settle.

Among them were Rabbi Meir of Premishlan and Rabbi Nachman of Horodenke.

There couldn't have been two men whose natures were more unalike! Rabbi Meir of Premishlan was well-built and had a thick chestnut beard and large, piercing black eyes. He was hearty, impulsive, loud. He had a strong, vibrant voice, and he prayed loudly, talked and argued loudly, praised and scolded his congregation loudly. He was a man famed for both his wisdom and his irrepressible outbursts of joy or anger.

Rabbi Nachman of Horodenke, on the other hand, was thin and had a black, straggly beard and colourless eyes. It was as if he were timid and trying to hide. He was taciturn, pensive. His voice was soft and low, and he recited his prayers in a whisper, praised and scolded his congregation in a whisper, almost as if he were begging their forgiveness for praising or scolding them.

As it happened, the two rabbis were passengers aboard the same ship, along with another nineteen scholars of the Book, from the lands of Russia and the Ukraine, from the lands of the Poles, and from the lands of the Moldavians and Wallachians. They boarded that rather rickety wooden ship in the port of

Ismailia and, their souls overflowing with hope, they set sail for the Land of Israel.

It so fell out that taken together Rabbi Meir of Premishlan, Rabbi Nachman of Horodenke, and the other nineteen scholars made up a full court of twenty-one judges, or what is known as a Lesser Sanhedrin.

But after seven days of quiet sailing on the Black Sea, a terrifying storm suddenly blew up. The waves furiously lashed the rickety sides of the ship. Rabbi Meir of Premishlan and the nineteen wise men from the lands of Russia and the Ukraine, from the lands of the Poles, from the lands of the Moldavians and Wallachians, began to pray in loud voices. The voice of Rabbi Meir thundered above the voices of the others, even above the roar of the waves. But Rabbi Nachman sat apart in a corner of the hold, and he did not pray; he did not utter a word.

The storm paid no heed to the prayers of the twenty scholars. Nor to the silence of the Rabbi of Horodenke. The waves struck both sides of the ship with a fury, they lashed its rickety ribs. The black timbers creaked. The ship was about to be shattered into splinters. Rabbi Meir shouted and prayed, with the nineteen adding their voices in a chorus.

The ship was about to break up and plunge all twenty praying wise men and the ship's crew into the sea.

It was then that Rabbi Nachman of Horodenke lost his temper. He rose up in wrath and clenching his fists he brandished them at the sky; he shouted as he had never shouted in his entire life:

'We are on our way to Eretz Israel! Since you in the Court Up Above have decided to drown us, know then that we in the Court Down Below do not agree with your decision!'

The waves, which were about to engulf the ship and deal the death blow, suddenly froze, as if in amazement. Within moments, the waves withdrew, as if ashamed of the deed they were about to commit, and spread out calm and smooth over the face of the sea.

And the ship sailed on its way, over that calm sea, now as smooth as a mirror; it passed through the Bosporus and the Dardanelles and reached the port of Jaffa.

Thence, Rabbi Meir of Premishlan and the nineteen rabbinic scholars from Russia and the Ukraine, from Poland and the lands of Moldavia and Wallachia, made their way to Jerusalem, where Rabbi Meir founded a thriving, boisterous congregation and became famed throughout Israel and the lands of the diaspora for his noisy disputations and wise answers.

And Rabbi Nachman of Horodenke settled in the holy city of Tveria on the bank of the Kineret, where all trace of him was lost. Nothing was heard of him again, and nothing more is known of him. It is said that he lived his life modestly, hidden away among other anonymous Jews.

2. TO SHEPETOVKA AND BACK

Rabbi Zainvel of Shepetovka, after living for years in the Land of Israel, enduring hardships, living almost entirely on bread and water, dwelling in a ramshackle house next to the wall of Jerusalem, which had a single room whose roof leaked in winter when it rained and which was like a cauldron in summer, decided to return to Shepetovka in northern Ukraine to bring the rest of his family to Israel.

He had had enough of living by himself without his wife and three children. He wasn't able to send money home to Shepetovka from Jerusalem because he didn't really have any. In which case, why shouldn't they all live there together?

And Rabbi Zainvel of Shepetovka set off on his journey. And he reached the great city of Istanbul, which the Jews respectfully call Kushta. There he spent the night in an inn at the edge of the city. In the morning, as he was about to continue his journey, washing his face in a basin with a black metal bottom, he suddenly saw his reflection in the water. And he was shaken. His face was bony, haggard, the yellow skin stretched taut over protruding cheekbones. His eyes were dull, his beard sparse, untidy. There was no doubt about it, he couldn't arrive in Shepetovka looking like that, otherwise people would say it was true that Israel is the land that eats its inhabitants: *eretz ochelet yoshveha*. No, Rabbi Zainvel of Shepetovka could not lend the Holy Land such a repute.

And so, he remained in that inn at the edge of the city of Istanbul. He preached in the neighbourhood synagogue, he hired himself out to teach children, he ate his meals at the houses of his pupils and of the city's rich men. He stuffed himself with everything he could lay hands on. Seven months passed. Rabbi Zainvel looked at his reflection in the basin with the black metal bottom and said to himself it was time to continue his journey to Shepetovka.

When he arrived there, on seeing his ruddy cheeks, as bulbous as a full moon, his gleaming eyes, and his tidy beard, the folk greeted him joyfully and said:

'A good life you lead there, in the Land of Israel!'

And they were happy that there was some small corner of this world where life was good for the likes of them.

And the people greeted him respectfully and said:

'A good life you lead there, in Eretz Israel!'

'God be thanked,' replied the Rabbi of Shepetovka.

And he took his wife and three children and returned to Jerusalem, where he lived in poverty and honour until advanced old age.

3. THE PROTECTOR

Rabbi Avraham Beer was an enterprising young man. Tall, strong, with black hair, a square black beard, and black, lively eyes, he made a success of his Talmudic studies at the yeshiva and mindful of what the wise man said, namely, 'im ein qemah, ein Torah'—if there is no flour, that is, bread, there is no learning—he also learned a trade, that of a carpenter.

Having completed his studies, the young rabbi and carpenter therefore went before his teacher, Rabbi Mordechai of Chernobyl, and told him that he wanted to go to live and work and study in Eretz Israel, and asked him to provide him with protection for the journey, particularly the journey by sea, since he'd never before left dry land, and finally he asked him to bless him so that he would reach the Land of Israel safely.

The rabbi regarded him pensively for a while, since after all he was his favourite student, before saying:

'Very well, my son! Your protector will be waiting for you in the port at Odessa. So that you will arrive safely in Eretz Israel,' said the Rabbi of Chernobyl, before murmuring once more, 'In Eretz Israel ...'

The young Avraham Beer remained rooted to the spot in surprise. Never would he have expected such a thing, to have a personal protector waiting for him in the port at Odessa. Where would the Rabbi of Chernobyl find a protector for a member of his congregation when he travelled? Avraham Beer had expected the rabbi to give him a locket, an amulet, or a written prayer to protect him from harm, particularly during the journey by sea, of which he was rather afraid, as he had never before left dry land.

But if Rabbi Mordechai of Chernobyl said that a protector would be waiting for him in Odessa, he must know what he was talking about. He therefore thanked his rabbi and teacher warmly, bid him farewell, and early the next morning, he put a few items of clothing and some food in his bag and set off for Odessa by mail coach.

Arriving in the large port of Odessa, he looked right and left, but saw no protector.

He waited and waited on the dock, but nobody approached him. People were embarking. The brass bell on the deck of the ship was rung, calling the passengers aboard, but still no protector came.

If Rabbi Mordechai told me that I would arrive safely, I should board the boat, for unless I set off, I'll never arrive, reasoned Avraham Beer. And he stepped onto the narrow gangplank. He sensed footsteps behind him. Somebody was coming up the gangplank after him, another late-boarding traveller.

On deck, as the ship began to weigh anchor and slowly move away from the quay, a Jew approached him. He was as slender as a mast, on which his dusty faded blue caftan fluttered like a sail in a sluggish breeze. The man had a long, dusty white face and watery blue eyes. He stretched out his hand to the young Rabbi Avraham Beer, as if asking for a *neduve*, a handout. Avraham Beer looked at him in amazement, hesitated, but since if a person begs, it means he's in need, he took his purse from his girdle and gave him a silver coin: a quarter rouble.

The man with the dusty white face and watery blue eyes took the coin, looked at it, and seemed very dissatisfied.

'I can't give you more than that,' said Avraham Beer in annoyance. 'I'm on my way to Eretz Israel ... I'll need all the money I have when I get there ...'

Having taken the silver coin, the man disappeared.

The next day, the winds were fair and the ship glided smoothly over a calm sea. After Rabbi Avraham Beer finished saying his morning prayer, the beggar with the white face and watery blue eyes appeared at his side once more, his hand outstretched.

'Yesterday, I gave you a silver rouble and told you I'm on my way to Eretz Israel, where I'm to start a new life, don't you understand, my good man?' But Avraham Beer took the purse from his girdle once more and gave him another silver rouble, so as not to embarrass him.

The beggar took the coin with something of a frown and vanished.

The sea was calm as the ship arrived in the port of Küstendje, in the Dobrudja region, the city which the local Wallachians and Moldavians call Constanţa. Avraham Beer looked from the deck of the ship at the city's silver spires and cupolas. And he looked at the hustle and bustle of the port, at the people selling halva and baklava and millet beer and grapes and plums. 'A big city,' Avraham Beer said to himself, 'people must live well here ...'

The Jew with the dusty white face who was as slender as a mast appeared next to him, his hand outstretched.

'Didn't I tell you I'm on my way to Eretz Israel? I'm going to Eretz Israel!' Avraham Beer shouted at the beggar, barely restraining his annoyance. But even so, he took another silver coin from his purse and gave it to him. Whereupon the beggar vanished.

Once passengers had disembarked and others embarked, the ship weighed anchor and left the port of Küstendje, heading south.

The sea was calm and there was a pleasant breeze. After he said his morning prayer, in the first rays of the rising sun there appeared on the horizon the golden spires and cupolas of the city of Istanbul. Avraham Beer gazed in enchantment at the city that the Jews call Kushta. Who hasn't heard of the community of Kushta, its distinguished men, its wealthy families, such as the houses of Nasi and Navon and Capsali, its great merchants, who deal in spices and silks and velvet, and its brokers, who trade with all four corners of the world, east and west, north and south? Who hasn't heard of Kushta, which sends money and aid to the communities in the Land of Israel? Who doesn't know that every Jew of Kushta donates one Turkish para a week to help the Holy City of Jerusalem and the other holy cities of Hebron and Tveria and Tsfat, which are in need. 'How good it must be to live in Kushta, in this golden city!' Avraham Beer said to himself and was unable to tear his eyes away from the city's gilded spires and cupolas.

The beggar suddenly appeared next to him, his hand outstretched:

'What is it now? What do you want from me?' yelled Avraham Beer in a rage. 'Didn't I tell you I'm on my way to Eretz Israel?'

His gaze fell on the beggar's translucent white face and, all of a sudden, he felt a sense of peace settle on his soul. He took out his purse and without regret gave him a silver quarter rouble.

Passengers disembarked and others embarked in the port of Israel, the ship took on supplies of water and provisions, and it set sail down the Bosporus and Dardanelles into the Mediterranean.

The sea was calm and the winds were fair. The ship arrived in the port of Kushta. Avraham Beer looked at the yellow stones of the city and the yellow sand of the beach, and his eyes filled with tears. He had arrived safely in the Land of Israel.

All of a sudden, the beggar appeared next to him, and for the first time, Avraham Beer thought to see a slight smile of satisfaction on the translucent white face and in the watery blue eyes. The man stretched out his hand, but this time not to beg. In his hand he held the four silver coins, the four quarter roubles, which he now returned to him. Avraham Beer looked in amazement at the silver coins the man had placed in his palm. But when he looked up to ask the reason why, the pale blue-eyed Jew had vanished.

He had seen no one else on deck apart from the beggar, thought Avraham Beer. And the beggar had not asked alms from anybody but him ... 'The protector sent by Rabbi Morde-chai of Chernobyl!' he exclaimed, slapping his forehead. The whole point had been that every day Avraham Beer would repeat where he was going. Lest he forget. Lest he be led astray. So that he would arrive safely in Eretz Israel.

Along with some other passengers, the young rabbi and carpenter Avraham Beer rented a cart to take his baggage and set off toward the Holy City of Jerusalem.

The Loan

Rabbi Mordchele of Nadvorna, that last Baal Shem Tov, or Master of the Good Name, that miracle worker, used to read people's souls as if they were a book open only to him. And this was why a heavy burden weighed on his shoulders.

For what seemed to be a good deed in the eyes of everybody else, who viewed it as if from aloft, might turn out not to be a good deed at all when Rabbi Mordchele of Nadvorna dissected it with the sharp blade of his mind; it might even turn out to be a bad deed, a sin—may the Merciful Lord protect us from the like!

The time was the mid-nineteenth century, and the same as he did every year before the high holidays of Rosh Hashanah and Yom Kippur, before the ten days of fear and judgement, which begin with the New Year and end on the Day of Atonement, Mr Kalonimos-Kalman Berg, a cloth wholesaler and retailer from Sighet, arrived in the village of Bushtino in the Carpathians to stay with Reb Mordchele Nadverner, that he might beg forgiveness for the sins he had committed without knowing, for he had no other sins that either he or others knew of. In truth, Mr Kalonimos-Kalman used to arrive at the Rabbi of Nadvorna's with a soul that was serene and at peace. He had always been honest in his business dealings, he had given sizeable sums of money to the poor, and with the same generous hand he had also fulfilled the commandment of *gmilas khesed*, the granting of loans to those in need without charging interest—he did not engage in usury, God forbid!—and without demanding guarantees. On the eve of the high holidays, during the fearful days between Rosh Hashanah and Yom Kippur, the same as ever, he did not arrive at the rabbi's empty-handed. With pious humility, he laid a pouch containing fifty silver crowns on the rough, time-weathered boards of the rabbi's table. It was the middle of the afternoon, but inside, in the room with the low ceiling and soot-blackened beams, whose windows had been covered so that not one sliver of light might pierce from outside, hundreds of candles were burning on the cracked dark wood of the table, candles of the purest wax, which a master chandler made especially for the rabbi's household. Mr Kalonimos-Kalman Berg, the respectable wholesaler and retailer of cloth, therefore laid the heavy pouch of silver crowns on the table, piously, modestly finding room for it among the candles. He knew that money never passed the night in the house of the Rabbi of Nadvorna, for the very same day the rabbi would scatter it to the four winds, making sure it reached those homes where there was a greater need of it.

But on this occasion Rabbi Mordchele of Nadvorna sadly gazed at the pouch on the table. To Kalonimos-Kalman it even seemed that he wore a slight frown. Might the rabbi be upset, he wondered fearfully? But if so, then why? Perhaps he had given too little? But the rabbi had no way of knowing how many silver pieces were in the pouch. And besides, who could gauge what was too much and what too little? It all depended on who was doing the giving, on how he did so and when. A small donation from a rich man going down in the world is greater than a large donation from a poor man going up in the world. Who can know the paths life will take? Who can know how high and for how long one man will rise and when and how low he might fall? The Good Lord knew that he, Kalonimos-Kalman, had always given according to his means, even above and beyond his means.

Finally, Reb Mordchele Nadverner looked up with a frown and asked:

'Did you give a loan to Moti-Leizer, the coachman, without interest and without demanding a guarantee?'

'Yes, I did, Rabbi!' Kalonimos-Kalman was quick to reply, taken aback by the question. 'It was after his horse died suddenly.'

'And what term did you set on the loan?'

'The term he asked for, Rabbi! Six months.'

'But now the six months have elapsed! And he hasn't come to pay you back!'

The cloth merchant nodded.

'And how long has elapsed since the debt came due?' insisted the rabbi.

'Three weeks ... only three weeks,' answered Mr Kalonimos-Kalman Berg, more and more amazed.

'Three weeks, only three weeks ...' murmured Reb Mordchele Nadverner, pained. 'Three long weeks ... Twenty-one days during which you have not been to see him or demand the money you lent him ...'

'But how can I demand the money from him, Rabbi? I don't understand!'

'In your heart you were more than happy that he didn't pay you back the loan. For you thought to yourself: "If he gives me the money back, then tomorrow or the day after, he'll come back for another *gmilas khesed*, another loan, probably a larger one ... but if he doesn't pay me back the debt, he'll leave me in peace and won't bother me any more ..."'

Mr Kalonimos-Kalman was left bewildered for a moment, as if struck over the head. But then, he himself had to admit that he had had that very same thought, without realising it. Such are the unworthy thoughts that often creep into a man's mind.

The Rabbi of Nadvorna went on:

'And all this time, you thought yourself a good man for not demanding repayment of the loan, a charitable and a merciful man ... And for three weeks, you have put Moti-Leizer the coachman to shame, so that now he hides from you, he avoids you if he sees you in the distance on the street, he darts down a side alley, so as not to come face to face with you ...'

'But I am the one who pretends not to see him!' said Kalonimos-Kalman in his own defence.

But Rabbi Mordchele raised his voice:

'Rosh Hashanah and the Day of Atonement are almost upon us, and in the house of prayer, you, Reb Kalonimos-Kalman, will seat yourself by the east wall, in the place of honour, before the whole congregation, while he, Moti-Leizer the coachman, your debtor, will be forced to hide at the back of the synagogue, behind everybody else, lest you see him ... Better you had never given him the loan! The Merciful Lord would have found another means to help him!' the Rabbi of Nadvorna cried in wrath.

'What should I have done, Rabbi? And what should I do now? Instruct me!' implored Kalonimos-Kalman in despair.

'After the lapse of the six months, when you saw that he did not come to pay back the loan, you, Reb Kalonimos-Kalman, should have gone to him in person to demand your money.'

'But how could I demand the money, Rabbi, when I knew he didn't have it, since otherwise he would have come to me!'

'All the more reason! If you were certain, then you had all the more reason to go to him and extend the term of payment, to give him a respite, to let him breathe ... you should have given him a fresh loan, to help him honestly to pay off the first one ...'

After a pause, the rabbi added in a calmer voice:

'Not even now is it too late!'

And with that the Rabbi of Nadvorna said no more. He merely cast a meaningful glance at the pouch fat with silver coins that rested on the table among the candles.

Mr Kalonimos-Kalman Berg, the cloth wholesaler and retailer, caught the gist. He took the pouch, murmured a word of thanks to the rabbi, and left.

The Guarantee

To my father, Mordechai ben Moise,
that little candle of the soul.

Around the middle of the last century, Rabbi Mordechai ben Isachar Beer, the Rabbi of Nadvorna, arrived in the village of Bushtino in the Carpathians, where he then settled.

This large-souled and modest rabbi, a man of strange habits, who ate only once a day, but who gave others food with a generous hand, who went around in a frayed, tattered caftan, but who gave others heavy bolts of silk to make themselves clothes, this rabbi whom the folk named simply Reb Mordchele Nadverner, was in fact the last Baal Shem Tov, or Master of the Good Name, and he was a miracle worker.

Like his forerunner, the wise and very modest Rabbi Israel Baal Shem Tov, who lived around a hundred years before him, Rabbi Mordchele Nadverner also roamed the land ceaselessly, restlessly; he roamed the villages and towns on both sides of the Carpathians, always appearing as if by miracle when least expected and most needed; he brought a wise parable here, a word of comfort there; he cured a patient suffering from an unknown illness here, he uttered a good prophecy there, which would be fulfilled without fail; he brought dowries and trousseaux to a poor but deserving maiden who had reached marriageable age; he gave money to a carter who had been left without his mare and therefore bread to put on the table. And everywhere he appeared with his raucous and motley retinue, he would say prayers with followers from dozens of villages, amid dancing and merrymaking, amid the light of hundreds of candles, whose living, flickering flames banished the darkness from souls and gave hope and strength for the grey days of toil to come.

For it is true that Rabbi Mordchele Nadverner lived in his own time the same as his forerunner, Rabbi Israel, the miracle-working first Baal Shem Tov, had lived in his time.

Rabbi Israel had been wont to travel in the one-horse cart of Reb Mendel Balegule, accompanied by his scribe, Reb Hirsch Soyfer, and his faithful disciple Reb Volf Kitzes, and perhaps another two or three followers.

'Reb Mendel, harness the horse to the cart!' Rabbi Israel Baal Shem Tov would say, out of the blue. And Mendel the carter would ask no questions, but harness the horse, and off they would go. They rode up and down roads familiar and unfamiliar, and it was as if Mendel Balegule's mare, left to her own devices, always knew the way. The Hassidim, the disciples of the Baal Shem Tov, would be filled with wonder at this, but never did they dare ask aloud how it could be. The rabbi would keep his silence, and that silence was deep and full of meaning, until finally they arrived in a place where the mare, having wearied, would come to a stop all by herself. And it would turn out that right in that very place, there was need of redemption, of a miracle.

Then, some hundred years later, Rabbi Mordchele Nadverner, the last miracle-working Baal Shem Tov, travelled the same roads, but this time with a raucous procession of fifteen carts laden with bread and salt, with bolts of white silk for bridal gowns and black silk for grooms' caftans, with prayer shawls and candles. And he was accompanied by scribes to indite the *ketubot*—marriage agreements—and scribes to write out phylacteries, and copyists of *mezuzot*—blessings to place on the right shoulder—and weavers and braiders of prayer shawl tassels, which are called *tzitzit*, and a host of other right-believers, who served no particular purpose, but came along in carts filled with people as thickly as bunches of grapes. And in the last cart came the housewives, who on the spot sewed the wedding dresses and grooms' caftans, and cooked the repast, and lit the candles to greet the Sabbath. And this raucous, motley retinue travelled all around, and it went by both the beaten path and untrodden ways, until it reached places where there was need of redemption, of a miracle.

And because over the last hundred years the number of people had multiplied, the number of needs had multiplied also, and there was an ever-greater number of miracles to be performed.

Bushtino was quite a wealthy village of ploughmen and woodcutters, of carters and traders, which lay on the country road that led to Tyachiv, Slatina and Sighet in the south. In the north it led to the town of Khust, below its castle, and thence to Mukatschewo and Pressburg, before veering south to Vienna, the capital of the empire. Along this much-travelled country road trundled carts laden with apples, timber, and flour from the Bushtino watermill; it was also by this road that the emperor and his courtiers arrived to hunt bears in Maramuresch. But above all it was the 'salt road', thus named because along it passed the heavy carts loaded with tablets of salt from the mines of Slatina and Bredenbad, arriving many days and nights later in Vienna, where the Emperor of Austria and King of Hungary, Bohemia, Moravia, Serbia, Bosnia and Herzegovina, etc., etc., when he wished to present another crowned head of Europe with a precious gift, would send a few carts laden with tablets and blocks of pure white salt from Maramuresch.

At one end of the village, the sluggish, sprawling waters of the Talabor trickled beneath the long wooden bridge, on which rafts glided down to the Tisza on their way to Szeged and beyond. It was to this river that the congregation came to mark Rosh Hashanah, the beginning of the new year, 'shedding their sins' by casting breadcrumbs to the fish amid the murmur of prayer.

At the edge of the country road, not far from the waters of the Talabor, stood a little cottage of unburnt mud bricks, painted blue, and which had a roof of time- and rain-blackened shingles. This was the cottage of Rabbi Mordchele Nadverner. And across the road, in another little cottage of unburnt mud bricks, plastered and painted ultramarine, and which likewise had a shingled roof, lived Moishe, the son of Israel Nathan-Alter, with his wife Sirca, of the house of Shapiro.

Rabbi Mordchele was approaching his seventies, a man recklessly generous and extraordinarily poor, a man who had but one God in heaven and but one tattered caftan here on earth. He felt great love for his neighbour across the way, who was a young, shy man, with a pale face, deep hazel eyes, and the beginnings of a chestnut beard. This young man and his young wife arrived from the east in that village beneath the Carpathians, borne on the wings of a love that repeats itself over the centuries but which is ever new to those who experience it. For Moishe son of Israel Nathan was not so simple a youth as he seemed at first sight: at the age of seventeen he was a man fully formed and in possession of solid book learning, the son, grandson and great-grandson of rabbinic scholars, writers of important works. His father, Israel Nathan-Alter, the Rabbi of Pistyn, was the author of *Minchat-Yisra'el* (Gift of Israel) and *Emunah Yisra'el* (Faith of Israel), profoundly mystical works on the Cabbala, of which a very learned man of the time said that only one in a thousand initiates would be able to understand them. Chaim-Josef, the father of Israel Nathan and grandfather of Moishe, was the author of *Tosafot Khayim* (Life Glosses), an elaborate commentary on the Pentateuch, and *Nishmat-Khayim* (The Breath of Life) an interpretation of the hidden meanings to be found in the Psalms of David. And so it went: generation after generation of scholars stretched back behind this pale, shy young man. But apart from their book learning and their love of books, all these ancestors shared another common feature: they were all dirt poor. Moishe's father, Israel Nathan, was also very sickly; important rabbis had blessed him and added to his name 'Alter' (Old Man) so that he would live to old age. But Israel Nathan-Alter, the Rabbi of Pistyn, had died young, barely having reached the age of thirty-one, passing down to his son Moishe, at the time a child of five, a good name and a chest full of manuscripts. 'I was left swaying as if atop a mast far out at sea,' as Moishe was later to write, in the preface to his father's *Gift of Israel*, which he published.

The young Moishe was taken into the house of his maternal grandfather, a famous scholar, a learned and pious man, Rabbi Eliezer Ipe of Scalit, where he lived until the age of thirteen, after which he became the sole master of his own deeds, be they good or—God forbid—bad.

In order to escape poverty, Moishe, the son of Israel Nathan, did not write books, but instead learned to be a bookkeeper and set off to find employment, walking from Pistyn, the town where his ancestors had served as rabbis, to Podkamin, where he was hired to keep the accounts of a wealthy grain merchant by the name of Elkanan Shapiro.

Reb Elkanan was an important man, the head of the Jewish community and of many companies, associations and charities; he kept a large house, open to guests and wayfarers. According to the custom of the time, young unmarried clerks received less pay, but by way of compensation ate at the master's table and had lodgings in an annex in his courtyard.

Fate had probably decreed that this Elkanan Shapiro should have a beautiful daughter, a slender, quiet, modest girl such as is seldom found in a rich man's house. Moishe son of Israel Nathan fell in love with her, and the girl loved this studious young man with the deep hazel eyes and the chestnut beard only just beginning to sprout from his pallid cheeks. The girl's parents were enraged; they would not hear of such a match. True, this Moishe, the son of the Rabbi of Pistyn, was a serious young man, a learned man, the son and grandson and great-grandson of famous writers; he was a good bookkeeper, hardworking, meticulous, he always wore a clean white shirt, his coat of cheap cloth was always carefully ironed, but even so ... even so, he was nothing but a bookkeeper, and his coat of cheap cloth was thin and shiny at the elbows.

But as has happened over the centuries, it was love and as ever it was too strong to be denied. The parents resigned themselves, the children were joined together, and, contrary to the custom that the young husband and wife live *oyf kest*, on the funds of the girl's parents, for a year or two, Moishe—wounded to the depths of his soul, without saying so aloud and without even admitting it to himself—left his parents-in-law's house with his wife Sirca immediately after the wedding and set off into the world to seek a living for himself. They crossed the Carpathians and arrived in the village of Bushtino, where they set up house in that little cottage whose mud bricks were painted ultramarine, with its tapering roof of old shingles, opposite the similar house of Rabbi Mordchele Nadverner, the last Baal Shem Tov and a worker of miracles.

Moishe never missed Sabbath prayers and meals at the rabbi's house. He always took the same modest place on the bench, at the end of the long table, and listened insatiably to the rabbi's wise words, behind which he could sense deeper and yet deeper meanings. 'Wherefore man shall leave his father and his mother and he shall cleave to his wife and they shall be a single body,' read the rabbi from the pericope for that week, taken from the Book of Genesis. For there comes a time and man must tear himself away from worldly things, from wellbeing, from stale warmth, from the safety of the parental home, and he must leave, raise himself up through love toward things spiritual … toward Learning, and Understanding, and Goodness toward his fellow men … 'And the man and his wife were naked and they were not ashamed,' the rabbi read on, and to Moishe ben Israel Nathan-Alter it seemed that he spoke of Sirca and himself… But how did the rabbi know? Podkamin was far away and he had never spoken to anybody of what had happened there. And he had complained to nobody.

Another time, Rabbi Mordchele examined the following verse from the Book of Exodus: 'The Lord said to Moishe, take up your staff … you will strike the rock, and water will flow therefrom, and the people will drink …' And if with the help of the Almighty water flows forth after you strike the rock with your staff, do not imagine that the feat is yours alone, or that the water is yours alone … you must give water to all those who would drink, explained the rabbi, and to Moishe again it seemed that the words were addressed to him. What did the rabbi mean to say? Moishe was unable to comprehend.

That Sabbath, a large yellow cake rested on the table, sent by Sirca, a cake in which the young wife had put much honey and many eggs, as well as much heart. After saying the blessing over a small glass of strong slivovitz, Rabbi Mordchele Nadverner broke off a piece of the cake and passed the tray to his followers, who sat around the long table. The tray was passed from hand to hand, each broke off a piece of the yellow cake, as it was a *mitzva* to eat from what the rabbi had left over, but when it reached Moishe at the far end of the table, nothing was left but crumbs. Moishe gazed ruefully at the tray, not knowing what to do. Rabbi Mordchele Nadverner then rose from his place, went to the end of the table, gathered up the crumbs of cake from the tray with his fingers and gave them to Moishe, saying these words: 'From the crumbs of the Tables of the Law was Moishe enriched.'

A Talmudic legend had it that Moishe Rabenu became a wealthy man thanks to the crumbs of the precious stones from which the Tables of the Law were carved on Mount Sinai.

And the miracle did indeed come to pass. From that day forth, says the family legend, Moishe ben Israel Nathan-Alter prospered and became a rich man, a man who had wealth, offspring, and people's esteem in abundance.

This miracle on the part of Rabbi Mordchele Nadverner, the last miracle-working Baal Shem Tov, in fact occurred in the form of a light, which lit up in the waking, searching mind of Moishe ben Israel Nathan-Alter.

Moishe was a bookkeeper at the time, a modestly paid accountant at a large timber enterprise, which cut down parcels of forest in the Maramuresch Carpathians. Many times, he had to take a bundle of food to last him a few days—Sirca would pack for him a loaf she had baked in the oven, a few hard-boiled eggs, a few apples—and set off into the forest where they were felling trees. When he got there, he counted the logs and kept a tally of the days worked by the men who cut and trimmed the trees and the carters who, with one or with two horses, then hauled the logs down into the valley. Moishe began to discover the life of the forest, which man entered so cruelly, with iron axes, jagged saws, and sharp hooks, to conquer it and bend it to his own uses. Moishe saw how in winter when the snow lay thick on the ground and the branches of the trees and life itself seemed frozen and still, men entered the forest to clear it, to thin out the stumps and stems and all the useless growth, so that in spring the trees would take up more sap and grow the better. These sticks and bushes, these lopped stumps, which the peasants called 'wood fall', were left there to rot, because they served no purpose and there was no money in clearing them away and carting them down the mountain.

One day, after Moishe blessed his bread and peeled a hard-boiled egg, sitting down on a log to eat and looking at those mounds of discarded sticks and stumps, which served no use, a light lit up in his mind: 'Take up thy staff, Moishe!' And he stood up and began to search among the wood fall. And he discovered a treasure trove: not a chest of gold coins or jewels and precious stones fashioned by others, but a treasure for which you would have to toil from dawn to dusk ... But still a treasure.

At the time, a fashion for canes was spreading around the world. Every self-respecting man carried a cane, and the most elegant among them had to have a whole collection, one to match each suit and pair of shoes, each collar and tie. Once gathered, sorted by length, thickness and type of wood, the wood fall could be sent to factories, which turned them into beautiful oak canes, with or without a knob, bone-tipped canes for summer or sharp steel caps for winter, light hazelnut canes, aromatic cherry-wood canes for young men in love, black canes with silver handles for respectable old gentlemen, walking sticks for hikers, canes with curved handles for invalids, straight staffs for scouts, sticks for skiers, umbrella handles, and all kinds of other useful items that could be produced from the litter left to rot in the woods.

Thus was born the Raw Canes Production and Export Company, which had its office in a little room of the cottage made of mud bricks painted ultramarine and roofed with old shingles, a room with a writing table, a chair, headed paper, a filing cabinet in one corner, and a press for copying letters. The company sent its products from Bushtino, that village in the Carpathians, all the way to Germany and England, to Austria and Switzerland, to Sweden and Italy, and to countries all over the world.

And Moishe ben Israel Nathan-Alter's yard expanded, store-rooms and sheds sprang up on every side, in which the canes were stored and sorted and bundled, and large ovens were built, with cauldrons for boiling the staffs to be peeled and bent. The yard was all a-bustle with people, horses, and the carts that brought brushwood from the forest and took bundles of canes to the station, where they were loaded onto railcars and dispatched all over the world.

And in that expanding yard there sprang up outbuildings of stone and brick, like the ones in the yard of his father-in-law, the wealthy grain merchant and leading citizen of Podkamin, Reb Elkanan Shapiro; outbuildings into which Moishe's sons and daughters moved one by one as they grew up.

But Moishe himself and his wife Sirca, of the house of Shapiro, lived to the end of their days in that little ultramarine cottage with the time-blackened shingle roof, across the way from the similar house of Rabbi Mordchele Nadverner.

'From the crumbs of the Tables of Law did Moise grow rich.'

From the litter of the forest did Moishe ben Israel Nathan-Alter grow rich.

And many were those who tried to steal his idea, to compete with him, to buy wood litter and sell it, but all they succeeded in doing was to lose money, and they quickly gave up. Was it because they were unskilled in sorting the canes? Or because they did not know the sizes, the kinds of wood, the different colours, the different shapes the canes had to have? Or was it because the miracle worked by Rabbi Mordchele Nadverner had to be complete? Who can say?

And Moishe increased in wealth, offspring, good works, and people's esteem. Sirca, his wife, of the house of Shapiro, small of body and beautiful of countenance, quiet and hardworking, gave him nine children—six sons and three daughters: Israel Nathan, the first born, named after Moishe's father, the author of the books *Gift of Israel* and *Creed of Israel*; Eliezer-Lippe, named after the grandfather in whose house Moishe had lived till the age of thirteen; Chaim-Josef, named after Moishe's paternal grandfather, the author of *Life Glosses* and *Breath of Life*; and Zindel, and Mordechai, and Aharon. And their daughters were Miriam, Sara and Yokevet.

Moishe ben Israel Nathan-Alter increased in wealth and offspring, but above all in good works. For according to the commandment of the Lord Above and following the example and the teachings of the great and pious Rabbi Mordchele Nadverner, he gave alms to the needy, helped widows and orphans, contributed to the dowries of poor maidens, and gave *gmilas khsodim*, loans without interest and without a due date, without usury (the Lord forbid!) and without fuss to those in need.

At the house of the Rabbi of Nadvorna, along both sides of the table in the large room whose walls were whitewashed and whose low ceiling beams were blackened by time and the smoke of candles, there sat crowded together believers from both sides of the Carpathians; there too sat wayfarers who knew that here they would find a roof and a table lit merrily by dozens of pure wax candles made especially for the rabbi's house, and a tot of pure plum brandy, and tasty food cooked by the hardworking and blessed hands of Haya, the rabbi's wife, and other housewives from the village. At those meals full of song and merriment, so full that everybody forgot their cares and misfortunes from the week that had gone before, so full that they even forgot themselves, Rabbi Mordchele of Nadvorna was in the habit of flinging out a question, which would fall like a bright thunderclap from a clear blue sky among the astonished guests, a question to which the answer seemed clear and easy to give, but which was not clear at all, and which in the mouth of the wise rabbi took on layer upon layer of meaning.

'That we must show kindness and understanding, that we must help our fellow man, that we must share what we have with those in need, all these things we know very well from the holy books and from the teachings of our sages. But tell me, which man is to be preferred, which is the more pleasing to the Lord and the more beneficial to his fellow man: he who gives out of mercy, because he has a good heart and takes pity on the needy? or he who gives against his will, he who is forced to do so by his fear of the Lord Above and His commandment?'

'Naturally, he who has a good heart is to be preferred, rabbi! He who gives out of mercy!' the disciples hastened to reply.

'You err greatly and commit a great injustice to think like this,' Rabbi Mordchele admonished them.

The guests looked at him in fear and amazement.

'But why, rabbi? We do not understand!'

'He who gives out of fear of the Lord is to be preferred, even if he gives against his own will!' said Rabbi Mordchele, almost in wrath. 'For he who gives out of mercy will give only when he sees a needy man on whom to take pity, while he who gives out of fear of the Lord and obeying His commandment will seek out the needy man to help and will never turn his gaze from him. He who gives out of charity will give only occasionally, he will even strive to avoid places and people that arouse his compassion, for pity is not a very pleasant feeling, whereas the other man will seek out places where there are people who need his help. Moreover, he who is generous only out of pity scorns in the depths of his soul him whom he helps, he demeans him by his very pity, whereas he who gives obeying the Lord's commandment will not be tainted by haughtiness or scorn or baseness in his heart, because he knows that he gives not of what is his but only of what he himself has received through the mercy of the Lord Above. And again, he who gives out of pity and a good heart finds it easy to give, he gives out of the urging of his good heart and good nature, whereas he who gives against his will and against his nature, but only in obedience to the commandment of the Lord, must always do battle with himself, must vanquish himself, which is a very hard thing to do ... to vanquish yourself is perhaps the hardest thing of all for any man to do ... and for this reason, his merit is without compare.'

Rabbi Mordchele Nadverner made a long pause, staring into space, gazing beyond the dozens of pure wax candles that flickered on the table like living jewels. Then he went on:

'By means of commandments and the fear of punishment, the worldly ruler, the emperor, the king, who is a man of flesh and blood, ensures that his subjects do not do evil unto each other. But also, through commandments and fear, the Lord in Heaven ensures that His subjects do good unto each other.'

And the disciples listened to the words of the rabbi, nodding in silence, deep in thought.

It came to the ears of the Great Rabbi of Sighet and the 'Galil', of the Comitatus of Maramuresch, Yekusiel Yehuda Teitelbaum, also known as Der Yetev Lev, from the books he wrote titled *Yetev Lev* and *Yetev Ponim—A Good Heart* and *A Good Welcome*—that a rabbi who worked miracles and did good deeds was roaming the villages and hamlets of Maramuresch with a motley procession of fifteen carts laden with people and candles, with bread and salt, with white silks for bridal gowns and black cloth for grooms' caftans. And on hearing all this, the human curiosity of Der Yetev Lev was awakened and he wished to meet this Reb Mordchele of Nadvorna and speak with him.

To meet him was easily said. But how? And where? They did not say their prayers in the same synagogue, they did not bathe in the same mikveh, they did not walk the same roads. The one was Rav Yekusiel Yehuda Teitelbaum, a head crowned with the golden wreath of learning, the author of indispensable treatises, of profound commentaries on the Torah and Talmud, a rabbi attested in the charters of a large, organised, official congregation that had trustees, administrators, and a temple of stone. The other was Reb Mordchele of Nadvorna, the unchartered and unofficial rabbi of a mass of people whose number was unknown, and who were scattered throughout the valleys and hills of Maramuresch; he was a *tzaddik* whose head was crowned with neither gold, nor laurels, nor thorns, since he sought to serve the Lord God with joy and in simple pleasures. Those two great men might go around and around that region for a hundred years or more without ever meeting. They were like stars, each with his own separate orbit, each his own radiance.

But nevertheless, how was he to meet Rabbi Mordchele? The thought tortured Rabbi Yetev Lev. Were he simply to invite him to come and see him, it might be interpreted as arrogance. Were he, the Rabbi of Sighet and of the Maramuresch Galil, to set off without an invitation to visit Rabbi Mordchele in the village of Bushtino beneath the Carpathians, it would be an act of extraordinary humility, which might ultimately still be construed as arrogance.

What then should he do?

Still wracking his brains, he decided to try a roundabout way, that is, first to invite a guest from the village of Bushtino beneath the Carpathians and to take counsel with him. And that guest was none other than Moishe ben Israel Nathan-Alter, who also happened to be related to the house of Teitelbaum. For a time, Moishe, while a young scholar at the Talmudic School in Sighet, had stayed in that house, where he was provided bed and board while he helped in the copying and preparation for the press of a commentary on the Psalms of David.

Rabbi Yekusiel Yehuda Teitelbaum therefore sent a trustee to summon him.

'How might I meet Rabbi Reb Mordchele Nadverner? Should I invite him on the Sabbath? Should I go to see him? You know him well, Moishe, you are his neighbour. Give me some advice!'

'Who can say that he knows Reb Mordchele well, when his words and deeds are so unexpected? When you expect him to go north, he goes south. When you expect him to say no, he says yes. I don't know whether it would be a good idea to invite him to come to see you without having a good reason, Rabbi. He might come simply not to offend Yetev Lev, but then again, he might not come, and then he would feel pain at not having come ... But one thing I know for sure: he has never refused to make a mitzvah journey, no matter how long or how hard the journey to do the good deed might be.'

'You are right, Moishe,' said the Rabbi of Sighet, and his face suddenly lit up. 'We will be having a *berit milah* for a new-born boy whose father died a month ago. The father was a tinsmith and fell from a roof. I will invite Rabbi Mordchele to be the *sandik* at this covenant of Abraham.'

And that was what he did.

That Tuesday, Reb Mordchele arrived in Sighet with his motley retinue, whereupon he entered the first house of prayer he came to and said his morning prayers.

At the other end of town, in the house of the new-born boy, the people had gathered for that solemn and painful ceremony. In the narrow bedroom, women crowded around the nursing mother and the child's cradle, they gathered around the withered old midwife, and they talked, they gossiped, they dipped burning coals in water which they then spat in the child's face to guard him against the evil eye, and they gave all kinds of useless advice to the mother. In the main room of the house, adjoining the bedroom, with its low ceiling and time-blackened oak beams, the men were waiting: the mohel, testing the sharpness of circumcision knife at the window, the cantor, clearing his throat, the trustees, the administrator, the beggars waiting for the meal, and others who were there simply as Jews. In their midst was the great and wise Yetev Lev. The table had been laid with a white cloth and on it were set white candles in gleaming brass candlesticks. All stood waiting for Reb Mordchele to appear, now that his arrival in town was known.

But Reb Mordchele was deep in prayer and oblivious to the passage of time. On seeing that he still did not arrive, Yetev-Lev sent two gabbaim, two of the community's most prominent trustees, to remind him, half seriously, half jokingly, that the boy was now eight days old and if his *sandik* tarried much longer, the day for fulfilling the Covenant would pass, at which Reb Mordchele sent his respect to the great Rabbi of Sighet and assured him that all would be completed in time, in accordance with the commandments of the Lord Above.

And so it was. Amid singing and merriment, Rabbi Morde-chai of Nadvorna finished his morning prayers and when he sensed the time was right, he arrived at the tinsmith's house and recited the sandik's blessing:

'Blessed be Thou, Our Lord God, pillar of the world, who with Thy Commandments hast blessed us and hast comman-ded us to bring him into the Covenant of Abraham.'

The Rabbi of Sighet and the Galil gave a start, as if he were hearing the prayer for the first time.

Cradling the child Rabbi Mordchele went on:

'Let his name in Israel be Reuven ben Reuven ... And let the father rejoice in Gan-Eden at him who issued from his loins and his mother at him who is the fruit of her womb ...'

Rabbi Mordchele then blessed a glass of plum brandy, he ate of the yellow cake baked by the mother, bid the Rabbi of Sighet farewell, and with his procession of fifteen carts quickly departed for a destination known only to him.

It was only once the creaking of the cartwheels and the tramping of the horses' hooves had faded into the distance that the Rabbi of Sighet, Yekusiel Yehuda Teitelbaum, realised that he hadn't exchanged a single word with the Rabbi of Nadvorna. And when Moishe ben Israel Nathan-Alter, who had arranged the whole meeting, asked him his opinion of Reb Mordchele, Rabbi Teitelbaum gave a mysterious smile and said only this:

'In all my life never have I heard such a sandik's blessing!'

And he said not a word more.

And when Moishe told the Rabbi of Nadvorna that the great Yetev Lev, who had heard so many prayers and blessings recited in so many ways, had never in all his life heard such a blessing as that spoken by Rabbi Mordchele, the latter also gave a mysterious smile, and said:

'Nor have I heard such a blessing in all my life ...'

At which Moishe looked at him in bewilderment and incomprehension.

Reb Mordchele went on:

'I wasn't the one who said it. It was spoken through me.'

Moishe could not suppress his curiosity:

'Rabbi, what will the child grow up to be, having been worthy of such a blessing?'

Rabbi Mordchele Nadverner knitted his eyebrows, pondered for a long while, and then said:

'What will he grow up to be, you ask? What will he grow up to be? Well, know that he will be a carter.'

Moishe looked at him in amazement, and in disappointment.

'What, a carter? Only a carter?'

'"Only" you say? "Only"?' And Reb Mordchele cast him a scolding look.

And so it was. The boy who in the tribe of Israel bore the name Reuven ben Reuven grew up to be big and strong, and he became a carter. A man who lived by the toil of his own hands, tended his horse, greased the axles of his cart. A hardworking man, a wise and waggish man. He enlivened travellers weary from the bumping of the cart with witty sayings cast over his shoulder from up on his box. He drove the Jews along the bumpy roads of Maramuresch, he drove them on their way to their *tzadikim*, he drove them on holidays, he drove them to weddings and name days. Only to funerals he did not drive them, for the dead were borne on men's shoulders, and the procession went on foot.

And when they built the railway and the first train arrived in Sighet, its locomotive proudly puffing and whistling, Reuven ben Reuven was in the station with his cart, waiting for the weary travellers, ready to take them and their luggage home.

He lived to a ripe old age and when he departed, he left behind sons and grandsons and great-grandsons.

And so it was that the Rabbi of Nadvorna read as if in a book open only to him the hidden thoughts of folk and was able to see their destinies from birth to death and beyond.

The Rabbi of Nadvorna worked miracles and his fame spread far and wide in the world.

The rabbi cured people's bodies and healed their souls with fervent, stubborn, sometimes desperate prayers, which strove with all their might and not seldom would they fly high, high above, all the way to the foot of His throne.

The rabbi cured the suffering with wise advice and all kinds of healing herbs, including those which the natives of those climes gave names such as 'Jew's cherry', 'Yid's grass', 'Rabbi's leaf', and so on; Reb Mordchele also cured the sick with all kinds of potions and ointments, whose secrets were known to him alone.

All the folk on both sides of the Carpathians were amused and even laughed till their sides ached at the miraculous cure of Itzhak Mendel of Poienii-Glodului, for example:

This Itzhak Mendel was a short, stocky man, who with his wife Beile kept a grocery store in the village. He was a cheerful, hardworking man, who was on his feet from early in the morning till late at night, eager to help all those in need. A patient man, he extended credit to those who needed it. He didn't smoke, drink, gamble, gossip, or take the Lord's name in vain. In short, he was a simple, God-fearing man, but he was awfully fond of eating and, like every other good Jew, on the Sabbath he was endowed with a veritable *neshamah yeterah*, and that 'second soul' demanded for itself a double helping of cholent, a dish of beans stewed in a clay pot and kept in the oven over the long night between Friday and the Sabbath; it demanded double portions of *kigel*—potato cake fried in goose grease—which, the way his wife Beile made it, was like manna from heaven, a dish suited to every taste.

One Sabbath afternoon, after a goodly portion of one such heavenly *kigel*, Itzhak Mendel was struck with a bellyache, with cramps so bad that they left him crawling up the wall.

Itzhak Mendel was scared. Beile didn't know what to do; her husband had never been ill before.

He writhed with the cramps the whole of that day, and then for two more days, after which he decided to go to Reb Mordchele in Bushtino.

The rabbi listened to him carefully, examined the man's greenish, suffering face for a long time, then suddenly cried out toward the kitchen:

'Sara, fetch that piece of *kigel* left over from the Great Sabbath!'

Rabbi Mordchele ate only once a day, other than on the Sabbath, when, albeit with great temperance, he did the honour of eating three meals. But food, no matter how old it might be, was never thrown away in the rabbi's house.

Itzhak Mendel was amazed. *Kigel* left over from the Great Sabbath? And in his head, he totted it up: six weeks had elapsed since then. What would the rabbi be doing with such an old *kigel*?

Sara came in from the kitchen holding a blackened frying pan in which there was a potato cake covered with a fluffy green beard of mould. Rabbi Mordchele cut a large slice of the *kigel* and gave it to Itzhak Mendel to eat.

Itzhak Mendel's eyes bulged wide. But if the *kigel* is from the Rabbi of Nadvorna, you murmur the blessing, 'I thank Thee Lord God, Master of the World, for all things come about by Thy will,' you close your eyes, and you swallow.

Which is what Itzhak Mendel did. He felt his stomach turning inside out, but he valiantly ate the whole slice of mouldy potato cake. Barely had he swallowed the last mouthful when he saw to his horror that the rabbi was cutting another slice … 'Come what may,' Itzhak Mendel thought to himself, he closed his eyes and ate the second slice. He muttered an inaudible thank you to the rabbi and went out, reeling like a drunk man.

Back home, he tossed and turned in bed the whole night, he was nauseous, he had spasms, and finally he threw up, after which he fell into a deep sleep, a sleep as dense as a stone.

In the morning he woke up amazed. He felt himself all over, but not a single ache anywhere. He was as sound as a bell. And everybody laughed and was amazed at the miraculous cure of the 'old kigel with the green beard'.

The fame of Rabbi Mordechai of Nadvorna had even travelled far to the West, to that great city named Pressburg, where at the time there lived an enlightened Jew who loved scholars and held rabbis in great esteem, but who did not believe in miracles. On hearing of a miracle-working rabbi at the end of the nineteenth century, his curiosity was aroused and he wished to meet him.

Yehiel Halevy Pressburger, as the man was called, made the long journey to Bushtino by mail coach and went to say his prayers in the synagogue of Rabbi Mordchele. As he prayed, mingling with the crowd, he fixed his eyes on Rabbi Mordchele and said to himself: 'Nothing out of the ordinary. An eastern Jew, with a beard ... A man like any other ...' And in his disappointment, he couldn't help but think: 'I've made a long journey, a shame about the fare.'

That evening, when according to the custom, Yehiel Halevy Pressburger went into Rabbi Mordchele's room to bid him farewell, to his amazement the rabbi refused to take his donation for the poor, and instead opened a drawer and counted out two silver florins and thirty brass kreuzers, which he laid on the table. It was the exact fare that Yehiel Halevy Pressburger had paid for his journey.

Yehiel Halevy Pressburger froze in amazement, but he said not a word aloud to anybody about it. He stammered an apology, tried to refuse the money. However, the rabbi, gently but very determinedly insisted that he take it.

The man left with his head lowered, ashamed and humiliated, and it is said that thereafter he began to believe in miracles.

One evening, Moishe ben Israel Nathan-Alter went into Rabbi Mordchele Nadverner's room.

The rabbi was alone, bowed over a book. However, he was not reading, but gazing into space with tearful eyes.

Noticing him, the rabbi said to him sorrowfully:

'Moishe, Moishe, it is very hard for me ... I hear people's thoughts as if I were listening to them from behind a door. And I see their journey from birth till the end ... And I pray to the All-Merciful to relieve me of it ... it is so hard to carry this burden ... so hard ... so hard ...'

And Reb Mordchele suddenly leapt up from his chair, ran outside, and melted into the night.

And Moishe, the son of Israel Nathan-Alter, grew in good deeds and charity, and in the commandments of the Lord, and this Moishe was made worthy of a great and unheard-of privilege: he was to be the only one of whom the great Rabbi Mordchele Nadverner asked a *gmilas khesed*, which is to say a loan, and this with a guarantee, for until the end of his life Moishe thereby became the keeper of the rabbi's tallit.

And this is how it came about:

Money never spent the night in the house of Rabbi Nadverner, for what he received he distributed among the poor the very same day. One Friday, Haya, the rabbi's wife, went to Rabbi Mordchele in despair. He was deep in a book, oblivious to all else, he had forgotten what day it was, he had forgotten that it was the Sabbath the next day, he had even forgotten what world he lived in. But Haya could not forget what world she lived in or what day it was, and she was in despair: it was almost the eve of the Sabbath and in the house, they had neither candles to sanctify, nor wine to bless, nor ring loaves with which to thank the Lord, let alone fish—not so much as a herring. Thanks to the rabbi's reckless generosity, Haya had been left without a single penny for housekeeping.

Alarmed at his wife's desperation, Rabbi Mordchele set about searching: there had to be a stray penny somewhere in the house. He looked in the drawer, he looked on top of the cupboard, he looked underneath it: maybe some coin had rolled into a corner. Nothing anywhere. Now there really was need of a miracle, but the miracle-working rabbi had never been known to work a miracle for his own benefit and, more to the point, he had never been heard to work the miracle of producing money.

Rabbi Mordchele Nadverner stood a while in thought, then he sent for Moishe ben Israel Nathan-Alter, his neighbour from across the road, who was now a wealthy man.

'Lend me seventy kreuzers, Moishe, and I will give you my tallit as a guarantee.'

Moishe looked at the rabbi in wide-eyed astonishment:

'What, Rabbi, a loan you want? And with a guarantee? Did you not teach us that we do not give what is ours, but that money is from the Lord when we use it to do good and from the Unclean One when we use it in the wrong way? And besides, look at all I owe you—'

'I won't take a loan unless it's secured with a guarantee!' interrupted Rabbi Mordchele in a determined voice.

'Very well, so be it! A loan,' said Moishe, in resignation. 'But at least let it be without a guarantee, Rabbi, I don't doubt that you'll pay me back.'

'I won't take it without giving a guarantee! Who knows what might happen to me? At any moment I might be called to the Next World and I don't wish to leave a debt behind me here on earth.'

Knowing the rabbi's stubbornness, Moishe counted out seventy brass kreuzers onto the table and in return received the rabbi's rather threadbare, fraying, everyday prayer shawl as a guarantee.

That evening, after the Havdalah, the prayer of parting from the Sabbath, Rabbi Mordchele still did not have the money to redeem his guarantee, but he had need of his everyday tallit. He therefore sent his best Sabbath prayer shawl to Moishe and asked for his threadbare everyday one back.

After which, for the whole of that week, the Rabbi of Nadvorna roamed the countryside with his raucous, motley procession of fifteen carts laden with bread and salt, with bolts of white silk for bridal gowns and black silk for grooms' caftans, with tasselled prayer shawls, with books and candles, accompanied by scribes to indite wedding agreements, and scribes to write out phylacteries, and scribes to inscribe the blessings to place on the right shoulder, and braiders of tassels, and other disciples both with a purpose in the procession and without any at all, and in the carts that came behind were the housewives and seamstresses, ready to sew the brides' gowns and the grooms' caftans and to cook the repast for the wedding feast. And the rabbi travelled the roads on both sides of the Maramuresch Carpathians, distributing gifts of money right and left, for there was always a widow or orphan to help, always a poor girl in need of a dowry, always a horse to buy for a carter whose nag had dropped dead in the road, there were always places and folk in great need of money, and thank the Lord, Moishe ben Israel Nathan-Alter could afford to wait for his seventy kreuzers.

So it was written that Moishe should endlessly obey the commandment of *gmilas khesed*, the commandment to give a loan without interest or due date, without usury, Lord forbid! and also that he should be the custodian of the wise and pious Rabbi Mordchele Nadverner's tallit, of his best Sabbath shawl during the week and his tatty, fraying everyday shawl on the Sabbath and high holy days.

And Rabbi Mordchele Nadverner taught his disciples to obey the laws of the country and public property.

But it so happened that none other than Rabbi Mordchele Nadverner was to be entangled in public affairs without wishing it and without realising it. For at the time a new *stuhlrichter* had been appointed to the Teutschenau district of Mara-muresch County, who had never heard of Rabbi Mordchele.

Rabbi Mordchele of Nadvorna was now of advanced old age and weary in days, his beard had turned grey, but his eyesight had not weakened and his strength had not ebbed, and the same as every year, on the eve of Sukkot, the Feast of Tabernacles, he insisted on erecting his own tabernacle in the yard of his house in Bushtyno. He therefore beat the poles into the ground, wove the walls of rushes, roofed the tabernacle with green fir branches, and, the same as every year, the children of the village came to decorate it with walnuts wrapped in gold and silver foil, and with red, green, and yellow apples, which they hung from the branches of the roof. The rabbi's congregation of worshippers had grown over the years, but the yard of his house had remained as small as ever. Every year, the tabernacle had to be built bigger and bigger to accommodate more and more people. Somehow or other, without the Rabbi of Nadvorna wishing it and without him realising it in the fervour of building the booth, one end of the tabernacle ended up jutting onto public property, which is to say, the road.

And it so happened that the new *stuhlrichter* appointed to the Teutschenau district, who had never heard of Rabbi Mordchele, decided to take a ride in his carriage to inspect the lands of which he was in charge. Passing through Bushtyno he all of a sudden saw a booth jutting a few *zollen* into the street. And he turned scarlet with rage:

'How dare he? Who gave him leave? Does he have a permit? What is the meaning of such disorder?'

His underlings did not dare to open their mouths to answer him, to provide an explanation. The new *stuhlrichter* was a stern, vindictive man, a stickler, and he was determined to preserve peace and order in his district at all costs. 'Peace and order!' was his motto, and his underlings knew it all too well.

And there and then, the *stuhlrichter* gave an order to the secretary of the district and the head of the gendarmes, who were among those accompanying him:

'If within eight days, this ... this lean-to, this shed is not demolished, then I shall expel him from the village!'

Gathered around the rabbi, the congregation, the women, the children, were left pale with fright. What? Expel him from the village? The word landed with a thud, it reawakened dark memories. To expel him from the village? To expel their rabbi? The light of their minds and the joy of their hearts? And for what? For obeying the beautiful commandment to erect a Sukkot tabernacle? Impossible! The Lord Who sees and hears all could never allow such a thing! And they all turned their eyes to Rabbi Mordchele, eyes filled with both fear and hope. What would he do? What would he say?

But the rabbi was silent. Instead, the zealous voice of the district secretary made itself heard:

'Understood, Your Worship, Herr Stuhlrichter!' he cried and then quickly made a note of the order.

The head of the gendarmes stood to attention, loudly clicking the heels of his boots, and cried:

'At your order, Herr Stuhlrichter!'

The *stuhlrichter* of Teutschenau quickly climbed back into his carriage, followed by his secretary and staff. The captain of the gendarmes mounted the bench at the back of the carriage along with a sergeant. The coachman whipped the chestnut stallions and the carriage, carrying its important passengers, hurtled off down the dusty road.

Without a word, the Rabbi of Nadvorna watched them depart. His disciples even thought to glimpse the flicker of a smile on his face. A vague, playful smile, it seemed.

It was only then that they realised their rabbi had worked yet another miracle. A silent, unobtrusive miracle, but a miracle none the less. In his blind, stickler's fury, the *stuhlrichter* of Teutschenau might have granted three days for the dismantling of the tabernacle, or five days, or six days. He might, Lord forbid, even have issued a *gezerah*, an order to demolish the booth right then and there, on the eve of Sukkot, and Rabbi Mordchele and his congregation would have been left without a Sukkot Tabernacle, for there would have been no time to erect a new one. But no, the Lord had illumined the rage-darkened mind of the *stuhlrichter* and he had decreed: eight days.

And eight days later, the feast of Sukkot passed and the tabernacle was dismantled, this time not by Rabbi Mordchele himself, but by his faithful disciples, with mourning in their souls.

The Lord was with Rabbi Mordchele Nadverner and Rabbi Mordchele Nadverner was with the people his whole life. And as he himself prophesied, this last Baal Shem Tov, this Master of the Good Name and worker of miracles, the day arrived when he too was called to the Next World. It was the first day of Sukkot, the Feast of the Tabernacles, in the year 5655 from the Creation of the World, or the autumn of 1893, according to the new reckoning. In Bushtyno below the Maramuresch Carpathians 'lies hidden the legacy of the Lawmaker,' it was here that he was laid to eternal rest, accompanied by every last living soul among his disciples in the Land of Maramuresch and the adjacent lands of Bereg and Galicia and Bukowina, and farther afield.

And as Rabbi Mordchele Nadverner had willed, Moishe ben Israel Nathan-Alter, his neighbour from across the road, did not remain unpaid. Before he closed his eyes, the rabbi left word that since he was to be returned to the soil on the first day of Chol HaMoed Sukkot, which was in fact a working day, it was meet that he be wrapped in his everyday tallit, and that Moishe ben Israel Nathan-Alter keep his Sabbath prayer shawl, in exchange for the seventy kreuzers in good coin that he owed him.

For thirty-five years Moishe had kept the precious guarantee, the Sabbath tallit of the great and modest Rabbi Mordchele Nadverner, the Master of the Good Name, when the time came to follow him. He took with him the rabbi's Sabbath prayer shawl, perhaps with the secret thought of exchanging it in the New World for the rabbi's everyday prayer shawl.

Or perhaps in the Next World there are no Sabbaths and no working days of the week.

And perhaps there are neither days nor nights, perhaps there are neither prayer shawls nor prayers. Perhaps there is only silence and serenity, emptiness and light.

That same year, the 5655th since the Creation of the World, or the autumn of the year 1893 according to the new reckoning, Sirka of the house of Shapiro gave birth to Moishe ben Israel Nathan-Alter, the fifth son to bear the name of Mordechai, after the Rabbi Mordchele of Nadvorna.

'And Mordechai was illustrious among the Jews and beloved of all men, for he sought good for men and toiled for their happiness,' as is written in the Book of Esther.

And this is the scion of the family of Moishe, who his whole life kept the prayer shawl of the Rabbi of Nadvorna: Avraham, of the tribe of Yehuda, the author of *Yerach ha-eitanim* (The Month of the Strong), sired Yehoshua-Itzhak, who sired Chaim-Josef, who wrote the books *Tosafot Chaim* (Life Glosses) and *Nishmat Chaim* (Soul of Life).

Chaim-Josef sired Pinchas and Israel Nathan, who was nicknamed Alter, the old man, that he might live to a ripe old age, but who died at the age of thirty-one, after writing the works of cabbala *Gift of Israel* and *Creed of Israel*, and other books still in manuscript. And Israel Nathan-Alter sired Moishe.

And Moishe had six sons and three daughters. And the sons were Israel-Nathan, Eliezer-Lipe, Chaim-Josef, Zingel, Mordechai, and Aharon, and the daughters Miriam, Sara and Yochevet.

And all of them had sons and daughters.

Around the middle of the last century, a new and modern wind began to blow through these Carpathian climes and with it came the surnames law, namely that every person must have both a first name and a last name. It was then that Moishe ben Israel Nathan-Alter chose the name Bruckstein, which is to say, Bridgestone. Why? To this day, nobody knows.

PART TWO

The Earthly Tribunal

Semi-historical Tales

Rabbeinu Yaakov
of Orléans

Around the year 4900 since the Creation of the World, which coincided with the end of the twelfth century by the new reckoning, Rabbi Yaakov of Orléans left France and came to London, where he had been called to serve as the rabbi and head of the Yeshiva, or Talmudic School.

Some still called him Rabbeinu Yaakov Tam of Orléans, as he was one of the brilliant disciples and continuers of the work of the great Rabbi Yaakov ben Meir of Troyes, known as Rabbeinu Tam, which is to say, 'our righteous teacher,' after the passage in the Book of Genesis: 'And Jacob was a righteous man' ... And Rabbeinu Tam was in his turn the disciple of the famous Rabbi Shlomo Itzhaki, abbreviated to Rashi, thanks to whom we are today able to fathom many of the secrets of the teachings of the Torah and Talmud.

And they were right to call him Rabbeinu Yaakov Tam of Orléans, for he was honest and modest; educated in the school of his great teacher, he taught all his life, and he wrote his *tosafot*, his marginal glosses, under the name of his teacher. The name Yaakov of Orléans is mentioned only some thirty times in all the voluminous tractates of the Talmud, and in a few places in the commentaries on the Books of Moses; other than that, all that he wrote and taught by word of mouth to others was under the name and in the shadow of his great teacher. 'Kol hamevi davar beshem omro mevi geula leolam'—whosoever tells a thing in the name of him who said it brings redemption to the world. Yaakov of Orléans knew the deeper meaning of these words of the wise men of the Talmud. And since he could not know which of the ideas and commentaries that entered his mind were his own and which of them he had heard from his teacher, he attributed all to his teacher, Rabbi Tam of Troyes.

It was therefore with good reason that they called Rabbeinu Yaakov of Orléans 'Tam', which is to say, 'The Righteous', just as it was with good, but also sad, reason that he was named Rabbeinu Yaakov Ha-Kadosh, 'the Saint', for it was fated that he should end his life as a martyr for the holiness of the Name of God and for the Jewish people.

Rabbi Yaakov left France, above which there still hovered the black shadow cast by the trial for ritual murder in Blois—a town near Orléans—the first trial of its kind to be held in Europe: a strange, tragic, and at the same time risible trial, in which the Jews of an entire town were accused of having killed a Christian child to use its blood in the Passover ritual, even though the body of no child had been found, even though no parent had claimed a child was missing, even though no child was missing from any house in all of Blois, in all of France. But this deterred neither the Comte de Blois, Theobald V, known as 'the Good', nor the town's judges; it did not prevent every last one of the town's Jews from being sentenced to burn at the stake: the rabbi, the synagogue caretakers, the congregation, the women, the children. All that was needed was the sole testimony of an ordinary soldier, who on the eve of the Jewish Passover had taken his master's horse to the river to water it and found there a caretaker from the synagogue, who was watering his nag; the soldier's horse had taken fright at something, perhaps the white sheepskin that the Jew was wearing, it reared up, neighed, refused to enter the water; the soldier had galloped back to his master and told him exactly what he knew he liked to hear, namely that he had seen a Jew cast the body of a dead infant into the river: a white, innocent body, drained of blood ... And the judges believed this tale, forgetting that in order for there to be a murder there had to be a dead body or at least for someone among the living to be missing.

At the time, England seemed an oasis of peace and tranquillity in comparison with a France that was consumed with hatred. Trade, the crafts, and navigation were beginning to develop. London, York, and other cities were flourishing. The treasury of the king, who was preparing a third Crusade to liberate the Holy Sepulchre in Jerusalem, was eager for gold; the nobility, the owners of castles and large tracts of land, were desperate for loans; the Jews needed to lend and many others needed to borrow. And where there is lending there is also usury.

'If thou lend money to any of my people that is poor by thee, thou shalt not be to him as an usurer, neither shalt thou lay upon him usury,' as it is written in the Book of Exodus (22:25). Rabbi Yaakov, newly arrived from Orléans, saw that this sin, committed in full knowledge and in resignation, as if in the face of a natural calamity, had spread among the people and he knew that he had to call them back to charitable works and at the same time to alleviate the sense of sinfulness that vainly weighed on their consciences; on the other hand, it was also clear to him that he ought to preach against loans and the interest that went hand in hand with them, but that it would be like preaching to the Thames to flow back to its source, for who would then give a loan to the needy, if it was without fee or interest? And without the institution of lending, the world would be the poorer rather than the richer, the worse rather than the better, for 'lending is greater than giving,' as our wise men somewhere say. It is to be understood that giving humiliates, whereas lending, when practised at compassionate interest, helps the poor man pull himself out of his predicament with his pride intact. Rabbi Yaakov knew all this, and it was then that, anonymously as ever, that daring policy text appeared, which opened the way to progress, allowing people to live today on their income from tomorrow, the said text stirring amazement and even heated arguments among the commentators of the Law: 'I the undersigned acknowledge with full acknowledgement that I am in debt to so-and-so from the town of so-and-so. And so long as I am unable to make payment, I shall give him a gift, for every week from the day of the loan to the day of payment, such-and-such a sum in such-and-such a currency, which I undertake to bring so-and-so in the town of so-and-so within fifteen days of his summons ... The which I have acknowledged and signed that it might serve me as proof and evidence the same as a hundred honest testimonies ...'

There in England, the same as in every other place, the nobles and commons never saw the Jews ploughing the land and growing wheat, because the Jews did not own land and were not allowed to buy land. Nor did they see Jews toiling, as they did elsewhere, working as craftsmen, weavers, tinsmiths, cobblers, tailors; nor did they see the Jews peddling or going from place to place as day labourers; nor did they see them working as carters, porters, water carriers, woodcutters. Nobles and commons alike knew the Jews only as brokers rich in gold coins, as usurers who lent at a high rate of interest. But no matter what the rate of interest might be, it is always too high. And brokers, whatever their race, are not loved when they lend, and they are hated when the time comes for them to demand repayment of a loan. And when such brokers were of the Jewish people, they were hated with a deadly hatred when they lent, and hated with a deadly hatred when they received repayment of the borrowed money. And thus did the name of Jew become synonymous with that of usurer.

Nor was any account taken of the fact that such usury, or rather the trade in money, encouraged the development of manufacturing, of agriculture, of trade and navigation, which were so vital to the England of that time, and to the England of all times, so much so that the country adopted the motto, 'Navigare necesse est, vivere non!' History was to recognise it only centuries later, when those who had granted the loans were no longer able to enjoy anything of that recognition.

Yaakov of Orléans was a tall, strong man, with a gentle, smiling face framed by a wavy chestnut beard, with hazel eyes that were always screwed up, as if squinting to read tiny letters. His wife, Dora, was a tall woman, with thin lips, an ambitious woman, who urged her husband to shepherd the flock that lived in the capital of England. Their daughter, Esther, was a slender girl of seventeen, with long black hair gathered in a bun on the top of her head. Yaakov took up residence in the house by the synagogue on old Jews Lane, which had existed since the time of William the Conqueror, but according to others ever since Julius Caesar conquered England.

The new Rabbi of London worked tirelessly, and his labours were both fruitful for his congregation and satisfying to himself. He settled the order of the prayers in the synagogue and houses of prayer, he organised teaching at different levels for children of all ages, beginning with the aleph-bet, which is to say, basic reading and writing, continuing with the Books of Moses, then passages from the Book of Kings, the Prophets, the Psalms of David, the Proverbs of Solomon. Nor did the subjects that were taught omit worldly matters such as arithmetic and the rudiments of geometry, geography and astronomy. Rabbi Yaakov taught and closely supervised the teaching at the Talmudic school, where he educated disciples who insatiably drank their master's every word, before augmenting those words with their own ideas. And in addition to all these works, during the quiet London nights, Rabbi Yaakov of Orléans continued to write his *tosafot* in the margins of the Babylonian Talmud.

Whereas Europe was wracked by conflict, laid waste by hatred, in England there was universal peace and tranquillity. And for the Jews, this was a miracle. The weavers wove cloth, the tanners tanned hides, the teachers taught pupils, the brokers lent money, the porters carried burdens, and in this wise the year 4903 since the Creation of the World arrived, or 1189 by the Christian reckoning, when a new King of England was to be crowned, a young, ambitious, courageous ruler, Richard by name, also known as Lionheart.

The coronation of Richard was to take place in September, and the whole of England eagerly awaited the event. The Jewish districts of London, York, Norwich, Lynn, and other towns of the kingdom began to fret. They would have to send an emissary bearing a precious gift to the new King of England in order to show their fealty and win his goodwill.

Delegates from all the communities met in London. It was not easy to choose the embassy. Four prestigious men were to be part of the mission, and as to them there could be no debate: the Rabbi of London, Yaakov of Orléans; Rabbi Yom-Tov ben Itzhak of Joigny, the Rabbi of York; and the King's two bankers, both citizens of York, whose names were Baruch and Joicy. In fact, Joicy was really called Yossi, but his name had acquired an English ring and an English spelling. As for the other members of the embassy, there was heated discussion; quarrels even broke out. If Chaim ben Menashe, the tanner from York, was to be included, then why not Aaron ben Pinhas, the tanner from London? And why only master weaver Aharon ben Yeshayahu, a manufacturer from London? Why not also Nathaniel Vives, the owner of a weaving factory and velvet dye works in Lincoln? And whereas in the beginning, an embassy of five, seven, or at most nine men had been intended, finally a list of twenty-nine delegates was drawn up, who, bearing a joint gift, would go to pay homage to King Richard the Lion-heart at his coronation.

But the quarrel was still not over. The question arose as to what gift they should take to the King, what offering would be worthy of the ruler of England and of that country's long-standing and respectable Jewish community. The gift would have to be neither too cheap, lest it insult him, God forbid, nor too expensive, lest it blatantly create an obligation on the part of its recipient, lest it stand out and be considered to be arrogant and scornful of others. It was no easy task. There were proposals and counterproposals, and the discussion became heated. The weavers proposed a purple cloak stitched with gold thread; the tanners a coat of fine chammy leather, lined with ermine; the cobblers a pair of shoes with golden buckles; the smiths a steel broadsword with a wrought silver handle. Finally, after many other proposals were made, the assembly listened to the advice of Baruch of York, the king's banker and the Jew most respected by the young sovereign: he proposed that they commission a golden goblet weighing thirty-ounces—no more, no less, on which should be engraved ... And here Baruch cast a questioning look at the rabbis ... 'And they anointed David the King of Israel,' Rabbi Yaakov of Orléans, the Rabbi of London, quoted from the Book of the Prophet Samuel. Rabbi Yom-Tov of Joigny, the Rabbi of York, a tall, thin, agile man with large dark eyes set in a bony face framed by a straggly black beard, interjected that the verses that follow the coronation should also be engraved: 'The King went with his men to Jerusalem ... this is the city of David.' And the Rabbi of

York then cast the Rabbi of London a meaningful look, blinking his dark, lively eyes.

But who would make this goblet? Who else but master Bentzion Levi of London, renowned throughout the world as the best goldsmith ... But if the king was to be given a gold goblet fashioned by master Bentzion Levi, was it fitting that Bentzion Levi should be left out of the delegation?

The delegation therefore added another member, reaching thirty in number.

True, at the last moment, the trustee of the Norwich community tried his hand, saying that if the London goldsmith was going, then why not Menachem Cohen, the Norwich goldsmith? 'Because he's not making the goblet,' came the curt, annoyed reply from every side. 'But the London goldsmith is lame in one leg,' the trustee attempted to object, 'and what would it look like if he dragged his leg when he walked before the king as part of the embassy?' Rabbi Yaakov of Orléans then gave a gentle smile: 'If the Lord wished to make him the way he is, then what right do we mortals have to punish him for it?'

And so, it turned out that the embassy bearing the message of good will and the thirty-ounce gold goblet to the king remained settled at the round number of thirty men.

History tells of great men and important events. It recounts at length the life and deeds of Richard the Lionheart, it also tells of the rabbis Yaakov of Orléans and Yom-Tov of Joigny, who left us important glosses on the Talmud, it even tells of the great bankers Baruch and Joicy of York, but it breathes not a single word about Yehuda ben Mordechai, although he too lived in those times and in the city of London.

Yehuda, the son of Mordechai, was a blond, blue-eyed young man, an apprentice weaver, and hopelessly in love with Esther, the beautiful daughter of Rabbi Yaakov of Orléans. It so happened that one fine spring day, Dora, the wife of the Rabbi of London, went with her daughter Esther to the shop of master weaver Avraham ben Yeshaiahu, to pick out a velvet dress for her daughter.

Master Avraham shouted to Yehuda to fetch some bolts of silk. The two youngsters exchanged a few words with each other. Yehuda also provided a few explanations about the weave and the colour of the different bolts of velvet. After which, the youngsters met on the street a few times, near the Talmudic school, since Yehuda ben Mordechai liked to listen to the lectures and commentaries of the Rabbi of Orléans, and when he had the time, he would slip inside the yeshiva, sit on the corner of a bench at the back, and listen. Yehuda and Esther also met on the Sabbath, after prayers, in the courtyard of the synagogue. In the garden behind the synagogue, they would then sometimes sit on a bench in the dusk. Esther had a delicate profile, a long, slender neck, like a swan's, and thick black hair gathered in a tall bun on the top of her head.

And like young men of all times and all places, the weaver's apprentice Yehuda ben Mordechai had his own opinions and ideas, of which he spoke passionately.

And one autumn evening in the year of the coronation, as they sat embracing on their bench in the garden behind the synagogue, Yehuda told the girl, half in jest, half in earnest:

'Why do the senior members of our congregation expend so much zeal and anxiety on the king's gift? It is a fine gesture, of that there can be no denying. But were they really invited to the coronation?'

'I don't know!' said the girl, amazed at the question. 'But what is in your mind? I doubt that anybody has thought about it. Nobody expects such an invitation ...'

'Maybe they ought to have thought about it ... All honour to the kings of England, but we had our own great kings, thousands of years before them. And it would not have dented the royal honour one bit if the descendants of King Saul, of King David, of King Solomon had received an invitation ...'

And Yehuda ben Mordechai gave a soft laugh before continuing:

'Today, the Rabbi of London, your father, spoke beautiful words to us about Jacob and his brother Esau. Esau was angry. As Jacob was afraid to meet him, he prepared in three ways: *ledoron*, with gifts to mollify Esau, *letfila*, with pleas to make him relent, and if those did not work, *ulemilchama*, for battle, that he might be able to defend himself if need be. We listen to this teaching with pleasure, we repeat it countless times, but we do not follow it. We are always prepared with gifts; we are always prepared to fall on our knees and beg. But then we leave it at that. We pay large sums of money, heavy taxes to equip the King of England's army, but it never crosses our minds to equip ourselves for battle to be able to defend ourselves if need be.'

'What are you saying, Yehuda?' exclaimed the girl in fright, but with a tinge of admiration in her voice.

Yehuda ben Mordechai burst out laughing:

'My master, Abraham ben Yeshayahu, took fright exactly the same as you do now when I told him that around us is being built a wall of mute, smouldering anger, and that we stand before it holding a prayerbook, when we ought to prepare ourselves ... "Let me never hear you speak like this again," he interrupted, his face pale, frightened. And he told me that only a few years before, King Henry II, Richard's father, decreed that the Jews should surrender to the army any weapons they might have, in exchange for the king's protection. But on the day of wrath, the king is far, and those who wish us harm are near. Baruch and Yossi of York, the notables of London, Lynn, Norwich and other towns, have built themselves houses of stone surrounded by high walls, and within them they feel safe. But they do not realise that first they need to defend their walls before the walls can defend them ...'

Esther gazed at him once more her large dark eyes wide in amazement. The young apprentice weaver continued in a bitter voice:

'And the strangest thing of all is that with our heavy taxes and our gifts to the crown, we pay toward equipping the army of the Cross, which goes to liberate the holy places conquered by the armies of the Half Moon, commanded by Sultan Saladin. We keep our distance, we mind our own business, we look after our own affairs, as if those events did not concern us, when in fact what is at stake is our holy places, the Wall of our Temple, our land, the tombs of our ancestors and our future life ... From the East they came with pennants emblazoned with the half moon, from the West they set off with the Cross emblazoned on their chests ... We ought to amass from all four corners of the world and with the Magen David on our chests, we ought to make our way back there ...'

Esther looked at him speechless. And all of a sudden, in the autumn twilight, she thought to glimpse a Yehuda ben Mordechai in the shining chainmail of a knight, with tall blue plumes on his helmet, holding a broadsword in one hand and the shield of David in the other: Yehuda, her proud, strong, fearless knight.

But History has recorded nothing of the words of Yehuda ben Mordechai or the visions of Esther of Orléans.

History has no time to spare for young people in love such as Yehuda and Esther, for their secret meetings in the back gardens of synagogues, for their embraces, for their childlike, fantastical dreams.

The third day of September in the year 1189 by the Christian reckoning finally arrived: the great day when Richard, known as the Lionheart for his valour and fearlessness, was to be crowned King of England and the provinces of Normandy, Brittany, Anjou, Poitou, Gascony, and so on, and so on.

In the large square in front of the royal palace had gathered a crowd of commoners dressed in their best, and among them stood out the tall, broad-backed figure of Peter the Hermit, wearing his black habit of coarse sackcloth, with the hood drawn low over his black, feverishly burning eyes, and from the darkness of that hood jutted an aquiline nose and a prominent chin. After gawping at and cheering the resplendent procession headed by the young king, followed by prelates, nobles and knights, on their way back from the coronation at Canterbury, the crowd now craned their necks at the emissaries from every corner of the land, from the distant provinces ruled by England, from the kingdoms of France and Spain, from the German principalities, from the Italian city states, emissaries who wore rich garments tailored according to the local custom, made of velvet, silk and other costly materials in every colour of the rainbow, stitched with gold and silver thread. Then came the delegates of the guilds, bearing flags emblazoned with their insignia, then the representatives of the merchants and sea-farers, who brought an abundance of spices from the distant lands of the East. The crowd stared in wonder and let out cries of admiration, whoops of joy.

All of a sudden, Peter the Hermit jerked his head back. His eyes flashed with fury, the nostrils of his aquiline nose distended as he sniffed the air. 'Heretics,' he snarled ... 'The cru-cifiers of the Son of God! The sons of the Devil! What are they doing here?' An angry murmur spread throughout the crowd.

The delegation of Jews from London, York, Stanford, Nor-wich and other towns of England had arrived: the thirty dele-gates, headed by Baruch of York, bearing a magnificent goblet of engraved gold, which flashed in the sun.

'The sons of the Devil! Look at them in their finery!' shouted a ragged man from the crowd.

The Jewish emissaries were not garbed any more richly than those who went before them in the procession or those who came after them. The two rabbis, Yaakov of Orléans and Yom-Tov of Joigny, in their best black cloaks, white shirts, and high-crowned hats, the master craftsmen, the weavers from London and York, the shoemaker, the goldsmith, whose limp was barely perceptible, and the leather maker, in a black deerskin jerkin, all of them wore their best, to do honour to that great day, in which with all their hearts they wished to take part alongside the whole of the English people, and only the two bankers, Baruch and Joicy of York, wore garments of rich, brightly coloured velvet and silk, stitched with gold and silver thread, the attire in which they were wont to appear at court. But with their eyes on the two bankers alone, the crowd muttered enviously:

'Look at them in all their finery!'

'Nought but gold, from head to toe!'

'The sons of the Devil! The crucifiers of Christ!'

As always, the crowd did not see the many who did not own land or houses, the hardworking Jews, the tinsmiths, the tanners, the weavers, the pedlars who took their wares from place to place, the day labourers who went from place to place to hire out the strength of their arms, the porters, the water carriers, the woodcutters, who were as ragged as their fellow men of every nation and every creed. They saw only the thirty, who crossed the square in front of the royal palace in their best clothes, with the thirty-ounce gold goblet borne before them.

The Jewish delegation crossed the courtyard and arrived in front of the steps to the royal palace.

Within, the young King Richard sat in the throne room, a man of medium height, although his leonine mane made him look taller, broad in the back, wearing silver chainmail, his chest emblazoned with a cross, and draped in a purple cloak lined with ermine, which fell in folds around him. To his left stood the nobles of the court and knights in armour, among them Lord Richard de Malbys, Count Percy, and Viscount Pudsey, to his right, Archbishop Baldwin of Canterbury, William Longchamps Bishop of Ely, and other high prelates in white cassocks fastened with broad red and blue belts, wearing tall mitres and holding the crooks of their pastorship, and behind them monks and abbots in brown and black habits.

The king received the delegations from England, the royal provinces, and foreign lands.

When the court chamberlain, Ranulph de Granville, announced the arrival of the delegation representing the Jewish community of His Majesty's Kingdom, Richard started in pleasant surprise. A smile of amusement quickly appeared on his lips. The surprise was pleasant because they were his Jews after all, they were under his protection, they were his secret allies, by whom he kept in check the nobles and even the high prelates of the Church, who were eager for him to wage holy war, but who meted out their donations to that war with a thriftiness that verged on the niggardly. They even made sure to augment their own wealth and influence by means of their donations to the war that would liberate the road to the Holy Sepulchre and the road for spices from the East, from which they stood to profit. And he also tempered his nobles with the help of those secret allies of his. The nobles borrowed from the Jews, and he, as king, guaranteed the loans, a large share of which filled the coffers of the royal treasury. The king therefore had a stake in the timely repayment of loans to his bankers and at rates of interest that were as high as possible, as thereby he weakened the power and the impertinence of the nobility.

King Richard was about to tell the chamberlain to usher in the Jewish emissaries, when, pale with rage, Archbishop Baldwin of Canterbury exclaimed:

'The King of England cannot receive this embassy of the deniers of Christ on the day the Crown is sanctified!'

The King was astonished at this unexpected interruption. In his confusion, he was unwilling to make any immediate response, even less so to provoke a quarrel with the head of the Church, who had anointed him and placed the crown of England on his head. Therefore, in order to buy time, rather than to satisfy his curiosity, he asked the chamberlain:

'Who are the emissaries and what gift do they bring?'

'There are thirty of them, including rabbis from London and York, headed by the bankers Baruch and Joicy of York, and they bring a golden goblet with an inscription concerning the coronation of King David, and which weighs thirty ounces.'

Richard felt the urge to see and accept this gift on the part of subjects who could be said to be solely his, since all his others were also subjects of the Church, perhaps even more so than they were the king's. But Archbishop Baldwin cried out in a fury:

'Thirty heretics bring thirty ounces of gold, and Judas Iscariot once took thirty pieces of silver! Saint Paul the Apostle spoke aright in his Epistle to the Hebrews when he said, "Wherefore I was grieved with that generation, and said, They do always err in their heart, and they have not known my ways. So I sware in my wrath, They shall not enter into my rest."*

The Bishop of Ely, William Longchamps, a friend of Prince Richard's since his youth, attempted to quell the archbishop's fanatical rage:

'But in the same epistle, Saint Paul the Apostle then says to the Jews: "But, beloved, we are persuaded better things of you,

---

*   Hebrews, 3:11.

and things that accompany salvation, though we thus speak. For God is not unrighteous to forget your work and labour of love, which ye have shewed toward his name, in that ye have ministered to the saints, and do minister."* And this they do now, in aiding the holy work of liberating Jerusalem.'

'But without any faith in their souls! For their souls are in thrall to Hell! And the soil that they water brings forth only thorns,' cried the aged archbishop, his voice trembling with hatred.

Lord de Malbys respectfully approached the king:

'Sire, we too believe that they are not worthy to be received in this place on a day such as this.'

The Viscount of Pudsey and Count Percy nodded in silent agreement.

'The debtors do not find it pleasing to come face to face with their creditors,' thought the king to himself. 'They would prefer not to set eyes on them at all.' And then, in order to assert his kingly authority from the very outset of his reign, he said aloud:

'I have listened to your opinions and now I, your king, will decide!'

The king was seething with anger. He felt a mad urge to defy them, to receive the delegation of Jews, to show these lords who was the ruler of England! But he hesitated. He was even gripped by an obscure fear. King Richard of England, the fearless, valiant knight known as the Lionheart, even he, was gripped with fear. In battle, or when jousting, or in a duel, he had never been afraid. In such combat, you could see the enemy in front of you, you could gauge his strength, the weapons he wielded against you. But here, you could not know from which direction the blow would come or how to parry it. His brother, John without a Land, a fugitive in France, was plotting with

* Hebrews, 6:9-10.

King Philip Augustus, who was anything but a friend, and with obscure Norman barons, waiting for his chance to return to England and usurp his throne. And even now, before setting off to fight the war that would open Christendom's road to the Holy Sepulchre and England's road to the spices of the East, even now, was he to leave his back unguarded? Was he to be at odds with the heads of the Church and the lords who would stay behind and with the knights who would accompany him in battle? To what end? So as not to offend a delegation of Jews?

And so it was that the Jews, caught between the hammer of the king and the anvil of the lords, were dealt a crushing blow, a blow more powerful than those who dealt it had been expecting, a true coup de grâce.

The King turned to his chamberlain, Ranulph de Granville, and said:

'Tell the Jewish emissaries that the King of England cannot receive them today ... not today ...'

Richard emphasised the final words to let it be understood that the next day, or the day after that, he would be able to receive them. But the emphasis the king laid on those words was not heard outside the palace, and disaster ensued, sweeping over all the Jews of England like an avalanche.

With regal smiles and greetings, the king was still receiving the splendid delegations and precious gifts from England, the royal provinces, and foreign lands, when suddenly a tide of savage yells rolled into the throne room from the square outside. The crowd was in an uproar. The king dispatched his chamberlain to find out what had come to pass. On his return, the chamberlain went to the throne and whispered something in the king's ear. The king gave the order to the captain of the guard, but he soon returned, shrugging his shoulders in helplessness. Once unleashed, the fury of the crowd could no longer be quelled.

When the chamberlain informed the delegation that the king could not receive them, the thirty Jews had turned pale and remained rooted to the spot for a moment, and then, not understanding what was happening, ashamed and humiliated, they had walked with slow steps back to the palace doors.

Here, they encountered a few overly zealous soldiers of the guard, who pushed them from behind, hitting them with the flat of their swords, to make them leave the palace with greater haste.

The crowd saw it. And the news spread like wildfire throughout the square: The King had rejected the gift of the heretics, the deniers and crucifiers of Christ, the sons of the Devil! And the mob bayed in joy and hatred, they rushed upon the thirty old men, they ripped their best coats from their backs, leaving them in only their shirts, which were also soon reduced to tatters; they were left barefoot, unshod. Peter the Hermit, the monk in the black habit, with a voice of thunder, took command and the Jews were dragged to the bank of the Thames.

With terrifying zeal, the crowd obeyed the orders of the hermit, cutting firewood from nearby gardens to build a huge pyre. And between the waters of the Thames and flames of the kindled pyre, Peter the Hermit set up a makeshift court of law: barrels and crates were brought, and the black monk seated himself in the middle, surrounded by ragged, grinning vagabonds. The first to be tried was the Rabbi of London, Yaakov of Orléans.

In a solemn voice, Peter the Hermit pronounced:

'Yaakov of Orléans, choose between the water of baptism and the fire of Gehenna!'

'And for the sins we have sinned knowingly and unknowingly, forgive us! Spare us, Lord God,' Rabbi Yaakov's lips murmured soundlessly.

'Speak, Yaakov of Orléans!' resounded the stern voice of the hermit.

'I broke off the writing of a *tosefah*, an important gloss on the Pesachim tractate, about the sacrifice of the exodus from bondage, to bring a gift to an earthly king,' Yaakov said to himself. 'How could I have done such a thing? And for the sins we have sinned knowingly and unknowingly, forgive us, Lord God!'

'Yaakov of Orléans, for the third time I ask you: the water of baptism or the fire of Gehenna? Answer!'

The black monk, affronted by the rabbi's silence, was howling like a wounded animal. He wanted to hold a disputation with the rabbi, to preach to him the miracles of the Son of the Lord, the healing of the leper, the miracle of the loaves, the Transfiguration; he wanted the rabbi to defy him, curse him, insult him, but the Yaakov of Orléans was silent, he deigned to speak not a word, he would not even look at him, but gazed through him as if he were not there, as if he were nothing.

But Rabbi Yaakov saw the monk; he saw the face distorted by hatred. And all of a sudden, he was afraid. He would have wished to speak, to debate with him, to defend his faith and his life ... But what hope did he have, when the sentence had been pronounced in advance? But maybe his life could still be saved, came a thought, a temptation, from unknown depths ... Maybe his mouth could repudiate his faith, only his mouth ... And within him, his faith burned hot, hotter than ever before. Yaakov felt his brow beaded with a cold sweat.

If the spirit of evil should tempt you, drive it out by learning the Torah, he remembered the wise men of the Talmud had said. And if the unclean one should prevent you from concentrating on learning, utter the summons, 'Shema Israel! Hearken, Israel, our Lord God is one...' And if even this should not help you to rid yourself of the appetites of the flesh, the appetite to live at all costs, then ... then think of the day of death.

Of the day that will arrive in the end, sooner or later ... then what does it matter when and how it arrives, if sooner or later it will arrive, come what may?

The gentle face of Yaakov of Orléans, framed by its chestnut beard, suddenly became radiant, his eyes shone from between half-closed lids: Yes, the answer to the question that had pre-occupied him for so many years, the question concerning a judgement of the great Sanhedrion, here it was ... But why care, why pay attention to judgements concerning life?

... And yet another answer rose in his mind, concerning the question of the unnatural pairing of two things: two different kinds of animal under the same yoke, two different plants in the same furrow, a woollen and a hemp thread ... The hith-erto concealed meanings of Creation now appeared to him limpidly ... Thousands of answers that he had sought, flashed through his mind ... And he abruptly felt a sharp pain in his back, he would not be able to set down any of this on parch-ment ... He had no parchment, no goose quill, no ink, and the many questions would remain without answers, his work would remain unfinished ... A boundless sadness filled his soul ... His cheeks turned red with shame. 'Lord God, why do you punish me? Why do you lead me into the sin of pride? Was I alone called to provide answers and to write glosses in the margins of learning? Will there be nothing after me? Who am I, after all? And what am I but a speck of dust on the endless path of learning? *Lo alekha ham'lakhah ligmor!* It is not demanded of thee that thou finish the work, said our wise men, may their memory be blessed! In His mercy, the Lord will illumine the mind of another, of one of your descendants, who will write the answers to your questions. And perhaps he will do so better than you yourself would have been able to. You need only begin where others left off the work and write your own part. Then others will come after you to carry on the learning from where you left off. Others will come and they will write glosses, gloss after gloss. And the Work will never end ...'

Our teacher, Rabbi Jacob of Orléans, felt a sharp pain in his back, like the cut of a knife. 'When I have Thee, how should I rely on a king of flesh and blood?' A warmth flooded his body, smoke filled his eyes. He felt hot tears well between his half-closed eyes. The smoke was now suffocating him. 'Hear, O Israel, the Lord Our God is One ...' he murmured. Beside him, he heard howls of pain. Then other voices took up the prayer: 'Hear, O Israel, the Lord Our God is One ...'

That day, twenty-seven of the thirty were tortured, their living flesh was hacked with knives and swords, and then they were burned on the huge pyre that had been erected on the bank of the Thames.

Only twenty-seven of the thirty delegates were burned at the stake, as two of them, Rabbi Yom-Tov of Joigny and the king's banker Joicy of York managed to escape the clutches of the mob, and as nobody stopped to count how many had been caught or how many burned, the two finally made their way to York. But the third, Baruch of York, also one of the king's bankers, was caught but did not end up burned on the pyre.

Did Peter the Hermit deliberately leave Baruch till last because he was a banker and a moneylender, and consequently the most envied and the most hated of Jews? Was it so that he would first see the judgement passed on the other emissaries and would be terrified? But who could divine the thoughts of that monk?

'Choose, Baruch of York! Which is it to be, the water of holy baptism or the fire of Gehenna?'

His eyes starting from his head, his mouth dry, delirious from the sight of the blood, the smell of the burning flesh, the muffled groans that still wafted from the flames, Baruch murmured as if lost:

'Water ... water ... water ...'

Peter the Hermit raised his head in triumph, his pointed chin proudly jabbed the air, the nostrils of his aquiline nose dilated avidly, his dark eyes flashed with joy.

The hermit was wearing a black habit of harsh sackcloth and he went barefoot.

Baruch's white shirt hung in tatters and he was also barefoot, his shoes having been torn from his feet.

The hermit clasped his hand, as if he were a good and obedient child, and with slow solemn steps he led him into the water of the Thames until both stood knee deep. The monk cupped his hands and thrice poured river water over Baruch's head, muttering the words of John the Baptist all in a rush, 'I indeed baptise you with water unto repentance, but he that cometh after me is mightier than I, whose shoes I am not worthy to bear: he shall baptise you with the Holy Ghost and with fire ... in the name of the Father and of the Son and of the Holy Ghost ... let Benedict be your name in the Lord ...'

And the mob rejoiced that Benedict of York, the King's Jew, had become one of them.

And leaving him there, barefoot in the water of the Thames, with the hermit at their head the mob set out for London's 'Jews Street' to finish the work that had begun so auspiciously.

They slaughtered and burned at the stake countless Jews and they looted their houses.

The contagion spread to Norwich and Lynn, to Lincoln and Stanford, and to every town of England where there were Jews.

In York, having been warned by the two fugitives, Rabbi Yom-Tov of Joigny and Joicy the King's banker, the Jews took refuge inside the walls of the castle. But the words of the young weaver Yehuda ben Mordechai proved to be true: walls alone were no defence when they needed armed men to defend them. Seeing there was no escape, lest they fall into the hands of the furious mob and be humiliated before dying an agonising death, Rabbi Yom-Tov of Joigny gave permission for the Jews to kill each other, and he himself took his own life by the sharp blade of the kosher knife.

After the mob, whooping for joy at having won the soul of a Jew, left him barefoot in the water of the Thames, Benedict burst into sobs.

He perhaps wept because of the terror he had endured, perhaps because he was overjoyed at having escaped with his life, perhaps because he was bitter at having sold his soul to a God unknown to him.

He slowly emerged from the mud of the Thames, he passed a still smouldering body, and barefoot as he was, his fine shirt hanging in tatters, he wandered the streets of London that whole day and the whole of the night that followed it. Morning found him exhausted, lying on the stone steps in front of the gates of the royal palace.

Benedict kissed the top step and begged the soldier on guard to admit him to His Royal Majesty.

Astonished at the sight of that wretched man, the solider called for the officer of the guard. The officer called for the king's chamberlain, who recognised him for Baruch of York; he knew that he was under the king's protection and immediately went to announce him.

The King was sitting in his first council to be held since the coronation and there was heated discussion on how to quash the unexpected disorder or at least hold it in check, lest it spread yet further and take a different direction: in exile in France, John Without a Land might seize upon the unrest in England and use it to usurp the throne.

When he heard from the mouth of his chamberlain that his banker, Baruch of York, was at the gates of the palace in so wretched a state, King Richard ordered that he immediately be brought before him.

Benedict was brought into the council chamber, he fell at the King's feet, and said:

'Sire, I was baptised by force in the water of the Thames and I cannot live like this. I cannot return home to my family like this. What will I tell my wife, my son, my daughters? I feel estranged from myself, a liar before the world. And I feel a liar before you, my brave and just king. Day and night, I would be a liar, were I to remain like this. Merciful King, permit me to return to the faith of my ancestors!'

The king cast a reproachful glance at Archbishop Baldwin of Canterbury. And William Longchamps, Bishop of Ely, the friend of the king's youth, who aspired to the archbishop's see, also gave the stiff, emaciated old prelate a long and ironic look. The archbishop sensed that it was time to yield, that it was not wise to stretch the bowstring to breaking point. With barely constrained rage, he therefore said:

'If he does not wish to be a man of Christ, then let him be what he once was: a man of the Devil! We shall not stand opposed!'

And that day, Benedict, becoming Baruch once more, was released from his baptism and he departed from the king with his soul reconciled.

King Richard of England placed at his disposal a carriage with two grey horses and a guard of ten riders. Baruch of York, the king's banker, set off home. But on the way, jolted by the carriage as it travelled the bumpy road, he fell into a deep sleep from which he was never to awake. His heart gave out, ceasing to beat.

Baruch of York did not reach his home, he did not see his wife, his son, and his two daughters, who had been slaughtered; he did not see his ransacked house.

Perhaps it was his reward from the Lord Above for having repented.

The tide of blind rage had ebbed.

Those Jews still alive had buried their dead. The burnt wreckage of their looted homes had ceased to smoke.

King Richard, the valiant and large-hearted, was in a hurry to set off to war, eager to do battle with the Grand Sultan of Egypt and Syria, Yussuf Ibn-Ayyub, known as Saladin, or Gift of Religion, and to wrest from his clutches the holy places of Jerusalem.

Before going off on his crusade, King Richard appointed William Longchamps, Bishop of Ely, as his regent, the guardian of his throne. Among the many other high affairs of state with which the king charged him, William was to find and punish those responsible for the uprising, those who had slain the Jews under the King's protection.

The regent appointed a commission of venerable judges and notables, headed by the palace chamberlain, Ranulph of Granville.

The commission worked for a long time, for months and years it worked, as it was hard to discover the guilty parties: some of them had left the country, having joined the army of King Richard the Lionheart's crusaders, and those who remained cast the whole blame on those who had departed.

But even so, guilty men were found and they received their punishment: a fine of twenty shillings for every Jew they had killed.

Nobles too were fined, with a view to compensating the royal treasury for the Jews that would never return to their estates: twenty shillings for every Jew.

The lords Malbys, Percy and Pudsey were fined, but it seems that they still managed to turn a profit from the whole affair, since the loan contracts and the ledgers of their debts to bankers Joicy and Baruch of York had burned along with the bankers. These nobles, and many others, emerged from the chaos and confusion without a single debt, as pure as newborn babes.

Three members of the mob were hanged for the crime of looting Christian homes by mistake.

Many things are recorded in History and many things are omitted therefrom. Which does not mean that the things that are not recorded are any the less true.

For example, not one jot is recorded of the heated and rather strange discussions that took place on London's 'Jews Street', when some Jews sought to cast the blame for the catastrophe on other Jews ... 'How could they make such a mistake?' they asked querulously. 'How could they hand them reasons on a plate? Why did thirty men have to go? Why not twenty-nine? Or thirty-one? Why did the golden goblet have to weigh precisely thirty ounces?'

On hearing suchlike, Yehuda ben Mordechai gave a bitter, hooting laugh:

'Reasons! As if they needed reasons! In Blois, they said that the Jews had killed a Christian child to use its blood during Pesach ... There were accusers, there were accused, there were judges, there was a trial, but there was no murdered child ... Not one child was missing from any house in that town ...'

True, without caring about reasons and without encountering any impediment, the mob led by the black monk, Peter the Hermit, had attacked the Jews in their homes, they had slaughtered, looted, burned at will.

But in London's old 'Jews Street', which had existed since the time of William the Conqueror, or according to some even since the time of Julius Caesar, the mob met with a surprise.

In front of the synagogue and the rabbi's house next door—in which Dora, the widow of Jacob of Orléans and his daughter Esther sat deep in mourning—a band of young journeymen and apprentices, weavers, tanners, cobblers, Yeshiva students, was waiting for them, armed with sharpened iron rods, with knives and axes, with makeshift swords hastily forged in the smithy, and with heaps of stones ready to throw.

'Stop! Not one step further!' cried Yehuda ben Mordechai to the mob.

The mob paused for a moment, amazed at such boldness. But recovering from his surprise, the black monk shouted:

'Behold, the sons of the Devil have risen up! Send them to hell!'

And the mob rushed forward, baying in fury.

Yehuda ben Mordechai flung his sharpened iron rod with all his might. A bestial howl split the air and the hermit fell like a black sack down onto the cobblestones. The mob stopped short. A deep silence descended on 'Jews Street'. The mob was astonished that one of their own could be killed. Or maybe they were shocked that the blood which flowed from the chest of that holy monk was as red as that of the sons of the Devil?

Presently, the mob began to fall back, dragging with them the heavy, bony body of the hermit.

Dora, the widow of Rabbi Jacob of Orléans, and her daughter Esther hid for a while in a house outside London until the fury abated, and then, accompanied by a few of the rabbi's disciples, they crossed the Channel and returned to Orléans, where they still had relatives. Esther and Yehuda separated, without words, with pain in their souls and with a glimmer of hope that once and for all, maybe, just maybe, they would see each other again in a better world.

And the band led by weaver's journeyman Yehuda ben Mordechai wandered for a while in the forests on the outskirts of London. After which, these knights without horses, without chainmail and helmets, but with the Shield of David in their hearts, made their way to the south coast of England, where, in a fishing village, they boarded three boats and reached Europe. There, they wandered the north of France, the German duchies, they crossed the plains of Hungary, the land of the Wallachians and Moldavians, and finally they boarded a ship and with a fair wind filling its three sails, they reached the shore of the land of Israel. On the beach at Acre they set foot on land, and mingling with the armies of the Cross and the Half Moon, they walked to the Western Wall of the Temple. Small, lost, bewildered, they stood before the huge stones of the eternal Wall. Yehuda ben Mordechai approached with slow steps, he pressed his burning brow to the cold stone and in tears, he recited the confession: 'Shema Israel ... Hearken, O Israel: The Lord Our God is One ...'

And the others did likewise.

It was on the day of Yom Kippur.

But the year from the Creation of the World is not known.

History has not recorded the date.

The Book of Mordechai

also known as

The Book of Fates,

*compiled from the Purim scroll of the most learned and
pious Rabbi Shmuel ibn Sid-Sidilyo and other writings
with glosses from the things heard and thought by
Mordechai ben Moshe, descended from the houses of
Aboab and Galante*

It was in the time of Sultan Suleyman, known also as the
Magnificent, thanks to his noble and lofty deeds, and as the
Lawmaker, thanks to the good laws and regulations that he
drew up; it was in the time of that same Suleyman who ruled
countless lands and provinces, open cities and closed for-
tresses, islands in both the eastern and western seas, the lands
of Egypt and Syria, the regions on the near and far banks of
the Jordan, and the land of Persia as far as the city of Baghdad,
conquering the Isle of Rhodes and other Greek islands, then the
city of Belgrade, extending his dominion by fire and sword, de-
stroying Hungarian Mohacs, subjugating the lands of Moldavia
and Wallachia, and the merchant city of Venice, reaching the
heart of Europe, as far as Buda and Vienna and beyond.

The Emperor Suleyman ruled from his imperial throne in
Istanbul, the capital of Ottoman Turkey, the large city that the
Christians called Constantinople. It was in the year 900 from
the Hegira, that is, the journey of the Prophet Mohammed
from Mecca to Medina, which corresponded with the year 5282

from the Creation of the World in the Jewish calendar and the year 1522 according to the reckoning of the believers in the Prophet Jeshu of Nazareth. After conquering the Isle of Rhodes and driving out the Johannite knights, Suleyman imposed a new tax on his subjects and appointed high governors, lieutenants and judges in every land, province and island of his empire to rule and sit in judgement of the people in his name, and that they might act justly, impartially and wisely.

In the land of Egypt, too, in his capital Missr, or Cahir, he sent as his lieutenant Ahmed Shaitan Pasha, the valiant conqueror of the Isle of Rhodes, and placing him in higher honour than all the governors of the other lands and provinces and islands of his empire, before Ahmed Shaitan set out on his journey, the Sultan called him before him and said:

'The Land of Egypt I have given to you, slave of Allah, Ahmed Shaitan, brother, that you might dwell therein and rule it in my name, and that you might guide the people according to my word and judge them according to my laws. By this imperial throne alone will I be greater than you. I give into your hands the people of Egypt, with its hardworking tillers of the soil and the masters of the land on which they toil, with its builders of houses and palaces, with its owners of houses and palaces, with its scribes who write out scrolls and its scholars who seek within books and in the stars, with its masters of Time and its sages who fathom the mysteries of the Earth and Heavens. I give into your hands the believers in Allah and his Prophet Mohammed, and the *giaours* who live by the creed of Moses and by the creed of Jesus the Nazarene and in other vain creeds, but may you be strong enough and brave enough to judge fairly and to divide the burden of taxes wisely. And I also give you Abraham of Castro the Jew, the skilled master coin engraver of Cahir, that in my name he might strike coins engraved with my head.'

'I will do everything in accordance with your command and I shall follow your guidance in all things! I will serve you loyally, master!' said Ahmed Shaitan Pasha and thrice bowed before the sultan.

Emperor Suleyman the Great embraced him like a brother and wished him a safe journey, a calm sea, and a fair wind in his sails. Ahmed Pasha boarded a ship fitted with sails and crewed with a hundred strong oarsmen lest the vessel be becalmed, a vessel adorned with gossamer-thin green and red silk flags emblazoned with the half-moon, fluttering in the wind. And behind him came his retinue of administrators and advisers, his harem and his eunuchs, and the soldiers of his guard, armoured in shining chainmail. Arriving in the port of Alexandria, he disembarked to the sound of trumpets and in a long procession of adorned carts and horsemen, camels, and asses of burden, he set out for Missr, the capital of that land, which some also called Cahir or Cairo.

'I will do everything in accordance with your command and I shall follow your guidance in all things! I will serve you loyally, master!' Ahmed Shaitan Pasha had said as he bid his sovereign farewell. And thrice he bowed before him. Yet even then, treachery had been lurking in his heart.

Allow me, dear reader, to interrupt this narrative that has barely begun so that I might write a few things about myself, who, with fear and humility, labours to compose this book, asking the help of the Almighty to guard me against the temptation of pride, for as my grandfather, the wise Rabbi Isaac Aboab wrote in the preface to his *The Menorah of Light*: 'He sees into the souls of each and He knows that it is not in order to pride myself or to purchase myself a name that I labour over this book, but that to the reader it might provide some instruction and be remembered .'

I, the scribe of this book, am called Mordechai ben Moshe, and I am descended from the house of Aboab by my mother, being the grandson of Rabbi Isaac Aboab, the author of *Menorat ha-Maor* (*The Menorah of Light*), a seven-branched candelabrum whose stem is a verse from the thirty-fourth Psalm of David: 'Depart from evil, and do good, seek peace, and pursue it,' and which was forged from the purest gold of the Aggadah, of the legends and proverbs and parables of the great scholars of the oral teaching, of the Mishnah and the Talmud, and of the Tosafot, which is to say, the Glosses on the great teaching. And he wrought that candelabrum in the image and the likeness of the Menorah, of the holy seven-branched candelabrum of the Temple of Jerusalem, in the image and the likeness of the seven planetary stars that illumine the firmament. A book of profound thought, but written in such a way that all who read it might understand: young and old, men and women, scholars and the ignorant alike.

Having lost my mother and father in terrible circumstances, I was raised from the age of seven in the house of my uncle, Rabbi Shmuel ibn Sid, or Sidilyo, as he was called in Spanish, and my Aunt Sara of the house of Aboab, my mother's elder sister.

Rachel Aboab, my mother, was married at a young age to Moshe ben Samson of the house of Galante, who was the grandson of scholars and himself a learned man, a great spice merchant of Toledo, the city of my birth. At the time, in that city, the same as in all the provinces and cities of Spain, trade flourished, ships brought spices and carpets and expensive silks and Arabian horses and blades—daggers, swords, yataghans, their handles inlaid with gold, silver and precious stones—and ivory and amber and other costly goods from the Near and Far East and from the coast of North Africa. The Jewish communities flourished, according to custom they celebrated their holidays, they circumcised their new-born males, they buried their dead amid weeping and held their marriages amid merry-making, they helped the poor, their teachers taught their pupils and their writers wrote their books—life flourished, cares lasted no more than a day, and it seemed as though things would never be any different.

For seven years I lived in that happy country of Spain, in my parents' house in Toledo, until catastrophe struck us, the same as it did the whole Jewish community. The pyre. Exile.

By means of terrifying torture, the pious monk Juan of Colivera, the inquisitor of the Kingdom of Aragon, extorted from a man and wife from the city of Saragossa, Marranos—Jews who had converted to Christianity, but who secretly kept their old religion—a confession that they had spent the evening of the Pesach in Toledo at the Seyder, the paschal table, of my father. After a summary, torturous trial, it was sufficient that my father and mother be handed over to the civil authorities, since it was not fitting that the merciful and forgiving Church should pronounce that they be sentenced to burn at the stake along with the two unknown Marranos, for the Church was determinedly against the shedding of blood. And my parents were burned at the stake, although they had never converted, although to be honest they did not really remember having met that couple, since their house was open to all wayfarers and they never turned away a wandering guest, be he from Saragossa or elsewhere, when they celebrated Pesach, and when he was a guest in their house, they never asked a tired and hungry traveller who he was or what was his religion ... But none of these arguments was to any avail.

Later, it turned out that they had been burned at the stake as a result of simple error. For they had been sent from Toledo to Saragossa only as witnesses rather than as the accused. But here in the city of Saragossa, the zealous inquisitor twisted first their words, and then the torturers twisted their every limb before breaking the bones, so that they found themselves confessing they were guilty of enticing, seducing, tempting the baptised to return to their ancestral faith. De Colivera, the pious inquisitor of Aragon, received a paternal admonishment from no less than the Grand Inquisitor Thomas Torquemada for the error of having burned a pair of unbaptised Jews.

And I, Mordechai ben Moshe, the writer of these words, a child of seven at the time, lame in the left leg since birth, was left orphaned thanks to that error; I was left all alone in the world, like a shipwrecked sailor clinging to a rotten board in the middle of a heaving ocean. Which was literally what was to happen to me not long afterward.

From the still smoking pyre of my parents, my uncle, the learned Rabbi Shmuel ben Sid-Sidilyo, and Aunt Sara, my mother's elder sister, took me to their home. It was the year when Spain drove out the Jews and the Mahommedans, the year 1492 by their reckoning. We embarked on an aged ship, paying a large sum of money to the captain: we had to pay him not only for the voyage, our food, and the oarsmen, but also for the wind in the sails and for days when the ship was becalmed. We sailed for North Africa, thinking to disembark in Tunisia and thence to take a merchant caravan to the Land of Egypt, where fleeing Jews found a good welcome.

On the ship crowded with refugees from Spain we travelled with the great scholar and poet Rabbi Moshe ben Isaac Alashkar and his granddaughter, Miriam-Mona, whose pet name was Ramona, or 'Wee Sprig', a girl of six with curly black hair and blue eyes as clear as crystal. The girl's mother had died during the journey of an unknown disease and was buried on the south coast of Spain, in the small Jewish cemetery in Almeria, Granada.

Rabbi Alashkar's wife had died long ago, and he had been left with his granddaughter, his only son, Abraham, having fled from Spain to the north: he was to wander Europe before reaching Egypt many years later, where he would become a rabbi and a judge.

At sea, we were crowded below deck, deep in the hold, as if bounded in a nutshell, lest the ship's motley and suspect cargo be seen by the lookouts of any other vessel it might pass. And for a time, we did not know whether we were passengers on a ship or prisoners of the shipmaster, who sought to extort as much money as he could from that cargo of people without a land ... But we were fated to pass through another great danger. We could hear the waves beating ever more violently against the rotten hull of the ship. We were not far from the coast of Tunisia when a storm blew up and we were almost drowned like mice trapped in the hold. My uncle, Rabbi Shmuel Sidilyo, who was known as a great cabbalist and miracle-working rabbi, recited a prayer, murmuring strange, unknown words. All of a sudden there was a loud cracking noise, the ship broke in two and we were hurled into the cold waves. But then as if by a miracle, the sea suddenly grew calm. The people grabbed on to planks, crates, masts and other timbers floating on the water after the ship broke apart. I found myself hanging onto a rope from the main mast and looking to my right I saw Miriam Mona, Rabbi Alashkar's daughter. She was clinging to the same rope as I was. Finally, the waves brought us both to the shore of Tunisia. At the time, I could not imagine that that rope would bind us together for all eternity.

Rabbi Moshe ben Isaac Alashkar wrote a beautiful poem about the shipwreck and that miracle, which begins with the words 'Berna akkadem':

'With what might I hail Thy works, O Lord God that abideth in the heavens ... For thou art the cause of all causes and art without beginning and without end ...

'For great is the good that Thou hast done Thy servant. From many wounds and many insults hast Thou delivered me ... And Thou hast guarded me from vicissitudes ... And from the depths of the sea didst Thou raise me up and from the pit of bondage didst Thou free me ...'

And I, Mordechai ben Moshe, have inserted these lines about my all too insignificant life in this book, as I have said, not from vainglory, God forbid, not to show how many things I have been fated to suffer from a very early age, but so that the things which happened to me and others like myself might be instructive to the good reader of this book, and so that they might make him reflect upon how a good and a safe life was cast into peril and misfortune, almost without our realising it, living as we did like the blind who see not and the deaf who hear not, and so that they might make him think about how you cannot rely on the masters of this world, be they as malevolent as Satan himself, be they as benevolent, just and wise as King Solomon, for even such rulers cannot always stand in the way of Satan and defend us when he rages.

After our miraculous escape from the shipwreck, we set off down the coast of Tunisia with a caravan of merchants and arrived in Cahir, the capital of Egypt, where I stayed in the house of my uncle, Rabbi Shmuel Ibn Sid-Sidilyo, studying in his school, where, since my calligraphy stood out, I became the scribe of his scrolls, letters and books.

And this book too I write according to the Purim scroll, which is to say the Book of Fates of my uncle, of my rabbi and teacher, Shmuel ibn Sid, adding to it from what I have experienced, what I have seen and heard and thought. For thrice in my life was it fated that I should see my family pass from wealth and happiness to the deepest misfortune, to burning pyres and exile, and then to joy once more, thence to sorrow and grief, and once more to joy and the blind childlike happiness of Purim, an inexplicable, wholly inexplicable happiness ...

Ahmed Shaitan Pasha arrived from Alexandria with his rich and motley retinue in train. He disembarked in Missr, which is to say, Cahir, and great was the rejoicing and celebration in the capital. Even to the Jews it was occasion for joy and gladness. For the emissary and lieutenant of the good Sultan Suleyman the Magnificent had arrived, the Maker of Just Laws, whom the Jews, altering the vowels of his name, called King Solomon, since he was a ruler as wise and as just as his Hebrew counterpart of old.

And in Cahir there was joy in every house; there was dancing and merrymaking in the streets. The folk of each tribe danced and sang in their own language and according to their own custom. The Jews sang songs of praise in the synagogue and the prayer houses, the Armenians and the Greeks did likewise, and the Fellaheen sang their ancient songs in sad, drawn-out voices, for they had no other songs:

'Thresh, thresh if you want grain,

Thresh, thresh, work hard,

Till the end, the evening will be cool ...'

And in the songs of all there glimmered a ray of hope, because Suleyman was an enlightened emperor and he had told the lieutenant he sent to Egypt: 'be strong and courageous enough to judge justly and to share the burden of taxes and levies wisely ...' And Ahmed Shaitan had replied to the Ottoman Emperor: 'I will do everything according to your command and I shall follow your wise guidance in all things, and I shall faithfully serve you!'

And at the time, nobody knew that treachery lurked in the heart of Shaitan Pasha when he spoke those words ...

Ahmed Shaitan was a short man and for that reason he wore high sandals and a turban taller than was usual; he had a sparse, pointed black beard, a bony face with protruding cheekbones, small, lively grey eyes, thin lips, and a thin nose as hooked as the blade of a Turkish dagger. His mien was harsh toward those beneath him and gentle, docile toward those above him, but his ambition and lust for wealth and glory ate away at him inside.

The appointment to rule and govern in the name of the sultan over the most important land in the Ottoman Empire would have been an honour to anybody except Ahmed Shaitan Pasha, who felt deeply offended. Now that the empire was extending ever further, conquering new lands to both east and west, the brilliant general and conqueror of Rhodes ought to have been appointed Grand Vizier, not to have been diverted from the road paved with glory and appointed governor of a province, even as important a province as Egypt. But Sultan Suleyman was mistaken if he reckoned that Ahmed Shaitan would sit in judgement over petty cases or supervise the moneys collected by the province's treasurers, taking care only to send the gold accumulated to Sultan Suleyman for his glorious wars. No, he had different plans. He would not be an ordinary governor, a docile lieutenant of the sultan, rather he would have himself proclaimed King of Egypt to start with, and then he would set off to conquer the East, advancing in a semicircle around the Mediterranean before defeating Turkey. Then, as Sultan of the Ottoman Empire, he would continue his conquests in the West, in Europe and North Africa.

In hatching these plans of his, he soon found a valuable ally in the person of Mohammed-Bey, the commander of the Mameluke army, the largest military force in Egypt. Kindred souls have a way of finding each other, they sound each other out, each senses the stuff the other is made of by means of allusions, casting verbal bait half in jest, half in earnest.

This man with a broad face framed by a thick, curly black beard, a face that might have been taken to be gentle, jovial, childlike even, had it not been for the scar left by a yataghan on the right cheek, which lent that half of the face a ferocious expression, so that whereas the left profile wore an innocent smile, while the right always looked furious, savage; this Mohammed, Bey of Cahir, was also discontented with Sultan Suleyman. But while Ahmed Shaitan Pasha was discontented, offended, at the sultan having appointed him governor of Egypt, Mohammed Bey was discontented at the sultan not having appointed him governor of Egypt ... So, for the time being, the hatred of the two men was directed not at each other but at the Ottoman Sultan; as soon as he learned of Ahmed Pasha's discontentment, of the fact that he had been sent to Egypt against his will, Mohammed ceased to see him as a usurper of the position that was rightfully his. It was only later, when he scented which way the wind was blowing, that the bey was to rise up against him, in the hope of replacing him.

Almost two years after he took up residence in the Missr Palace, with the help of his guards, his allies, the governors of various cities and provinces of Egypt, and above all the army of Mamelukes commanded by Mohammed Bey, Ahmed Shaitan proclaimed himself King of Egypt and commanded that there be rejoicing throughout the land.

And once more, there were celebrations in the streets and in people's homes, in obedience to the ruler's command. In mosques, temples and synagogues, prayers of thanksgiving were offered up, each tribe rejoiced and glorified the new ruler in their own tongues and according to their own customs; but this time, the joy was forced, and was filled with fear and disquiet.

After they had hailed him as King of Egypt, Lord of the Cities of Cahir and Alexandria, Guardian of the fertile Nile in the name of Allah and his Prophet Mohammed, Ahmed Shaitan gave a banquet for all the governors of the land and the generals of the army. Green, red and blue carpets were spread over the palace's marble, mother-of-pearl and black flagstones. The guests lolled on silk pillows next to tables of ebony, mahogany, and Lebanese cedar, drinking aromatic juices, unfermented beverages made from figs and dates, pomegranates and other rare fruits, and eating fine foods from platters of gold and silver, dishes both peppered and sweet, according to the taste of each. There were food and drink in abundance, but none was forced to eat or drink, since the newly proclaimed King Ahmed Shaitan had ordered all the servants of his house to treat each of his guests according to his own wishes.

And at intervals during the meal, King Ahmed Shaitan, who lolled three steps higher than his guests, with Mohammed Bey one step lower to his right, called out witticisms to the lower table in the left-hand corner, where the 'King's Jews' were seated, the holders of high official positions and the leaders of the Jewish community: Abraham Al-Kiultumant, the treasurer and overseer of the king's stables; Abraham de Castro, the skilled master minter of coins; Rabbi David ben Solomon ibn Abi-Zimra, the Grand Rabbi of the Community; Yaakov Berab, or Bey-rav, a scholar of the secrets of the Kabbalah and rich cereal merchant; Rabbi Abraham Ibn Shoshan and Isaac Acrish, both members of the rabbinic college; and also the poet Moshe Alashkar, a poor man, a wanderer, who after many years in Tunis and Morocco, had arrived with his daughter Miriam Mona in Cahir, having been summoned to take up the post of *dayan*, or judge. Seated at the same table was my uncle, Rabbi Shmuel Ibn Sid-Sidilyo, the head of the Tanachic and Talmudic school, and other dignitaries from the Jewish communities of Cahir and Alexandria, who attended that feast with expressions of joy on their faces and feelings of dread in their hearts. And so at intervals, Ahmed Shaitan called out to them, quoting from the Koran and other holy books: 'And the Jews and the Christians say: we are the children of Allah, His beloved sons ... But I, Ahmed Shaitan, the King, say to you that all the *giaours* will truly return to Him ...' And winking at them, he cried out: 'People of the Book! A Prophet is now come to bring you good news ... and to warn you!' And the guests seated at that table sensed a gust of danger.

It was now midnight, and the new King of Egypt brimming with joy and merriment. But all of a sudden, staring stiffly straight ahead of him, without turning his head to the master minter of coins, Ahmed Shaitan cried out: 'Abraham de Castro, regard well the left side of my face!'

Castro understood and he shuddered, but said nothing. Rather, he studied that profile, with its hooked nose that was as sharp as a Turkish dagger.

And on the other side of the king, the left side of Mohammed Bey's face smiled as gently as a child.

On the third day after his coronation, the new king gave a feast for the poor of Missr in the courtyard and gardens of the palace. And all sang and danced, each tribe according to its customs and its own language.

And I, Mordechai ben Moshe, descended from the house of Aboab and Galante, the writer of this work, mingled with the Fellaheen and I listened to their songs, the words of some of which I have set down. They sang their drawn-out songs, which were somewhat dolorous for such an occasion, but presumably they had no others:

> 'How many sheaves we have to carry,
> How bushels of barley every day,
> All the barns are full,
> And every barge is full
> To overflowing, spilling grain.

Thus, are we driven on,
Hungry, bent double,
Our shoulders almost breaking,
But our backs are made of iron,
Given the burdens we must bear ...'

Thus began the reign of Ahmed Shaitan.

And the new King of Egypt imposed new taxes and levies on the citizens of Cahir, Alexandria, and the towns along the fertile banks of the Nile, he collected customs fees in the ports and on the caravan routes.

After the days of celebration had passed, King Ahmed Shaitan of Egypt called the master minter of coins Abraham de Castro and ordered him to strike a gold coin to be accepted by all merchants, which would be stamped with his head and the inscription: 'Ahmed the First, King of Egypt by the will of Allah and his Prophet Mohammed.'

Abraham, a tall imposing man with a long face made longer by a pointed black beard streaked with silver strands, had been expecting this call since the feast in the palace and now he stood awkwardly before the usurping king. He was caught between hammer and anvil. He knew that he had to remain loyal to Sultan Suleyman of Ottoman Turkey and the lands over which he extended his rule; he had to remain loyal to the man who had sent him there, and therefore it would be treachery to strike a coin with any other head than the sultan's. On the other hand, he was wholly at the whim and mercy of this ambitious man, and he also knew full well that if he openly refused to strike the coin demanded by Ahmed Shaitan, his head would soon be parted from his body by a single stroke of the yataghan. There was nothing else to do except to play for time. He made a deep bow and answered the king: 'The striking of a new coin to be accepted by every merchant must rest on the written command of the king, which in turn must rest on a law whose parchment has been placed in the treasury archives. Give the command, O King of Egypt, and all that is needed shall be done …'

Ahmed Shaitan did not detect the equivocation of these words. On the contrary, he was overjoyed at the prospect of issuing the decree in writing. 'Rightly have you spoken, Abraham de Castro. I shall have the scribe indite the order for you.' And the very next day, he sent him the parchment. Abraham de Castro was now ready. He carefully wrapped the scroll and that same night, disguising himself as a merchant travelling with a caravan, he crossed the Sinai desert, travelled up the coast of Israel, Lebanon and Syria, and many weeks later arrived in Istanbul, where he delivered the parchment to Sultan Suleyman the Great, who from the mouth of Abraham de Castro thereby discovered the particulars of Ahmed Shaitan's treachery.

When Ahmed, the usurping King of Egypt, discovered Abraham's flight, rage darkened his mind. He was in a rage at the master coin minter who had defied his command, the command of no less than the King of Egypt, which he had both spoken and, at his request, issued as a sealed written decree; he was in a rage at Abraham de Castro for having vanished without trace from his kingdom. But Mohammed, the Bey of Cahir, deemed it too little that this rage should be directed at Abraham de Castro, the sultan's master coin minter, alone. He realised that Ahmed's blind rage was a vast force that could be exploited, that could be channelled in a particular direction, like a torrent that would finally sweep Ahmed Shaitan along with it and carry him into the abyss, while he, Bey Mohammed, would simultaneously be given fresh wind in his sails.

Mohammed Bey therefore said: 'Do not forget, Your Radiance, King Ahmed, that this fugitive, Ibrahim de Castro, is of the tribe of the Jews, and that this tribe of infidel *giaours* lives scattered throughout your kingdom and is set apart from other nations, that it has its own special laws and does not hold to the laws and commands of Your Radiance, and that it is not to your advantage to leave them undisturbed. By the help of Allah and his Prophet Mohammed, we have anointed you King of Egypt, Protector of the fertile Nile, Lord of the cities of Missr and Alexandria and all the towns of this land, and were Your Radiance to look kindly on our advice, he would command that this nation be removed from under your protection and be given into the hands of those loyal to you, that they might be annihilated, young and old, man, woman and child, and that in revenge, booty be taken from them, for they are destroyers and our enemies. And for this, we shall pay ten thousand gold talents into the royal treasury.'

And King Ahmed, blinded with rage, answered: 'I grant you both the gold and this cursed tribe, do with them what you will!'

When this news arrived, falling like a thunderbolt from a clear blue sky, the Jews were sitting peacefully in their houses, trade and the crafts were flourishing, caravans and ships were departing and arriving, laden with goods. When the news of this *gezerah*, this evil command, arrived, fear and grief overwhelmed the Jews, and they cried loudly to the heavens in their pain and despair. And Rabbi Shmuel Ibn Sid-Sidilyo, my uncle, who was peacefully working on his book *Klalei Shmuel*, an alphabetic compendium for study of the Talmud, on discovering what was in store, dropped his goose quill, rent his garments, put on sackcloth and sprinkled his head with ashes. He then went to his pupils in the Talmudic school and declared a fast to pray for annulment of the evil command. And he composed a prayer for that time of tribulation. For Rabbi Shmuel, the son of Sid, of the tribe of Sidlyo, was considered to be a *baal-nes*, which is to say, a worker of miracles by means of his prayers and fasts.

Rabbi David ben Solomon Ibn Abi-Zimra, the Grand Rabbi of the Cahir community, and the poet-judge Moshe Ibn Isaac Alashkar, and Rabbi Yaakov Berab, the learned cabbalist and important grain merchant, and Rabbi Isaac Akrish and Rabbi Abraham Ibn Shoshan kept a fast and recited prayers, and they called the people of Israel to fasting and prayer, to annul the evil command. The people fasted and prayed, and their weeping reached the heavens.

Messengers and runners were sent to Missr and every town and province, proclaiming that every Jew, young and old, man, woman and child, was to be slain by order of King Ahmed Shaitan. Some two thousand men gathered, soldiers, both Mamelukes and those who simply hated the Jews and loved to pillage. They swooped on the houses of the Jews, without fear of reprisal. And many, many houses were looted. That day, five Jews perished by the sword, and another died of terror before the looters could lift a finger against him.

And it was not as bad as it could have been only because a miracle took place that day, a miracle such as happens to the people of Israel, and which turned Ahmed Shaitan's order to the advantage of the Jews ...

At that time, in Missr, the capital of the kingdom, there lived a Jew by the name of Abraham Alkurkumani, who was overseer of the king's stables and whom the Lord chose to be of help and salvation to the Jews. The day when Ahmed Shaitan came to the royal stables to mount his sorrel thoroughbred Arabian horse, his servant Ibrahim Alkurkumani bowed, helped him mount, and grasping his ankle and kissing the sole of his sandal, plucked up courage and said, 'O King Ahmed, if I have found favour before Your Highness, hear me! Why do you not spare the Jews? What is their sin that you should deliver them to those who wish them harm and will destroy them? Your Highness was promised ten thousand talents in payment for the destruction of the Jews and the looting of their wealth. But it is a laughable bargain, for in truth what have they given you? The Jews are yours and their wealth is yours ... Revoke the command to destroy them, O King Ahmed, take them once more under your protection and in ransom they will pour into your coffers three times as much, thirty thousand gold talents, in addition to the usual taxes for their protection, which you will forfeit if they perish ... Take me as hostage for them and order the payment of the taxes and the ransom into your treasury ...'

Ahmed Shaitan looked down from his horse, surprised at this stableman, this small swarthy Jew whose eyes gleamed like a badger's. The man was right, he thought to himself. That Mohammed Bey, whom in the meantime he had appointed his vizier, had made a mockery of him. He had promised him the Jews' money in order to destroy the Jews, when in fact the Jews and their money were already his. He felt a smouldering rage at his vizier. But he would not say anything to him ... There was something insidious in the whole affair ... He had promised him ten thousand gold talents, but it would be inadvisable to accept the money, just as it would be inadvisable to take the booty from the soldiers once they had laid hands on it. It would have been highly dangerous, now of all times, when more than ever before he needed the unswerving loyalty of his soldiers and his vizier. By secret courier he had discovered that Emperor Suleyman was readying an army to invade Egypt. Ahmed Shaitan would need gold, much gold, to reinforce his army and ensure the loyalty of his soldiers, generals, and governors.

So, Ahmed, King of Egypt, looked down from the height of his saddle and said, 'Go, Ibrahim and do as you intend; do with your people as you see fit, for you have found favour in my eyes. And I will revoke the order and you will be the cashier of the Jews' payments.'

And then he spurred his chestnut Arabian horse.

Once more letters bearing the king's seal were sent out, runners and couriers took them to every town and village in the land, and the order was that the Jews, young and old, man, woman and child, be left in peace to go about their business.

Among the Jews there was rejoicing. They offered up prayers of praise and thanks to the Lord Above for this new miracle on behalf of His people.

Throughout the land, in every town and province where the king's order reached them, there was joy and celebration among the Jews.

Abraham Alkurkumani, the overseer of the king's stables and cashier of the Jews' payments, poured thirty thousand gold pieces into the treasury, in good coin accepted by merchants everywhere.

Mohammed Bey, the king's vizier, seethed with rage against Abraham Alkurkumani the Jew. He came before Ahmed Shaitan, made a low bow, and said, 'Allah would punish me cruelly if I were silent before Your Radiance and did not tell you all I have learned. There is a rumour that this Jew, Abraham Alkurkumani, the overseer of your stables, whom you have made treasurer and cashier of the Jews' taxes, has amassed a fortune. He has hidden away treasure. The booty taken from the Jews was taken to his house: precious stones, and carpets, silks, velvet, for he bought the booty from your soldiers for next to nothing and now there is discontent among the soldiers. And from your Jews, in your name and with your seal, he has wrung much gold, but only a small part has he paid into your treasury. Not a fifth part of the gold has he paid into your treasury.'

Ahmed Shaitan's heart was filled with rage. His small dark eyes flashed and his sparse beard trembled. He immediately sent for the overseer of his stables and the cashier of the Jews' payments. Abraham Alkurkumani thrice cast himself on the ground before the King of Egypt and kissed the white marble slab of the first step up to the throne. 'I await Your Radiance's command,' he said, feeling a heavy premonition in his heart.

Ahmed Shaitan was forthright: 'My command is that you bring to my treasury another one hundred and fifty thousand talents in good gold coin accepted by every merchant.'

Alkurkumani blinked his small badger-like eyes in fear. He said in a trembling voice, 'A hundred and fifty thousand gold talents ... the Jews have no such sum, Your Highness.'

'And bring the money quickly, Ibrahim Alkurkumani, otherwise the yataghan will part your cunning head from your unclean body in one blow.'

It was only now that Alkurkumani realised the trap in which he had unwittingly ensnared himself. Why should this cruel master avid for wealth and glory believe him? Why should he believe that where there was thirty thousand there was not also one hundred and fifty thousand? And thereafter larger and larger sums ... It was like a sack with a hole in it hanging over an abyss, in which you could pour and pour money without ever filling it.

'How much time will you need to collect the money?' asked Ahmed Shaitan harshly.

'So much time does not exist, Enlightened King, a whole lifetime would not be enough,' stammered Abraham in despair.

'Fetch dice,' Ahmed Shaitan suddenly called out to his servants. There was a mysterious glint in his eye. A servant brought two ivory dice in a crystal cup resting on a silver tray. Ahmed shook the cup and poured the dice on the floor. 'What luck!' he exclaimed in great merriment. 'Only a Jew such as yourself,

Ibrahim Alkurkumani, could have such luck. Double six. You therefore have twelve days to bring the money.'

'To demand this of us is as if you have already condemned us to death,' Alkurkumani murmured in despair.

And the King of Egypt convened all the palace scribes and dictated a letter that on a certain signal that he would give after leaving his bath, all the Jews, young and old, women and children, would be destroyed, slain, massacred, in the year 902 from the Hegira, from the Prophet Mohammed's journey from Mecca to Medina, starting on the nineteenth day of the twelfth month, which the Jews named Adar, of the year 5824 from the Creation of the World by the Jewish calendar—which, with the permission of Sultan Suleyman the Lawmaker, the Grand Rabbi of Cahir, David ben Solomon Ibn Abi-Zimra, had reintroduced, and which corresponded with the twenty-third day of the month of February in the year 1524 by the Christian calendar.

The wrath of King Ahmed Shaitan knew no bounds. In that same letter, he said that any Jew who tried to flee or hide was to be hanged from his own doorpost. And by way of a warning and public humiliation, every right-believer who concealed a *giaour* or helped him flee would be hanged along with that Jew from the Jew's doorpost.

Copied by the scribes, the letter containing the king's command urged the people of Missr and Alexandria and every town and village of the country wherein dwelled Jews to prepare for that day.

The runners and couriers set out with great haste bearing the command of the king. After which, King Ahmed told Abraham Alkurkumani, who stood with a sorrowing face and bowed neck before him, that if the one hundred and fifty thousand gold talents were not delivered to his royal treasury by the morning of that day, he would give the appropriate signal as he left his bath.

When this new evil command became known, there was once more great grief among the Jews. They fasted and they wept, they wept and they moaned, and many rent their garments and put on sackcloth and sprinkled their heads with ashes.

My uncle, Rabbi Shmuel Ibn Sid, descended from the house of Sidilyo, who was said to have the power to work miracles, once again gathered the pupils of the Tanakhic and Talmudic school of which he was the head, and together they spoke prayers and Psalms and Selichot, which is to say, pleas of forgiveness to avert the evil command.

But he was not able to stay with his pupils for long, since he was arrested and thrown in gaol. Before they took him away, he told me, his nephew, Mordechai Ibn Moshe, the writer of these words, that I should continue to say the prayers and the Selichot with the scholars and above all to sing thrice daily the seventieth Psalm, which begins with the verses:

Make haste, O God, to deliver me, make haste to help, me O Lord.

Let them be ashamed and confounded that seek after my soul; let them be turned backward, and put to confusion, that desire my hurt.

Let them be turned back for a reward of their shame that say, Aha, aha.

Rabbi Shmuel Ibn Sid-Sidilyo was taken to prison along with other notables and dignitaries of the Jewish community: Rabbi David ben Solomon Ibn Abi-Zimra, the Grand Rabbi of Cahir, poet and judge Moshe ben Isaac Alashkar, Yaakov Berab or Boyrav, the learned cabbalist and rich grain merchant, Rabbi Isaac Akrish and Rabbi William Ibn Shoshan of the rabbinic council, and spice merchants, master weavers, master stone and wood carvers, bronze casters. In all there were twelve leading citizens of the Jewish community, who were taken hostage and thrown in prison. For Mohammed, the Bey of Cahir and vizier of the king's army, had whispered in the king's ear that he should be vigilant lest any of them flee, as the master coin minter by the name of Abraham de Castro had done.

Abraham Alkurkumani was not thrown in gaol but left free so that he might collect the random. His house, his wife, and his seven children were kept under strict guard, however.

And I, Mordechai Ibn Moshe, descended from the house of Aboab by my mother and the house of Galante by my father, once again beg your indulgence, dear reader, to interrupt this story that I might write a few words about myself, praying to the Omniscient after every letter I set down on the page, that he guard me against the temptation to vanity and arrogance.

For as my maternal grandfather, the learned Rabbi Isaac Aboab, wrote in the preface to his *Seven-branched Candelabra*: 'The Lord sees into the soul of each man and knows that it is not in order to boast or to purchase myself a name that I labour over this book.'

And indeed, what do I, Mordechai ben Moshe, have to boast about, since I have never done anything worthy of note or praise? And if I insert into the pages of this book a few of the things that happened to me, it is because I deem they might be instructive and noteworthy.

I mean to say that during the time of rejoicing and thanksgiving, when Abraham Alkurkumani succeeded in stopping the massacre and pillage of the Jews, I became engaged to Miriam Mona of the house of Alashkar.

After he had wandered for some twenty years through various cities of Tunisia and Tripolitania and Greece, writing poems, judging cases as a *dayan*, and, due to his righteous, irascible, sensitive nature, becoming embroiled in disputes and even quarrels with other notable rabbis and judges in matters of the Halachah, of Judaic law and procedure, Moshe Ibn Isaac Alashkar returned to Cahir, accompanied by his slip of a niece; he returned just as honourable and as poor as he had left, having grown rich only in the manuscripts of his poems, which he kept in his niece's dowry chest.

Indeed, Miriam Mona Alashkar possessed no other dowry than her uncle's good name. As she wandered from place to place with her uncle, staying for a year here, two or three years there, keeping house for her widowed uncle, washing the dishes, cooking, cleaning, copying out his poems, time passed without her marrying and starting her own family. And when she returned to Cahir she was no longer very beautiful or very young—she was past her thirtieth year and was a year younger than I—she had a slender body, and her hair was no longer so curly as it had been when she was a girl, but rather it was straight and she wore it in a bun at the back of her neck; only her blue eyes had not lost their calm light, and were still as clear as crystal. And when we met again after so many years, I teased her, calling her Ramona, or 'wee sprig', the way I did on the ship. We remembered the mast to whose rigging we had clung and how we had been washed ashore, and we both laughed and felt well in each other's company. We were a perfect match: life had taught her to make do with little, while life had caused me to earn very little; she knew how to eke out what little she had as she ran her uncle's household, where, although there was not an abundance, there was no visible lack, while I earned a very modest wage from my three trades: copying books and scrolls, teaching in the Talmudic school, and repairing sandals, which I learned during my free hours, as and when I could.

We were therefore what is called a perfect match and as there was rejoicing and thanksgiving after Alkurkumani bought the peace of the community with thirty thousand gold talents, we became engaged. Her uncle, the poet Alashkar, and my uncle Ibn Sid and my Aunt Sara, my mother's elder sister, who had replaced my mother, set the date of our wedding for the seventeenth day of the month of Adar.

The rejoicing was short-lived. It had been proclaimed that the Jews were to be massacred and pillaged on the nineteenth day of the month of Adar … the third day after our wedding … And rejoicing turned to weeping and wailing, and the Jews fasted, they prayed, many rent their garments and put on sackcloth and ashes. Twelve of the community's notables were thrown into prison, including the uncle of the bride and the uncle of the groom, who was like a father to me. My Aunt Sara, who was like a mother to me, wept and wailed in fear and worry for her husband and the fate of the community.

Otherwise, it was as if we were all held within a gigantic prison; a wall had been built around us, an invisible wall of smouldering enmity, of indifference, but in places a wall that had hidden gaps of compassion. The other peoples, the Egyptians, the Greeks, the Armenians, avoided us; they either would not or dared not talk to us. They were terrified at the prospect of being hanged from a Jewish doorpost. And why would they talk to people removed from the protection of the law, people subject to the king's wrath? Why would they do business with them? Why would they buy from them, paying a fair price, if the next day they could help themselves to everything for free? Why would they sell at the day's price to those whose days and money no longer belonged to them? Why would they remain friends with those whose very souls had been left naked and no longer belonged to them? For in truth the Jews were nothing but living dead, who on the appointed day would become truly dead. Even if the signal for the slaughter had yet to be given, the Jews were all marked with the sign of Abel on their foreheads, the sign of the victim.

Given things were thus, I took counsel with Miriam Mona, whom when she was little and had curly black hair I had once nicknamed Ramona, or 'wee sprig', and we wept and decided that perhaps it was not fated that we should live together yet. We therefore decided to abandon the wedding, or to postpone it indefinitely.

I sent word through Abraham Alkurkumani, who had access to the gaol, and I received the determined and angry response of both Rabbi Sid-Sidilyo and Judge Alashkar: 'Do not postpone a wedding without cause!' 'Without cause?' I sent back: 'But there is weeping and wailing among the people of Israel.' 'Nobody has died yet, God forbid! Nothing has happened! A wedding is not postponed in Israel' was the reply that Alkurkumani brought back from the gaol.

Kol sason, ve-kol simha — Let a voice of joy and gladness redound in Israel!

Kol hatan ve-kol kala — The voice of a groom and a bride.

Na-ale et Yerushalaim al rosh simchateinu — We shall lift Jerusalem above our joy!

The wedding took place on the appointed day. The father of the bride rejoiced in prison; and the uncle of the groom rejoiced in prison. My Aunt Sara, acting as mother to both of us, accompanied us under the baldaquin, her eyes filled with tears of joy, of grief, of fear.

And in the souls of all the wedding guests, and of all the Jews in the land of Egypt, there was kindled a gleam of hope. 'If a wedding takes place in Israel ...' they said to themselves, without daring to finish the thought ...

Twelve notables of the Jewish community sat hostage in prison.

The house of Alkurkumani, with his wife and seven children within, was surrounded by soldiers and closely guarded.

Abraham Alkurkumani, the Jewish overseer of the king's stables, the treasurer who collected the Jewish taxes, was free to go where he willed. But he had to collect a hundred and fifty thousand gold talents.

Everywhere, the people looked at him with eyes glassy from weeping. His money collectors returned to the treasury empty-handed.

'The Jews do not have so much money, Your Radiance, Ahmed Shaitan!' said Alkurkumani, talking to himself, gesticulating as he walked. In his house and wherever else he might be, he talked to himself, addressing the king:

'O Enlightened King Ahmed Shaitan, I, Ibrahim, your servant, tell you that the Jews do not have so much money!'

'Oh, but they do! Oh, but they do!' sounded a cackle of laughter in his ears. Alkurkumani gave a start. That gurgling laugh was familiar to him. It was not Ahmed Shaitan, but Ahmed Satan ... the Devil ... the Adversary ... his swarthy face, his lively, beady grey eyes, his thin lips, and his curved nose, as sharp as a Turkish dagger ... and the domed forehead, the horns concealed beneath the tall turban ... Wishing to do good, Abraham Alkurkumani had sold his soul to Satan, to Hell. Henceforth, no matter how much gold he brought, it would never be enough. There was no escape from the clutches of Satan.

'They have the money! You only have to collect it, Ibrahim!'

Twelve thin-bladed gleaming yataghans whoosh through the air and twelve bearded heads fall to the ground. But the bodies remain standing.

'Here is your money, Your Darkness, Ahmed Satan, a hundred and fifty thousand! But mind you replace the heads!'

'Very well, Ibrahim, my son.'

And twelve palace servants replace the twelve heads on the twelve bodies, at random, without looking to see which head belongs to which body.

'Now bring me another three hundred thousand gold talents, Ibrahim, my son!'

'No such amount of gold exists!'

The yataghans whoosh and the heads once more fall to the ground, rolling across the paving slabs. And the bodies remain standing.

'Here are your three hundred thousand gold pieces, Your Darkness, Ahmed Satan!'

'Bring me five hundred thousand!'

The yataghans whoosh through the air ...

'Another five hundred thousand ...'

'Here is another seven hundred thousand ... another nine hundred thousand ...'

And in the house surrounded by soldiers, closely guarded, his wife and children weep. Abraham Alkurkumani has shut himself up in his room, he kneels, presses his forehead to the floor, talks to himself, gesticulates, mutters endless sums, as if bereft of his wits.

The day appointed by a roll of the dice arrived: the nineteenth day of the month of Adar, in the year 5824 from the Creation of the World, according to the Jewish calendar, which corresponded with the year 902 from the Hegira, the journey of the Prophet Mohammed from Mecca to Medina, and the year 1524, according to the reckoning of the believers in Jesus the Nazarene. Ahmed Shaitan, the King of Egypt, was in his bath, and Mohammed, the Bey of Cahir, whom he had appointed vizier, was nearby, with his men.

Ahmed Shaitan emerged from his bath, and the money, the fifty thousand gold talents, had not been delivered to the treasury. He was about to give the signal for all the Jews in his kingdom to be destroyed, to be slaughtered, when Mohammed Bey, whooshing his yataghan through the air, cut off his head.

Mohammed Bey had received a command from Suleyman the Great, the sultan in Istanbul, who by secret messengers had promised him a pardon and advancement.

In the ten days that followed, the army of the Ottoman Sultan reconquered Egypt and the city of Cahir; and the head of Ahmed Shaitan was impaled on a long spear and paraded through all the city as a terrible warning to any future traitors.

It was the twenty-eighth day of the month of Adar.

And Mohammed, the Bey of Cahir, gave a command in his own name and with the seal of Suleyman the Great, the Lawmaker, retracting letters sent out by Ahmed Shaitan, the treacherous, usurping king, by which all the Jews of Cahir and the land of Egypt would have been destroyed.

He issued a new command that the Jews be left in peace, that nobody should harm any Jew, young or old, man, woman or child, or take their property. And runners and messengers straight away set out with the ruler's command.

Emperor Suleyman the Great, the Maker of Just Laws, levied a new tax on the land of Egypt, and on all the lands, provinces, and islands of the sea under his rule. And all his deeds and accomplishments, all the particulars of his greatness, are inscribed in the chronicles of the Ottoman emperors.

For the Jews there was once more rejoicing and thanksgiving, merriment and praise. In their houses and on the streets, they sang and danced. In the houses of prayer and my uncle Ibn Sid-Sidilyo's synagogue in Cahir, they offered up prayers of thanksgiving for the miracle that the Lord had performed for the Jews. They declared the week between the nineteenth and the twenty-eighth of the month of Adar a holiday, and the twenty-seventh of the month was declared a day of fasting. The twenty-eighth of Adar became the Purim of Cahir, from the word Pur, or fate, since the dice were cast for the destruction of the Jews, but the Lord had turned fate toward their salvation, giving them days of rejoicing and celebration, a time for sending each other gifts.

My uncle, Rabbi Shmuel Ibn Sid-Sidilyo, and his wife, along with the poet Moshe Ibn Isaac Alashkar, his niece Miriam Mona, and myself, quickly sold all the items in our household that were not needful or were for ornament. On the backs of three asses, we loaded the things that were most needful, such as crockery and clothes, bread and dried fruit, and we set out for Jerusalem. The Great Rabbi David ben Solomon Ibn Abi-Zimra also went to the Land of Israel, settling in Tveria. But in those days, few were those who went to the Land of Israel. Most stayed behind in Cahir and Alexandria and the provinces of Egypt to rejoice and make merry.

For commerce and industry began to flourish once more. Caravans and ships arrived and departed laden with goods, and the Jews went on living in their houses as if nothing had happened.

And this is why I, Mordechai ben Moshe, descended from the house of Aboab and the house of Galante, have written this book, in sorrow and amazement, copying from the Purim scroll of my uncle and teacher Rabbi Shmuel Ibn Sid, and from other writings, adding things I myself saw, heard and thought, not from pride that I might make a name for myself, God forbid! but only in the hope that it might be something of a lesson and a reminder.

Nikolai's Soldiers

Velvele was among those captured by a *khaper*. That's what they called the child snatchers: *khapers*.

The lad was walking along early in the morning, on his way to the *cheyder* next to the synagogue, when out of the blue he was grabbed and bundled into the back of a closed wagon and taken to the recruitment office.

The Jewish community of Gorev, a village in the gubernia of Polonina, was required to send the tsar of Russia twenty-three recruits that year. The heralds had come beating their drums to announce the ukase issued by the Tsar of All Russia, Nicholas the First, which demanded that young men over the age of eighteen be sent to the military training camps and then serve as soldiers for twenty-five years. Every town and every village had its quota of soldiers to be handed over to the rulership.

But whom were the Jewish community to hand over? Married young men with children? Who then would feed their wives and children? Were they to hand over the baker's son, who baked the Sabbath ring loaves for the synagogue congregation? Or the timber merchant's son? Who then would support the community? And anyway, such folk paid ransom money, gold roubles in good coin, both to the community and the recruitment officers.

What other choice did the *khapers* have? They captured the likes of Velvele, the son of Zelda, an impoverished widow who took in laundry and had five mouths to feed, and the likes of Juda-Idele, the son of Hanoch, who cut firewood and drew water from the well and did all kinds of other chores for folk.

Nobody was going to check their teeth to see whether they were really eighteen years old. More often than not, the ones they captured were not even ten years old, not even eight, not even seven. But what did it matter? They were good enough to make up the head count of twenty-three that the community was required to hand over to the tsar in that Year of the Lord, 1825.

The snatchers rounded up twenty-three lads aged between seven and eighteen. And accompanied by a leading member of the community, they took them away in wagons that were like huge crates with tiny barred windows; they took them to the gubernia barracks.

Naturally, Zelda, Velvele's mother, wept. So too did Hanoch and his wife. And the other mothers wept. But what could be done? The twenty-three lads had been surrendered to the recruitment officer in exchange for a receipt, a piece of paper on which was inscribed the word 'Raspiska', and the whole Jewish community breathed a sigh of relief.

The young men and boys were given capes so baggy that the wind whistled between their scrawny bodies and the thick coarse cloth; they were given boots whose soles flapped open as they walked. And then the three hundred who had been rounded up from Gorev and the nearby villages were made to form a column and set out for Perm, in the Urals, which was where their 'cantonment' lay, and which was also why Nikolai's little soldiers-to-be were nicknamed 'cantonists'.

The journey on foot was long, endlessly long and snowy. It was a hard winter. And the hard, black rusks they ate were frozen solid. And when they did receive kasha, it was cold. The children began to drop like flies in the snow. Particularly those who were only seven or eight years old. Their boot soles flapped against the wet snow and their capes fluttered like dirty green drapes against their thin bodies. Velvele and Idel walked side by side, holding each other upright, shivering, and they dreamed of the *cheyder* next to the village synagogue, with its fire of dry twigs crackling on the hearth, where they would sit rocking back and forth, murmuring the old stories about the exodus from the bondage of Mitzraim, and about the parting of the waters, and about the sweet manna that fell from heaven every day, fresh, golden, tasty, like warm bread dipped in whey.

Juda-Idele, the son of Hanoch the water carrier and firewood cutter, was burning with fever. Velvele could feel his burning cheek against his own. Stagecoaches and large carts covered with awnings passed at rare intervals, but not one of them stopped, nobody climbed down to enquire about them. Once only, on what must have been the fourth or fifth day of the march, as Velvele remembered, a beautiful lacquered sleigh drawn by a troika of mettlesome black horses halted its headlong dash next to their column and a gentleman climbed down. He was a handsome gentleman, with long polished boots, an overcoat with a broad collar of gleaming brown fur, and a tall fur cap pulled down over his ears. The gentleman had a quite long brown bread, and his kind face was full of pity and amazement. He addressed the officer leading the column.

'Who are these children, lieutenant? And where are you taking them? Are they not too small to be malefactors?'

The officer gave a respectful salute, stood to attention, and answered:

'Your Excellency, they are Jewish boys aged eight or nine. They are cursed by fate. I'm taking them to join the army or marines, I don't know which exactly. At first, I had orders to take them to the cantonment in Perm, but then there was a change in the orders and now I'm taking them in the opposite direction, to Kazan. I had to make them march back the other way more than a hundred versts. What can I tell you, Your Excellency, it's awful: a third of them have dropped by the wayside ...' And here the lieutenant pointed at the ground. 'Not even half are going to reach their destination ...'

'There has been an outbreak of disease?' asked the man in furs, deeply moved.

'No, there's no outbreak,' laughed the officer. 'They quite simply drop like flies. Your Excellency ought to know that a Jewish boy is a creature as thin and delicate as a house cat. He's not used to walking ten hours a day in the snow and mud, with nothing but dry rusks to eat. All the more so when he's among strangers, without his father, without his mother, without any pampering. And then they start coughing, and they cough until they go down into the grave.'

The gentleman whom the officer addressed as Your Excellency said nothing more. He shook the lieutenant's hand and climbed back into his lacquered sleigh. The driver urged the three mettlesome horses into a gallop and the sleigh vanished into the distance.

'Who was that gentleman?' asked the sergeant.

'How should I know? Probably some important civil servant from Petersburg, with the rank of general,' replied the lieutenant. 'But I had to tell him! They ought to know about this in the capital' added the officer, without much conviction.

Not long after that, Juda-Idele, the son of Hanoch the woodcutter and water carrier, fell down in the snow and was never to get up again. He was seven years old and no longer able to resist. They buried him in the frozen earth at the side of the road. But Zelda's son Velvele, who was eight years old, stubbornly clung to life.

That gentleman, who was travelling through Russia in the lacquered sleigh drawn by a troika of mettlesome black horses, was not an important civil servant with the rank of general. His name was Alexander Ivanovitch Herzen, he was a writer and philosopher, a good man, a liberal, and back in Petersburg, he wrote about those 'pale, exhausted Israelite children with frightened faces, standing in that landscape of endless snow, in thick, comical soldier's capes, their lips blue and with blue rings around their eyes ... Horror that no brush could ever reproduce on canvas, no matter how much black pigment it might spread ...' Herzen thought that what he wrote would move even the stones to tears. But the stones did not weep. Nor did the people of Petersburg weep. Nor was the tsar's ukase revoked or altered. And the sun continued to rise and set, the same as before.

Once the 'cantonists' arrived at the military camp in Kazan, the military training of those young men and boys commenced. But training did not only entail instruction in the use of weapons: the Orthodox Christian tsar required devoted soldiers who were of the same faith as the father of their country.

The corporal in charge of the military and religious training of Zelda's son Velvele was a decent man by the name of Ivan Ivanovitch Dunyok. He was a simple man, short, stocky, and he wore a large black moustache with pointed ends. His task was to teach Velvele how to wield a rifle, how to march forward, how to throw himself to the ground in the event of danger, but also how to say the Lord's Prayer every morning and make the sign of the Cross at least three times a day. He even gave Velvele the nickname Volodya. Since Volodya Zeldovitch didn't sound right, he called him Volodya Zolotovitch, from *zoloto*, the word for gold. To flatter him. He had a soft spot for that tall thin lad with chestnut hair and lively dark eyes. But Velvele-Volodya didn't want to say, 'Our Father that art in Heaven,' and not for the life of him would he say, 'In the name of the Father and of the Son and of the Holy Ghost.' Instead, he kept saying, 'Shema Yisrael'—'Hearken, O Israel, the Lord is Our God, the One God'.

The order was that the young soldiers should convert to the faith of Tsar Nicholas the First 'voluntarily'. Which is to say, they should be asked nicely, combined with starvation, exhaustion and the whip.

One morning, when he had to say 'Our Father' and make the sign of the Cross, Volodya stubbornly said, 'Shema Yisrael', after which he was not given his rations for lunch. Another morning, he refused to say the Lord's Prayer and was given twenty-five lashes on the back and rump.

Corporal Ivan Ivanovitch Dunyok was a good man and he used to beg the stubborn Volodya Zolotovitch to say the prayer; he beseeched him as if were beseeching Christ Himself, and he would weep as he dealt him twenty lashes on the back.

As if a living miracle, Volodya grew up, and at the age of eighteen, he joined the army of Tsar Nicholas the First. He was a soldier tall and strong, a good soldier, who learned how to handle weapons, a soldier devoted to the tsar and the Russian homeland.

Zelda's son Velvele, nicknamed Volodya Zolotovitch, served for twenty-five years in the army of the tsar. He obeyed every order, he fought valiantly against the Cossacks and against the Turks, in the lands of Moldavia and Wallachia and in the Crimean War, at the siege of Sevastopol, and against all the tsar's enemies. But the one thing he would not do was say the Lord's Prayer and make the sign of the Cross, instead reciting 'Shema Yisrael' and a few other prayers he remembered from the *cheyder*, that school next to the synagogue in Gorev, a village in the Polonina gubernia.

After their years of 'cantonment' and military service, Nikolai's soldiers, although still Jews, nonetheless had the right to live anywhere in Russia, and therefore outside the Jewish settlements and ghettos. Many of those veterans, now old bachelors, settled in an outlying district of Petersburg, Russia's capital.

In 1855, a rumour spread throughout Russia and the world. The tsar and his government were preparing to pass a new law, a new ukase to oppress the Jews. The Jews were to be driven out of the places where they had lived so precariously hitherto, and there was also talk of bloody pogroms and suchlike.

A delegation of important writers and rabbis from Europe, from France, Germany and Austria-Hungary, travelled to the court of Tsar Nicholas I in an attempt to persuade him to relinquish his evil plan.

The delegation arrived on the eve of Yom Kippur, the Day of Atonement. Where was the delegation to stay if not in the district of the 'cantonists'? And where were they to pray if not in the synagogue of 'Nikolai's soldiers'?

So it was that in the synagogue of Nikolai's soldiers the Yom Kippur prayers were recited with Europe's most important rabbis at the pulpit. The Rabbi of Rothenburg was followed by the Rabbi of Pressburg, who was followed by the Rabbi of Vienna, each officiating in his own style, while Nikolai's veterans, the 'cantonists', listened attentively and repeated the prayers after them in a murmur, to the best of their understanding, reciting as many of the words as they could make out. But when the time came for the *ne'ila*, the prayer to conclude the Yom Kippur fast, and the Rabbi of Troyes proceeded to the pulpit, Nikolai's soldiers barred his way. No! The prayer to end the fast, during which the Lord Above sets the seal on his decisions regarding the fate of every man, would be recited by one of their own, as best he was able.

'But by whom?' asked the rabbis in astonishment.

'By Volodya Zolotovitch!'

And the soldiers seized Volodya, formerly Velvele, the son of Zelda, from the village of Gorev in the gubernia of Polonina, and there in the synagogue, they tore off his shirt. His body was covered in red welts left by the whip, scars that would never be erased.

The rabbis understood. Volodya Zolotovitch climbed the pulpit and as best he was able, he recited 'Shema Yisrael' and all the prayers he could remember from the Jewish school and the synagogue in his home village of Gorev, in the gubernia of and so on and so forth.

And the evil law, the new ukase against the Jews, was indeed never signed. Tsar Nicholas the First died before he could set his name to it.

Later, the Rabbi of Troyes could not refrain from praising Volodya Zolotovitch. He went to him and said:

'You did well not to let me climb the pulpit. As is plain to see, your prayer was answered.'

But Volodya angrily replied:

'But Rabbi, I didn't pray for that, I didn't pray for his death!'

Rabbi, Tsar, and Faith

Dr Isaac Iserovitch was an enlightened man and did not believe in miracles or tales of miracles.

Aged eighty-two, he was a tall, hale, imposing man with a silvery, leonine mane of hair and thick black eyebrows set above lively, restless eyes. Dr Iserovitch came from an old family of *Rizhiner Hassidim*, which is to say, followers of the Rabbi of Rizhin, but in his youth he had turned his eyes westward, travelling first to Vienna to study economics, then to Berlin to study mathematical logic, and then to Paris, where he gained a doctorate in philosophy at the Sorbonne. And in the end, he had stopped believing in miracles or tales of miracles.

I therefore found it all the more surprising when I met him in the Ramat Josef Park on the eve of Pesach and he took me by the arm and said:

'Let us sit down on this bench! I want to tell you a story which I think might interest you, the story of a kind of miracle that happened many, many years ago ...'

Strangely enough, I detected no hint of irony in his voice.

We sat down on the bench, Dr Iserovitch stubbed out his half-smoked cigarette, placed the butt in the matchbox he was twiddling, and began his story:

'In my little town, the same as many other little towns in Eastern Europe where large numbers of Jews lived, Easter never passed without a pogrom large or small. They would beat the Jews, throw stones at the Jews, break Jewish windows and heads, burn Jewish houses, yank Jewish sideburns and beards ... But I do not wish to bore you recounting things that are all too well known. One year, near the end of the last century, Rabbi Israel of Rizhin learned of a great calamity that was about to come down on the heads of the Jews. It was said that in great secret Tsar Nicholas and his ministers were preparing an ukase, an order to perpetrate a pogrom, a free pass to beat the Jews, to destroy and loot their property. Since the ukase was being prepared in such secrecy you will surely ask how it was that Rabbi Israel Rizhiner learned of it. And I will reply that I simply do not know. Perhaps he received a sign from heaven ... perhaps he had a presentiment, in which case how are we to explain it logically? But the fact is that the *tzadik* of Rizhin found out about the impending catastrophe almost at the very last moment. What was to be done? In such cases there is what might be called the usual, hierarchical way of going about things. In other words, given that all mortals, including rabbis and tsars, are subjects of the Almighty, the rabbi would have to make fervent prayers to the Lord Above as a means of swaying him, of begging Him to issue a heavenly counter-ukase to cancel the earthly ukase, the evil command of the tsar ... But the Rabbi of Rizhin realised that such a procedure would be too lengthy, too roundabout, for there was no longer any time for prayers and explanations and justifications; if, God forbid, the ukase had been signed, if the drums had been beaten and the trumpets blown for all the land to hear, then all was lost, for axes and scythes were always kept sharp, torches soaked in lamp oil were always at the ready, waiting to be lit and cast onto shingled roofs, and as for rocks, they lay scattered on every lane ... And anyway, how could you present yourself before the Heavenly Throne unprepared, without having carefully composed prayers that would go straight to the heart, without having thought out well-founded arguments? For it is well known that such a *gezerah*, God forbid, such a calamity, does not arrive without having some basis in sins great or small, known or unknown ... Think about the words of the Tocheichah, of the curse in the fifth Book of Moses: "But if ye will not hearken unto me, and will not do all these commandments ... I will make your cities waste ... And I will bring the land into desolation ... And ye shall perish among the heathen, and the land of your enemies shall eat you up."* Yes, yes, Rabbi Israel Rizhiner saw that there was no time left to pray, to beg forgiveness, and besides, he was impetuous, he was mercurial; he took the shortest path. He dressed up in clothes like the tsar wore: black trousers with a red stripe down the leg, a blue tunic with epaulettes, gold braid, and lots of medals and ribbons on the chest. Dressed like this, and given his chestnut beard, the rabbi was the very likeness of the tsar, *lehavdil*—separate, O Lord, the holy from the profane! And Rabbi Israel went to the capital, urgently summoned the tsar's ministers to the palace, and demanded the ukase. The document was ready for him to sign. Disguised as the tsar, the rabbi took the document, furiously ripped it to shreds, and ordered that there be no pogrom. The ministers were astounded by this change in the tsar, but they dared not say a thing. If their father the tsar gave an order, then theirs was to obey without comment. After which the Rabbi of Rizhin went back to his little town, shed his tsar's uniform, donned his caftan once more, and carried on with the customs to be performed on the eve of Pesach, such as baking the leavened bread, cleaning and rinsing the vessels in boiling water, poring

* Leviticus, 26.

over the holy scriptures concerning the holiday, and so on, as if absolutely nothing had happened.'

Here, Dr Iserovitch paused. I looked at him. The smile that flickered across his face showed no trace of irony. It was sooner a smile of vague satisfaction. After a short space, he continued his story:

'And there in the palace, what do you think happened? Around half an hour after Rabbi Israel left, the real Tsar Nicholas arrived, dressed in his black trousers with the broad red stripe down the leg, in his blue tunic with the epaulettes and gold braid, and with all his medals and ribbons pinned to the chest. He summoned his ministers and demanded the ukase in order to sign it. "Forgive us, Your Highness," stammered the ministers, pale with fear, "but only half an hour ago you demanded the ukase and then ripped it to shreds here in front of us ..." Well, what do you think the Tsar did? Do you imagine he frothed at the mouth with rage and demanded the heads of his ministers? Not at all! Tsar Nicholas burst out laughing and exclaimed in admiration: "Only Rabbi Israel of Rizhin could have played me a trick like that!" And he laughed heartily, he laughed harder than he had laughed in a long, long time.'

Dr Iserovitch also laughed, as heartily as the tsar in the story.

'But Doctor, do you really believe this story?' I asked him.

'How could I not believe it?' replied the doctor in all earnest.

And noticing my look of amazement, he went on:

'How could I not believe it? That year there really wasn't a pogrom, they didn't yank the Jews' beards and sideburns, they didn't throw stones at the Jews, they didn't burn down Jewish houses, they didn't break Jewish windows and Jewish heads ...'

Glossary

compiled by Alistair Ian Blyth

NOTE ON TRANSLITERATION

The Hebrew letters *chet* (ח) and *chaf* (כ), pronounced rather like a soft *k* (never like the *ch* in 'cheese') are transliterated *ch*, in keeping with the practice of transcribing Hebrew words that became established in English before the twentieth century, while the Yiddish letters *khes* (ח) and *khof* (כ) are rendered phonetically as *kh*. Thus, the word הצלחה in Hebrew is transliterated *hatzlachah*, while its pronunciation in Yiddish is rendered *hatzlokhe*.

1. TERMS FROM HEBREW, YIDDISH, AND OTHER LANGUAGES

Al netilat yadayim עַל נְטִילַת יָדַיִם (Hebrew) 'for the washing [lit. taking up] of the hands'. Prayer recited after the ritual hand-washing performed prior to any meal that includes bread or matzah (unleavened bread): 'Blessed are You, Lord our God, King of the universe, who has sanctified us with Your commandments, and commanded us concerning the washing of the hands.' ('The Seyder Evenings of Long Ago')

Alter אַלטער (Yiddish < German *älter* 'elder') 'old man, elder'.
('The Guarantee')

Avodah zarah עֲבוֹדָה זָרָה (Hebrew), *avoyde-zore* עבודה־זרה (Yiddish) 'idolatry', lit. 'strange worship'. The *Avodah Zarah* is the eighth volume of *Neziqin* (Damages), the fourth *Seder* (Order) of the *Mishnah*, the oldest collection of Jewish oral traditions, dating from the third century C.E., when such pagan festivals as the Saturnalia were still celebrated, and lays out the religious laws for interactions between Jews and idolaters, i.e., pagans of the Roman Empire. In Yiddish *avoyde-zore* also has the figurative meaning of 'misplaced zeal'.
('The Good Oil')

Baal-nes נֵס בַּעַל (Hebrew), *balnes* בעל־נס (Yiddish) 'miracle-worker', but also said of a person who has been miraculously cured. The title Baal ha-Nes, 'the Miracle Worker', was given to and is closely associated with Rabbi Meir (139–163 C.E.), a rabbinic sage from the time of the *Mishnah*.

('The Book of Mordechai')

Baal Shem Tov טוֹב שֵׁם בַּעַל (Hebrew), דער בעל־שם־טוב *Der Bal-Shem-Tov* (Yiddish) 'Master of the Good Name, or: He of the Good Name'. The title *Baal Shem*, 'Master of the Name, He of the Name', originated in the Middle Ages and was given to adepts who possessed esoteric knowledge of the Tetragrammaton (YHWH) and other Holy Names, which knowledge enabled them to perform miracles. Later, from the late thirteenth century, the term *bale-sheymes* (Yiddish בעלי־שמות) also came to be applied to those who inscribed amulets (*kemiyot*) with the Holy Names. In Germany and Poland, from the sixteenth century there were large numbers of rabbis and Talmudic scholars referred to as *Baalei shem* (Hebrew), who gained a popular following thanks to their powers of healing the sick by means of practical Kabbalah (*Kabalah maasit*), employing incantations and amulets that invoked the divine and angelic names, as well as by herbal and folk medicine. (See: Gershom Scholem, *Kabbalah*, Library of Jewish Knowledge, Jerusalem: Keter Publishing House, 1977, p. 311–2; *The Kabbalistic Tradition. An Anthology of Jewish Mysticism*, ed. and trans. Alan Unterman, Harmondsworth: Penguin, 2008)

Although others before him were also styled *Baal Shem Tov*, the title 'Master of the Good Name', often abbreviated as 'the Besht' (Yiddish דער בעשט *der Besht*), is now uniquely associated with Rabbi Israel ben Eliezer (1698–1760), the founder of Hassidic Judaism.

('The Fate of Yaakov Maggid', 'The Angel and the Bad Wife', 'For Ten's Sake', 'The Guarantee', 'The Loan')

Balegule בעל־עגלה (Yiddish < Hebrew בַּעַל־עֲגָלָה *ba'al 'agalah* 'cart master') 'coachman, driver, carter, wagoner'. From the eighteenth century, in Eastern Europe Jews made up a significant part of those whose occupation was the transportation of goods and people, so much so that the *balegule* became a distinct, often idealised, romantic figure in Yiddish folk tales, popular songs, and literature: strong, fearless, rough and uneducated but wise, often in contrast with the type of the cerebral but feeble Talmud student (*yeshive-bokher* ישיבֿה־ בחור). The trope of the rabbi and the *balegule* exchanging clothes can be found in the tale *Der rov un der balegule*, where a passenger in a cart asks a rabbi (the carter in disguise) a question regarding a thorny passage of the Talmud, and the latter replies that it is so simple that even the carter (the rabbi in disguise) could answer it. (See: Cornelia Aust, 'Balegule', *Enzyklopädie Jüdischer Geschichte und Kultur*, ed. Dan Diner, Vol. 1, Sächsische Akademie der Wissenschaften: Leipzig, 2011, p. 242)

In Yiddish, בעל־ *bal-*, בעלי־ *bale-* ('person characterised by, man/person of; responsible for; owner of; author of', *Arumnemik yidish-english werterbukh*, eds. Solon Beinfeld and Harry Bochner, Indiana University Press, p. 179) forms numerous compound nouns denoting occupations and categories of person, e.g. *balakhsanye* (innkeeper), *balboser* (fat person), *balhoze* (impudent person), *balkhaloymes* (idealist), *balkhshodim* (suspicious person), *baltakse* (official responsible for the tax on kosher meat in tsarist Russia), *balkaysn* (irascible person), *balmegazem* (exaggerator), *balmoyfes* (miracle worker), *baleytse* (giver of good advice), etc.

('The Guarantee')

Baruch haba בָּרוּךְ הַבָּא (Hebrew), *bor'khabo* ברוך הבא (Yiddish) 'welcome', lit. 'blessed be he who comes'. From Psalm 118:26, 'Blessed be he that cometh in the name of the Lord.'

('The Good Oil')

Beyodin ubelo yodin ביודעין ובלא יודעין (Hebrew) 'wittingly and unwittingly', with reference to the commission of sins. Part of the *Al Chet* (Hebrew עַל חֵטְא, 'for the sin [of]') or 'long confession' recited during Yom Kippur (the Day of Atonement), the holiest day in the Jewish calendar.

('The Inadvertent Sin')

Brit milah בְּרִית מִילָה (Hebrew), *brismile* ברית־מילה (Yiddish) 'covenant of circumcision', ceremony of the bris (*bris* being the Yiddish pronunciation of the Hebrew *berit* 'covenant').

('The Guarantee')

Chametz חָמֵץ (Hebrew), *khometz* חמץ (Yiddish) 'leaven, leavened bread', the eating of which is forbidden during Passover.

('The Silver Pocket Watch')

Chazaqah חֲזָקָה (Hebrew), *khazoke* חזקה (Yiddish) 'presumption; possession/pre-emption (of), claim (to)', lit. 'holding'. In Talmudic law, *chazaqah* is the presumption of title to property, particularly land, or the continued right to a benefit by virtue of use or enjoyment thereof over an uninterrupted period of time, defined in most cases as three years. *Chazaqah* is therefore similar to the concept of *usucapio* in Roman property law.

('The Inadvertent Sin')

Chevra Kadisha חֶבְרָה קַדִּישָׁא (Hebrew), *khevre kedishe* חברה־קדישא (Yiddish) 'holy society', funeral association acting on behalf of the Jewish community, whose purpose is to ensure the

dignified burial of the dead in accordance with Jewish law
and custom. ('The Inadvertent Sin')

Cheyder חדר (Yiddish), from Hebrew חֶדֶר *cheder* 'room', elemen-
tary school for Jewish children, where they learned the
alef-beys and to recite from the Pentateuch. The teacher at
a *cheyder* was called a *melamed* (q.v.).
('The Fate of Yaakov Maggid', 'Nikolai's Soldiers')

Chol ha-Moed חול המועד (Hebrew), *khalemoyd* חול־המועד (Yiddish) 'weekdays [of] the festival', i.e., the intermediate or
secular days that fall within the Passover and Sukkot pe-
riods, when the prohibitions that apply to the holy days
allow for certain exceptions, such as work to meet public
need or prevent individual financial loss.
('The Guarantee')

Chumash חֻמָש (Hebrew) *khumash* חומש (Yiddish), lit. 'fifth [part]',
the Torah (Pentateuch) in printed, book form, as opposed
to the Sefer Torah (סֵפֶר תּוֹרָה), which is a handwritten scroll.
('The Fate of Yaakov Maggid')

Dayan דַּיָן (Hebrew) דיין (Yiddish) '[rabbinical] judge, arbiter'.
('The Book of Mordechai')

Eliyahu HaNavi אֵלִיָהוּ הַנָּבִיא (Hebrew) 'Elijah the Prophet'. Hymn
sung after the Havdalah (q.v.) ceremony: 'May Elijah the
Prophet, Elijah of Tishbi, Elijah of Gilead, soon come to us
with the Messiah, Son of David.'
('The Silver Pocket Watch')

Emunah אֱמוּנָה (Hebrew), *emune* אמונה (Yiddish) 'faith, belief,
creed'. ('The Guarantee')

Eretz אֶרֶץ (Hebrew) 'land', with particular reference to the Promised Land (*Ha'aretz hamuvtakhat*) or Land of Israel (*Eretz Yisrael*). In Yiddish the word for 'land' is לאַנד *land*, and the Hebrew *eretz* is used only with specific reference to Israel: ארץ־ישראל *Ertsisról*.

('The Court Down Below', 'To Shepetovka and Back',
'The Protector')

Eretz ochelet yoshveha אֶרֶץ אֹכֶלֶת יוֹשְׁבֶיהָ (Hebrew) 'land that eats its inhabitants'. An allusion to the *Pentateuch* (Numbers, 13:32): 'And they brought up an evil report of the land which they had searched unto the children of Israel, saying, "The land, through which we have gone to search it, is a land that eateth up the inhabitants thereof, and all the people that we saw in it are men of a great stature."'

('To Shepetovka and Back')

Eshet chayil אֵשֶׁת חַיִל (Hebrew) 'virtuous woman', *eyshes-khayel* אשת־חיל (Yiddish) 'industrious and capable wife' (Beinfeld, Bochner). From the first verse of a passage from the Book of Proverbs (Prov. 31:10–31) that is traditionally sung or read after 'Shalom Aleichem' and prior to the Kiddush on the eve of the Sabbath: 'Who can find a virtuous woman? for her price is far above rubies.'

('The Good Oil')

Gabbai גַּבַּאי (Hebrew), *gabe* גבאי (Yiddish), the officer or trustee of a synagogue, appointed to supervise the order of services and to distribute charitable funds among the community, as is shown by the original meaning of the term *gabbai* ('collector [of dues]' < גָּבָה *gavah* 'to collect [dues, taxes]'). In Yiddish, a *gabe* is the adjunct or assistant of a Hassidic *rebbe* (q.v.).

('The Good Oil')

Gan-Eden גַּן־עֵדֶן (Hebrew) 'Garden of Eden'.   ('The Guarantee')

Gemara גְּמָרָא (Hebrew), *gemora* גמרא (Yiddish), lit. 'perfection; consummation', whence 'tradition; instruction'. Strictly speaking, the Gemara is the later Aramaic portion of the Talmud that follows the Mishnah and forms a commentary thereon, but in traditional Yiddish usage the word can refer to the whole of the Talmud.

('The Fate of Yaakov Maggid', 'The Seyder Evenings of Long Ago')

Gevir-adir גבִיר־אַדִיר (Yiddish) 'rich man'. A tautological expression (cf. *khamer-eyzl*, q.v.), lit. 'rich man-rich man', from Hebrew אַדִּיר *adir* 'mighty, powerful' and גְּבִיר *gevir* 'lord, master'. In Yiddish, the notions of wealth and power are closely intertwined, as shown by the proverb, *ver s'hot di mah hot di deh*: 'he who has the wealth [lit. hundred] has the authority', i.e., 'wealth is power'. Cf. *nagid* (q.v.).

('The Inadvertent Sin')

Gezerah גְּזֵרָה (Hebrew) *gzar* גזר (Yiddish) 'decree, command'. In Jewish law, the word came to have the connotation of 'evil decree', a command with no logical explanation and/or of nefarious effect, particularly with reference to anti-Semitic laws passed by the authorities of all the lands in which the Jews have lived in exile since Mitzraim (q.v.). In the Russian Empire, for example, any official decree that specifically named the Jews was automatically a *gezerah* in this sense inasmuch as it could be expected to bring persecution in one or another degree.

('The Fate of Yaakov Maggid', 'The Guarantee',
'The Book of Mordechai', 'Rabbi, Tsar and Faith')

Giaour (Turkish *gâvur* < Persian *gâwr*) 'infidel'. Pejorative term for non-Muslims living in the Ottoman Empire.

('The Book of Mordechai')

Gmilas khesed גמילות־חסד (Yiddish < Hebrew) 'bestowal [of] lovingkindness'. *Gmilas khsodim*, acts of disinterested kindness, may be monetary, such as the provision of a loan, but equally may entail visiting the sick or mediating a dispute. *Chesed* חֶסֶד (Hebrew) is a central concept of Jewish theology and ethics, and is the name of one of the ten Sephirot, or vehicles of divine emanation, in the Kabbalah.

('The Loan', 'The Guarantee')

Gubernia *губерния* (Russian < Latin *gubernator* 'governor'), *gubernie* גובערניע (Yiddish) 'governorate'. The main administrative territorial subdivision of the Russian Empire. In 1708 Russia was first divided into eight governorates consequent to an ukase (q.v.) issued by Peter the Great. The number of governorates subsequently increased and fluctuated, and the administrative term finally fell out of use in the 1920s, after the Bolshevik Revolution, when it was replaced by the territorial units of the *oblast*, *okrug* and *raion*.

('The Angel and the Bad Wife', 'Nikolai's Soldiers')

Hacham חָכָם (Hebrew), *hokhem* חכם (Yiddish) 'wise man, sage'

('The Fate of Yaakov Maggid')

Haggadah הַגָּדָה (Hebrew < *higgid* הִגִּיד 'narrate, expound'), *Hagode* הגדה (Yiddish), lit. 'the telling', (1) collection of texts, consisting of traditional tales and adages, psalms, hymns, and songs, all of which relate to the story of how God released the Israelites from bondage in Mitzraim (q.v.) and which are ritually recited during the festive meals held on the first two nights of Passover; (2) legend or parable illustrative of a point of the Law in the Talmud; (3) compilation of such allegorical passages from the Talmud, as opposed to *Halachah* (q.v.). '[A] parable, a tale, that pointed a moral and illustrated a question, that smoothed the billows of fierce debate, roused the slumbering attention, and was generally—to use its own phrase—a "comfort and a blessing."' (Emmanuel Deutsch, 'The Talmud', *The Quarterly Review*, Vol. 123, London, 1867, p. 430)   ('The Silver Pocket Watch')

Halachah הֲלָכָה (Hebrew < הָלְכָה *halchah* 'to walk', whence a man's conduct, his walk in life), *holokhe* הלכה (Yiddish). Jewish law, the part of the Talmud and rabbinic literature that deals with laws and regulations, as opposed to the *Haggadah* (q.v.).
                    ('The Fate of Yaakov Maggid', 'The Book of Mordechai')

Havdalah הַבְדָּלָה (Hebrew), *Havdole* הבדלה (Yiddish) 'separation, parting', the religious ceremony marking the end of the Sabbath, also the name of the prayer recited during this ceremony. The *Havdalah* praises God for making the distinction between the Sabbath and the six days of the week, between the sacred and the profane. Cf. *lehavdil* (q.v.).
                    ('The Fate of Yaakov Maggid', 'For Ten's Sake', 'The Guarantee')

Im ein qemach, ein Torah אם אין קמח אין תורה (Hebrew) 'without bread [lit. flour] there is no Torah' (*Pirke Avot*, 3:21)
                    ('The Protector')

Kadosh קָדוֹשׁ (Hebrew), *kodesh* קדוש (Yiddish) 'saint, martyr, holy man'.   ('Rabbeinu Yaakov of Orléans')

Kategor קָטֵגוֹר (Hebrew < Greek κατήγορος 'accuser, public prosecutor'), *kateyger* קטיגור (Yiddish) 'prosecuting angel'.

It is significant that *kategor* and *sanegor* (q.v.) are terms borrowed from Greek: the traditional Jewish court of law did not permit lawyers, as it was the task of the *dayan* (q.v.) alone to establish the truth of a case, unswayed by the rhetoric (and sophistry) of the professional pleaders who were an intrinsic part of the legal system of the Hellenic and Roman world. The image of the soul being tried in a heavenly court of law may therefore be said ultimately to derive from Hellenistic eschatologies rather than the Torah.

('The Angel and the Bad Wife')

Ketubot, כְּתֻבּוֹת pl., *ketubah* כְּתֻבָּה sg. (Hebrew), *ksubes* כתובות pl. *ksube* כתובה sg. (Yiddish) 'marriage contract(s)'. A Talmudic (rabbinic) rather than a Biblical institution, the *ketubah* was a contract laying down the groom's responsibilities to the bride, including financial obligations in the event of divorce or widowhood, and conjugal rights such as food, clothing and shelter. ('The Guarantee')

Khamer–eyzl חמור-אייזל (Yiddish) 'lecher, womaniser, libertine, debauchee, oysgelasener', lit. 'donkey-donkey'. A bilingual tautology, the expression compounds the Yiddish words for 'donkey', *khamer* (< Hebrew חֲמוֹר *khamor*) and *eyzl* (< German *Esel*), to create a humorous term of abuse—in its figurative sense of 'chucklehead', the word *khamer* is inherently humorous. Yiddish is particularly rich in tautological expressions; cf. *gevir-adir* (q.v.), Dov-Ber (דוב-בער 'Bear-Bear', q.v. Persons, Mezritscher Maggid), Ze'ev-Volf (זאב-וואָלף 'Wolf-Wolf', q.v. Persons, Ze'ev-Volf Kitzes).

An example of *khamer-eyzl* in context can be found in the following catalogue of epithets from the story 'Ab Jove principium' by twentieth-century Moldavian Yiddish writer Haim Goldenstein: '*Er hot zikh aroysgevizn der letster aferist, a gots-ganev, a khamereyzl, an opnarer, a paskudnyak , a vos-in-der-kort, volt men far dem ales gegebn dem nobel preyz, volt er im zikher geven gekrign'* (He turned out to be the ultimate swindler, a phoney, a skirt-chaser, a conman, a sleazeball, an out-and-out scoundrel: if there'd been a Nobel Prize for all that, he'd have won it) (Haim Goldenstein, *Regn-Boygns. Dertzeylungen* [Rainbows. Short Stories], Bucharest: Verlag Kriterion, 1981, p. 119).

('The Seyder Evenings of Long Ago')

Khaper כאַפּער (Yiddish) 'snatcher, grabber, catcher', man paid to kidnap Jewish boys younger than the official age of recruitment and force them into the army during the reign of Tsar Nicholas I (1825–55). (Cf. *izborshchik* איזבאַרשטשיק, name for a tax-collector from the same period who also abducted Jewish boys to press-gang them into the tsar's army.) Whereas a *khaper* was originally a childsnatcher, during the Holocaust the term came to be applied to children themselves, who in the ghettos snatched morsels of food from others in a desperate attempt to stave off starvation.

('Nikolai's Soldiers')

Khazern חזרן (Yiddish < Hebrew *chazar* חָזַר 'return [at regular intervals]') 'repeat [in order to learn], learn [by rote]'.

('The Fate of Yaakov Maggid')

Kidesh קדּוּשׁ (Hebrew) 'sanctification'. The blessing recited over the wine to commemorate the sanctity of the Sabbath or other holy day. ('The Seyder Evenings of Long Ago')

Kigel קוגל (Yiddish), the 'Unterland' (cf. Places, *Galil*, q.v.) pronunciation of *kugel*, a pudding made from *lokshn* (Yiddish לאָקשן, egg noodles), *farfel* (Yiddish פֿאַרפֿל, pasta pellets),

223

or potatoes, mixed with milk, flour, cottage cheese, and usually served on the Sabbath or festive occasions. The Yiddish word derives from the German *Kugel*, 'sphere, ball', probably with reference to the dish's puffed-up, soufflé-like appearance. In English, the word is first attested in the early nineteenth century, variously spelled *coogel*, *coogle*, and later *kugel*, for example in Lady Montefiore's *The Jewish Manual, or, Practical Information in Jewish and Modern Cookery, with a Collection of Valuable Recipes & Hints Relating to the Toilette* (London: T. & W. Boone, 1846), and in fiction it was to lend itself as the name of Jack Vance's puffed-up, picaresque anti-hero 'Cugel the Clever' in the novels *The Eyes of the Overworld* (1966) and *Cugel's Saga* (1983). **('The Guarantee')**

Kittel קיטל (Yiddish < German *Kittel* 'coat, smock'), white robe worn on holy days such as Yom Kippur, and sometimes used as a burial shroud. **('The Seyder Evenings of Long Ago')**

Klalei כְּלָלֵי (Hebrew) 'rules, precepts'. A term commonly used in the titles of systematising religious treatises.

('The Book of Mordechai')

Kol hamevi davar beshem omro mevi geula leolam כל המביא דבר בשם אומרו מביא גאולה לעולם (Hebrew) 'Whosoever tells a thing in the name of him who said it brings redemption to the world'. A precept from the *Pirkei Avot* (q.v.).

('Rabbeinu Yaakov of Orléans')

Kol sason, ve-kol simha, kol hatan ve-kol kala קוֹל שָׂשׂוֹן וְקוֹל שִׂמְחָה, קוֹל חָתָן וְקוֹל כַּלָּה (Hebrew) 'the voice of joy and the voice of gladness, the voice of the bridegroom and the voice of the bride' (Jeremiah 33:10–11).

Koyletch קוילעטש (Yiddish < Polish *kołacz* < *koło* 'wheel; Ukrainian *колач*, Czech *koláč*, etc.) *'challah'.* The Yiddish *koyletch* is an east-European synonym for *challah* (Hebrew חַלָּה, Yiddish *khale* חלה), a plaited loaf of leavened bread baked to celebrate the Sabbath. Customarily placed under a special cloth, two *koyletchn* (i.e., *challot*), together known as *lechem mishneh* (q.v.), symbolise the two portions of manna that fell in the wilderness on Friday in order to provide for the Sabbath. *Koyletchn*, which among the Slavs had a strong ritual association with prosperity and fertility, were also traditionally eaten during Jewish wedding feasts and at Purim.

('The Fate of Yaakov Maggid')

Komets-alef: o! אָ – קמץ־אַלף (Yiddish < Hebrew קָמָץ *qamats*, the name of a diacritical sign), the Yiddish letter אָ, pronounced *o*, as opposed to א *shtumer alef* (silent alef, used word-initially before ו *u*, וי *uy*, י *i*, וי *oy*, יי *ey*, ײ *ay*), and א *pasekh alef*, pronounced *a*. 'Komets-alef: o!' forms part of the refrain of 'Oyfn Pripetchik' [At the Hearthside] by Mark Warshawsky (1848–1907), one of the most famous Yiddish popular songs of pre-Holocaust Eastern Europe, in which a rabbi teaches children the *alef-beys* by the fire in his *cheyder*: '*Gedenkt zhe, kinderlekh, gedenkt zhe, teyere, / Vos ir lernt do; / Zogt zhe nokh a mol un take nokh a mol: / Komets-alef: o!*' (Remember, children, remember, dears, / What you learn here; / Say it once again and even once again, / Komets-alef: o!).

('The Fate of Yaakov Maggid')

Khremslakh, pl. כרעמזלעך, sg. כרעמזל *khremsl* (Yiddish), small, thick, potato or matzah (unleavened dough) fritters eaten at Passover.　　　　　('The Seyder Evenings of Long Ago')

Ledoron letfila ulemilchama לדורון לתפילה ולמלחמה (Hebrew) 'for gift-giving, for prayer, and for war'. The three ways in which Jacob prepared to meet his brother Esau as defined in rabbinical commentaries on the Book of Genesis.

('Rabbeinu Yaakov of Orléans')

Lechem mishneh לֶחֶם מִשְׁנֶה (Hebrew) 'double bread', collective term for the two loaves of leavened bread (*challah*, or *koyletch*, q.v.) that form part of the ritual of a Sabbath or holiday meal. At the start of the Sabbath meal, bread is broken over two unbroken loaves, the *lechem mishneh*, which commemorate the double portion of manna with which God provided the Israelites in the desert after the Exodus on the eve of every Sabbath so that they would not have to prepare manna on the Day of Rest: 'They must also spread on the table, a clean table-cloath, and set two loaves upon it; which loaves are baked on the Friday, and are called in Hebrew, חלות i.e. *Cholith*, and over the loaves must be spread a clean Napkin to cover them all over: and this is done, in memory of the *Manna* in the *wilderness*, which in like manner descended upon the earth, the dew falling beneath, and likewise a dew on top of it, but on the Sabbath it fell not at all, but on the Friday they gathered a double portion, therefore do they put two Loaves on the Sabbath' (David Levi, *A Succinct Account, of the Rites, and Ceremonies, of the Jews, As observed by them, in their different dispertions, throughout the world, at this Present Time*, London, 1782, p. 9). ('The Inadvertent Sin')

Lechem choq לֶחֶם חֻקִּ (Hebrew), 'rightful food', lit. 'law bread', with reference to Proverbs 30:8: 'Remove far from me vanity and lies: give me neither poverty nor riches; feed me with food convenient for me.' The Hebrew *choq*, which derives from the verb חָקַק *chaqaq* 'to carve [in stone]', whence 'to

226

legislate', is a theological term for a law in the sense of a divine commandment whose rationale may or may not be apparent or even intelligible, but to obey which is a necessary act of faith in the righteousness of God, Whose ways transcend all human understanding. Colloquially, *lechem choq* has come to mean a trait or habit essential to a person; a person's livelihood, his or her 'bread and butter'.

('A Monday of Fasting and Prayer')

Lehavdil להבדיל (Yiddish) 'make the distinction', from לְהַבְדִּיל *le-havdil* (Hebrew), imperative of הִבְדִּיל *hivdil* 'to separate, distinguish, make a distinction'. Originally, *lehavdil* was employed as an exhortation to make distinction between the sacred and the profane, the good and the bad. Colloquially, *lehavdil* is used in the sense of 'forgive the comparison' or 'not forgetting the difference' (Beinfeld and Bochner, *Arumnemik yidish-english verterbukh*, p. 363) when two things that are mutually exclusive are mentioned in succession, e.g. *a mentsh un lehavdl a malpe* 'a man and—not to compare the two—a monkey'. *Lehadvil* can be used for great ironic and humorous effect, as in the following example from Leo Rosten: 'I'm only starting in business, but *l'havdil*, at some point Rockefeller was only "starting in business"' (Leo Rosten, *The New Joys of Yiddish*, revised by Lawrence Bush, Three Rivers Press, New York, 2001, p. 208). ('Rabbi, Tsar, and Faith')

Lo alekha ham'lakhah ligmor לֹא עָלֶיךָ הַמְּלָאכָה לִגְמֹר (Hebrew) 'You are not duty bound to finish the work.' A teaching from the Talmud (*Pirkei Avot*, 2:19): 'You are not duty bound to finish the work, but neither are you free to desist therefrom.'

('Rabbeinu Yaakov of Orléans')

227

Maariv מַעֲרִיב (Hebrew), *mayrev* מעריב (Yiddish) evening prayer service. ('The Fate of Yaakov Maggid')

Maggid מַגִּיד (Hebrew), *maged* מגיד (Yiddish) 'teller, narrator'. (1) Itinerant preacher and storyteller. In Eastern Europe the *maggidim* were instrumental in the spread of new ideas, such as the Lurianic Kabbalah in the seventeenth century and Hassidism in the eighteenth and nineteenth centuries. (2) A *daemon* from the heavenly sphere that appeared to Kabbalists and conveyed messages regarding the divine mysteries. Rabbi Joseph Karo (1488–1575) wrote a work titled *Maggid Mesharim* [Preacher of Righteousness] (Lublin, 1646), a record of nocturnal visitations stretching over five decades by a *maggid* in this sense of the word. (3) Reciter of the answers to the Four Questions during the Passover Haggadah (q.v.). (4) Name of the section of the Passover Haggadah that introduces the Four Questions.

See also: *Dov Ber, Mezritscher Maggid* (Persons q.v.).

Mah nishtanah, ha–laylah ha–zeh, mi–kol ha–leylot

מַה נִּשְׁתַּנָּה, הַלַּיְלָה הַזֶּה מִכָּל הַלֵּילוֹת (Hebrew) 'What has changed, this night of all other nights?' The introduction to the Four Questions, part of the Maggid (q.v.) section of the Haggadah (q.v.), which tells the Passover story of the Exodus from bondage in Mitzraim (q.v.). It is customary for the youngest child present at the Seder to recite the questions.

('The Seyder Evenings of Long Ago')

Melamed מלמד (Yiddish, from Hebrew מְלַמֵּד) 'teacher, tutor'. In Yiddish, the word refers to a teacher of the youngest children, a *cheyder* (q.v.) teacher. A yeshiva teacher is a רבי *rebbe* (q.v.), while a (non-religious) teacher in general is a

לערער *lerer* (< German *Lehrer*). In Yiddish, *melamed* is also used ironically of an awkward, timid man.

('The Fate of Yaakov Maggid')

Melokhe melukhe מלוכה מלאָכה (Yiddish), shortened form of the saying: אַ מלוכה איז אַ מלאָכַה *a melokhe iz a melukhe* 'a trade is a kingdom', i.e., 'work is wealth'. The expression, as found in numerous Yiddish folk songs, was not without ironic overtones, as is evident for example in 'Melokhe Melukhe' by Moldavian songwriter Zelig Leib Bardichever (1903–1937), the song of an impoverished *stolyer* (carpenter), *shnayder* (tailor), and *shuster* (cobbler), with its refrain of *'Wer es veyst nit / Zol atsinder visn / Vi shver un biter / Karg un shiter / S'kumt undz on der bisn'* (He who doesn't know / Ought now to know / How heavily and bitterly / Meagrely and sparsely / We come by each morsel).

('For Ten's Sake')

Menorat ha-Maor מנורת המאור (Hebrew) 'The Illumining Menorah'. Title of a book by fourteenth-century Spanish Talmudist and Kabbalist Isaac Aboab (q.v. Persons), a collection of legends and moral homilies drawn from the *Talmud* and *Midrashim*.

('The Book of Mordechai')

Mezuzah מְזוּזָה 'doorpost', מְזוּזוֹת *mezuzot* pl., (Hebrew), *mezuze* מזוזה (Yiddish), whence the scroll inscribed with the verses from the Torah ('Hear, O Israel: The Lord our God is one Lord: And thou shalt love the Lord thy God with all thine heart, and with all thy soul, and with all thy might' Deut. 6: 4–5) that Jews place inside a special case attached to their doorposts in fulfilment of the *mitzvah* (q.v.) or religious commandment: 'And thou shalt write them upon the posts of thy house, and on thy gates' (Deut. 6: 9).

('The Guarantee')

Mikveh מִקְוֶה (Hebrew) 'ritual bath', lit. 'collection, or: mass [of water]'. In Judaism there are strict requirements as to the source and the purity of the water that fills a *mikveh* and as to its volume, which must allow complete immersion of the bather.   ('The Guarantee')

Minchah מִנְחָה (Hebrew) 'gift, offering'. *Minchat-Yisrael* 'Gift of Israel'.   ('The Guarantee')

Minyan מִנְיָן (Hebrew), מניין (Yiddish) 'number, quantity; quorum'. The quorum of ten males, over the age of thirteen, required for public worship.

('A Monday of Fasting and Prayer')

Mitzve מצווה (Yiddish < Hebrew מִצְוָה *mitzvah* 'commandment') 'charitable act, good deed'. In the proper sense, a *mitzvah* is a profound obligation passed down by God and which must be obeyed as a religious duty. In the *Mishneh Torah*, Maimonides (1138–1204) compiled and listed the 613 separate *mitzvot* to be found in the Torah, 248 of which are positive commandments, 365 negative commandments. By extension, a *mitzvah* is any selfless good deed.

('The Guarantee')

Mitzve tanz מצווה טאנץ (Yiddish). A Hassidic custom celebrated after the wedding feast once the guests have departed, during which the bride holds one end of a long sash as her close male relatives and often the rabbi take turns holding the other end as they dance before her, praying silently for the newly married couple's success.

('A Monday of Fasting and Prayer')

Mitzraim מִצְרַיִם (Hebrew), מצרים (Yiddish) 'Egypt', the land of bondage in the Book of Exodus. ('Nikolai's Soldiers')

Mohel מוֹהֵל (Hebrew), מוהל (Yiddish), man who performs the rite of circumcision. ('The Guarantee')

Mussaf מוּסָף (Hebrew), *Musef* מוסף (Yiddish), additional service recited on the Sabbath and the Chol ha-Moed (q.v.), lit. 'supplement'. ('For Ten's Sake')

Naggid, *noged* נגיד (Yiddish) 'wealthy man, powerful man', by extension, 'benefactor, philanthropist', from the Hebrew נָגִיד *nagid* 'prince, leader, ruler'. Cf. *gevir-adir* (q.v.). ('A Monday of Fasting and Prayer')

Neduve, nedove נדבה (Yiddish, from Hebrew נְדָבָה *nedovah*) 'alms, charity, donation, offering'. In Eastern Europe, שענקט א נדבה (*shenkt a neduve* 'spare some alms!') was the traditional cry of the mendicant, a collocation that lent itself as the title of a number of popular songs, such as the famous *Schenkt a neduwe!* (1906) by Anschel Schor with music by Arnold Perlmutter and Herman Wohl, which was a plea for Jews in the United States to send financial aid to 'die opfer fin der rusischer tiranei' (the victims of Russian tyranny) in the wake of that year's pogroms in Kishinev (now Chişinău). In Jacob Gordin's *The Yiddish King Lear*, produced by the Independent Yiddish Art Company, New York, in 1892, and starring Jacob P. Adler, Dovid Moishele, a wealthy merchant brought low by his monstrously grasping daughters, famously pleads, '*Shenkt a neduve der Yiddisher Kenig Lir*' (Give alms to the Yiddish King Lear) (Gerald Bordman, Thomas S. Hischak, *The Oxford Companion to American Theatre*, 3rd ed., Oxford: Oxford UP, 2004, p. 11). ('The Protector')

Ne'ila נְעִילָה (Hebrew), *Nile* נעילה (Yiddish) 'lit. locking, closure'. The fifth and final prayer service of Yom Kippur, the Day of Atonement, the holiest day in the Jewish calendar.

('Nikolai's Soldiers')

Neiro yair נֵרוֹ יָאִיר (Hebrew) *neyre yoer* נרו יאיר (Yiddish) 'may his [lit. lamp] shine', 'shine on', a traditional expression of respect for a party not present. ('The Inadvertent Sin')

('The Inadvertent Sin')

Neshamah yeterah נְשָׁמָה יְתֵרָה (Hebrew), *neshome-yeseyre* נשמה יתירה (Yiddish) 'additional soul'. The Jewish conception of the soul is threefold: the *nefesh* is the vital soul animating all living creatures, the *ruach* is the spirit, or man's intellectual dimension, and the *neshamah* is the higher soul, whereby man communicates with the celestial and the divine. In the Talmud (Beẓah 16a), Shimon ben Lakish (third century C.E.) says that God endows man with an additional *neshamah* on the eve of the Sabbath, withdrawing it at the Sabbath's close. This gave rise to a popular belief in the *neshamah yetarah*, which was elaborated upon in Jewish mysticism. In Yiddish, *neshome-yeseyre* may also refer to the joy of the Sabbath, its special mood.

('The Guarantee')

Nishmat-Chayim נִשְׁמַת חַיִּים (Hebrew) 'soul [or: breath] of life'. Rather like *De Anima* in Latin, *Nishmat-Chayim* is a generic title for treatises dealing with the nature and immortality of the soul. A famous example is the *Nishmat-Chayim* (Amsterdam, 1651) of Rabbi Menasseh ben Yisrael (1604–1657), a work contemporary with *The Immortality of the Soul* (London, 1659) by Cambridge Platonist Henry More (1614–1687), one of the philosemite intellectuals whom Menasseh ben Israel met during the two years he spent in London after attending the Whitehall Conference of December 1655 to debate the readmission of the Jews to England and the legality of the 1290 Edict of Expulsion. ('The Guarantee')

Oberlichter (German) 'skylights'.

('The Fate of Yaakov Maggid')

Olam keminhago noheg אולם כמינהגו נוהג (Hebrew) 'but as is its wont'. ('For Ten's Sake')

Oyf kest אויף קעסט (Yiddish) lit. 'on the chest, box, coffer', used of a dependent within a family, typically a husband living on his father-in-law's resources: אויף קעסט ביים שווער *oyf kest baym shver* 'in the keep of his father-in-law'. A child who is made a ward is a קעסטקינד *kestkind*. Cf. קעסטלעך *kestlekh* adj., 'expensive, pricey', lit. 'boxy'. ('The Guarantee')

Pamalia פָּמַלְיָה (Hebrew) 'retinue, entourage', *pamalye* פמליה (Yiddish). The Talmud makes reference to the 'heavenly *pamalia*' of angels that each minister to a nation on earth, strife among whom causes wars among men.

('The Angel and the Bad Wife', 'A Monday of Fasting and Prayer')

Parnose פרנסה (Yiddish) 'source of income, living, job, wage' (< Hebrew פַּרְנָסָה *parnasah* 'need; subsistence, a living; occupation, livelihood'). *Gebn parnose* געבן פרנסה, provide someone with a living, support someone financially.

('The Fate of Yaakov Maggid')

Pericope περικοπή (Greek), lit. 'cut-around', section of a religious text appointed for reading as part of public worship. ('For Ten's Sake')

Pesachim פְּסָחִים (Hebrew) 'Paschal Lambs', third tractate of the *Seder Moed* (Order of Festivals)

('Rabbeinu Yaakov of Orléans')

Pilpul פִּלְפּוּל (Hebrew), *pilpl* פילפול (Yiddish), in the proper sense, 'exegesis', i.e., close textual analysis of the Talmud, but the word also came to acquire the pejorative sense of 'sophistry, to split hairs, quibbling, casuistry'. *Pilplen zikh* (Yiddish) 'to split hairs'.

('The Fate of Yaakov Maggid')

Pirkei Avot פִּרְקֵי אָבוֹת (Hebrew), *Pirke-Oves* פירקי־אָבֿות (Yiddish) 'Chapters [of the] Fathers', a collection of rabbinic ethical and moral teachings.

('The Fate of Yaakov Maggid')

Rabbeinu רַבֵּנוּ (Hebrew) 'our teacher'.

('Rabbeinu Yaakov of Orléans')

Raspiska расписка (Russian), 'receipt, written acknowledgement'

('Nikolai's Soldiers')

Rebbe רבי (Yiddish). In Yiddish there is a distinction between a Hassidic rebbe and a traditional rabbi, or רבֿ *rov*.

('The Fate of Yaakov Maggid')

Sandek סנדק (Yiddish < Hebrew *sandak* סַנְדָּק < Greek σύνδικος < Latin *syndicus* 'representative, patron, advocate'), 'godfather'. A term found in the Talmud. The *sandik* is the *baal berit ha-milah* ('master of the covenant of circumcision'), who assists the *mohel* (q.v.) during the rite by holding the child, an office attended with special marks of honour and reserved for men of the highest moral character and religious standing, and is also the godfather in the sense of *ab sheni* ('second father') to the child as he grows up.

('The Guarantee')

Sanegor סָנֵגוֹר (Hebrew < Greek συνήγορος 'public advocate') 'counsel for the defence'. See *Kategor*.

('The Angel and the Bad Wife')

Sanhedrin סַנְהֶדְרִין (Hebrew < Greek συνέδριον 'assembly', lit. 'sitting together'), סנהדרין (Yiddish) 'council, court'. Historically, the Great Sanhedrin was the highest court of justice at ancient Jerusalem. ('The Court Down Below')

Shema Yisrael שְׁמַע יִשְׂרָאֵל (Hebrew) 'Hear, O Israel'. Prayer recited at morning and evening services, whose opening words are a statement of the monotheism that is the essence of Judaism: 'Hear, O Israel, the Lord [Hebrew יְהוָה *YHWH*] is our God, the Lord is one' (Deuteronomy, 6:4).

('Rabbeinu Yaakov of Orléans', 'Nikolai's Soldiers')

Selichot סְלִיחוֹת pl. (Hebrew), *Slikhes* סליחות (Yiddish) penitential poems and prayers recited before and during the High Holidays. ('The Guarantee')

Seyder סדר (Yiddish), from Hebrew פֶּסַח סֵדֶר *Seder Pesach* 'order [of the] Passover'. The religious service and ritual meal held on the first or the first two nights of the Passover.

('The Silver Pocket Watch', 'The Seyder Evenings of Long Ago',
'The Book of Mordechai')

Shadkhen שדכן (Yiddish < Hebrew *shadchan* שַׁדְכָן) 'matchmaker, marriage broker'. ('For Ten's Sake')

Shaleshides, shaloshudes שלש־סעודות (Yiddish < Hebrew שָׁלֹשׁ סְעֻדּוֹת 'three meals'), the third of the three meals of the Sabbath, eaten in the evening, before the end of the Sabbath.

('The Fate of Yaakov Maggid', 'The Inadvertent Sin', 'For Ten's Sake', 'A Monday of Fasting and Prayer')

Shemoneh-esrei שמנה עשרה (Hebrew) 'eighteen'. Name for the *Amidah*, the main prayer of the Jewish liturgy, with reference to the number of blessings it contains.

('The Angel and the Bad Wife')

Shallah lahmeka 'al-hammayim ki-berob hayyamim timsa'ennu שַׁלַּח לַחְמְךָ עַל הַמַּיִם כִּי־בְרֹב הַיָּמִים תִּמְצָאֶנּוּ (Hebrew), 'Cast your bread upon the waters, for in the abundance of days, you will find it' (Ecclesiastes 11:1). ('The Good Oil')

Shubat-Teshuvah שַׁבַּת תְּשׁוּבָה (Hebrew) 'Sabbath [of] Repentance'. The Sabbath that falls between Rosh Hashanah and Yom Kippur, during the Ten Days of Repentance.

('The Inadvertent Sin')

Stuhlrichter (German) 'district justice', a local official in Hungary under the Habsburg Empire. In his novel *A falu jegyzője* [The Village Notary] (1845), a satire of the old Hungary, Joseph Baron von Eötvös (1813–1871) describes the vast judicial and administrative powers of the *Stuhlrichter* in the following terms: 'A district justice is a firm pillar of the state; he upholds public order,—he protects both rich and poor,—he is the judge and the father of his neighbourhood; without him there is no justice—or, at the least, no judicature. All complaints of the people pass through his hands;

all decrees of the powers that be are promulgated and ad-
ministered by him. The district judge regulates the rivers,
makes roads, and constructs bridges. He is the representative of the poor, the inspector of the schools; he is lord chief
forester whenever a wolf happens to make its appearance;
he is "protomedicus" in the case of an epidemic; he is justice
of the peace, the king's advocate in criminal cases, commis-
sioner of the police, of war, of hospitals; in short, he is all in
all,—the man in whom we live, move and have our being'
(Baron Eötvös, *The Village Notary; A Romance of Hungarian Life*,
Vol. 1, trans. Otto Wenckstern, London: Longman, Brown,
Green, and Longmans, 1850, p. 14).

('The Guarantee')

Tallit טַלִּית (Hebrew), *tallis* טלית (Yiddish), 'prayer shawl'.

('The Guarantee')

Tam תָּם (Hebrew) 'honest, straightforward, innocent'. Epithet
suffixed to the name of twelfth-century French Tosafist
Rabbeinu Yaakov Tam (Persons q.v.).

('Rabbeinu Yaakov of Orléans')

Tanakh תְּנַ"ךְ (Hebrew) acronym (*TaNaKh*) for the Hebrew Bible,
from its three parts: *Torah* (Pentateuch), *Nevi'im* (Prophets),
and *Ketuvim* (Writings, i.e., the religious poems, wisdom
literature, the books of Daniel, Ezra and Nehemiah, and
Chronicles). ('The Book of Mordechai')

Thilim, pl. תְּהִלִּים (Hebrew), *Tilim* תהילים (Yiddish) 'Psalms', lit.
'praises'. ('The Inadvertent Sin')

Tiferet תִּפְאֶרֶת (Hebrew) 'glory, splendour, majesty'. The sixth of the ten *sefirot*, or vehicles for the emanation of the divine, in the Kabbala. ('The Inadvertent Sin')

Tocheichah תּוֹכֵחָה (Hebrew), *Toykhekhe* תוכחה (Yiddish) lit. 'admonition, reproof'. The name given to the section of Leviticus, Chapter 26, that lists the punishments that Israel would incur in disobeying the Lord's commandments, and which begins, 'I will even appoint over you terror, consumption, and the burning ague, that shall consume the eyes, and cause sorrow of heart: and ye shall sow your seed in vain, for your enemies shall eat it' (Lev. 26, 16). The Yiddish *toykhekhe* can also mean a 'series of calamities' more generally. ('Rabbi, Tsar, and Faith')

Tosafot, pl., תּוֹסָפֹת (Hebrew), sg. *tosafah*, lit. 'additions, glosses'. The term used for commentaries on the Talmud, originally written in the margins of the manuscript. After the invention of the printing press, *tosafot* were arranged in columns to either side of the main text. ('The Fate of Yaakov Maggid', 'The Guarantee')

Tzadik צַדִּיק (Hebrew) *tzadek* צדיק (Yiddish) 'righteous, saintly man'; title for a Hassidic master (Yiddish). ('The Guarantee')

Tzedakah צְדָקָה (Hebrew), *tsdoke* (Yiddish) 'righteousness', 'justice' (in the sense of just conduct), 'charity' (as a religiously prescribed ethical obligation). ('A Monday of Fasting and Prayer')

Tzitze ציצה (Yiddish) 'tassel'. ('The Guarantee')

Ukase указ (Russian), אוּקאַז (Yiddish) decree issued by the tsar or Russian government. ('Nikolai's Soldiers')

Urchatz וּרְחַץ (Hebrew), the ritual washing of hands at the beginning of the Passover Seder, after the Kiddush and first cup of wine. ('The Seyder Evenings of Long Ago')

Ve-el chet shichatnu וְעַל חֵטְא שֶׁחָטָאנוּ (Hebrew) 'and the sin we have committed'. From the *Al Chet*, or Great Confession: 'The sin we have committed against you under duress or by choice, / the sin we have committed against you consciously or unconsciously, / and the sin we have committed against you openly or secretly.' ('The Inadvertent Sin')

Yerach ha-eitanim יֶרַח הָאֵתָנִים (Hebrew) 'month of Ethanim', from 1 Kings 8: 'And all the men of Israel assembled themselves unto King Solomon at the feast in the month Ethanim, which is the seventh month.' In the Hebrew calendar, the seventh month of the ecclesiastical year is Tishrei (September-October in the Gregorian calendar). It is the month of the holiest days in the Jewish religious calendar: Rosh Hashanah (1–2 Tishrei), Yom Kippur (10 Tishrei), and Sukkot (15–21 Tishrei). ('The Guarantee')

Zeh dor dorshav זֶה, דּוֹר דֹּרְשָׁו (Hebrew) 'Such is the generation of them that seek after Him' (Psalm 24:6)
('The Fate of Yaakov Maggid')

Ze hasefer זה הספר (Hebrew) 'this is the book'
('The Inadvertent Sin')

Ze haparohet זה הפארוחת (Hebrew) 'this is the meal'
('The Inadvertent Sin')

Zimrah זְמִירָה (Hebrew), pl. *Zemirot* (Hebrew) 'hymn', *zmires* זמירות (Yiddish) 'Sabbath hymns sung at table'

('A Monday of Fasting and Prayer')

Zollen, pl. (German), Prussian unit of measurement. The *Zoll* was equal to 0.02615475 metres or 1.029715 inches.

('The Guarantee')

Barditschew (Yiddish: באַרדיטשעוו *Barditshev*; Polish: Berdyczów; Ukrainian: *Бердичів Berdychiv*). The present-day town of Berdychiv in the Zhytomyr Oblast of northern Ukraine.

Although the Jews of Barditschew were largely secular and embraced the values of the Haskalah, or Jewish Enlightenment, the town was to become an important Hassidic centre thanks to Rabbi Levi Yitzchak (1740–1809), a disciple of the Maggid of Mezeritch (q.v. Persons, Dov Ber), who lived in the town from 1785 until his death, founding a Hassidic court to which followers from all over Eastern Europe flocked in search of guidance. Berditchev was the birthplace of important Jewish writers Mendele Mocher Sforim (1836–1917) and Abraham Goldfaden (1840–1908); novelist Joseph Conrad (1857–1924); and Jewish-Russian novelist Vasily Grossman (1905–1964).

The city was part of the Polish-Lithuanian Commonwealth from 1569 to 1793, during which period it developed into an important commercial and banking centre. By the late eighteenth century, three quarters of the city's population were Jewish. Having become part of the Russian Empire after the Second Partition of Poland, from 1793 to 1917 Berdichev fell on hard times, however, chiefly because its banking institutions were relocated to Odessa, founded by decree of Catherine the Great in 1794 and granted the status of free port in 1818. By the 1860s, the Jewish share of the town's population was among the highest in the Russian Empire, at eighty per cent, despite steady emigration. In July 1941, during the German invasion of the Soviet Union, the S.S. herded the town's Jews into a ghetto and in September carried out mass executions in retaliation for anonymous anti-Nazi pamphlets that had been circulating among the community. In October, a twenty-five-man extermination squad, assisted by local Ukrainian auxiliaries, shot every last inhabitant of the ghetto, a number estimated at more than thirty thousand. The atrocity is described in the novel *Life and Fate* (1959, first published in 1980) by Vasily Grossman, whose mother perished in the massacre.

Bereg (Hungarian). A comitatus of the Kingdom of Hungary, bordering Galicia to the north and Máramaros to the east. The administrative seat of the county was Beregszász (Yiddish: בערעגסאַז *Beregsaz*, German: Bergsaß), present-day Berehove, Zakarpattia Oblast, western Ukraine. The large town of Munkatsch (q.v.) was part of Bereg County.

Borscha (Yiddish: באָרשע *Borshe*, Romanian: Borşa, German: Borscha, Hungarian: Borsa,). The present-day town of Borşa in eastern Maramureş County, Romania.

There was a strong Hassidic tradition in Borscha and local legend has it that the Baal Shem Tov himself used to visit the village.

The town dates back to the fourteenth century, when it was part of the estate of a Romanian boyar. By the mid-eighteenth century, a sizeable Jewish community had developed in Borscha. Local Jews were mainly employed as manual labourers in the local timber industry, although a wealthier few owned lumber mills and connected businesses. In the anti-Semitic climate of the Greater Romania, of which Maramuresch became part in 1918 after the disintegration of the Austro-Hungarian Empire, the Jewish quarter of Borscha was destroyed in an arson attack instigated by the Iron Guard. After the annexation of Maramuresch and northern Transylvania by Hungary in September 1940 and subsequent German occupation in 1941, the Jews of Borscha, who made up twenty-two per cent of the town's population, were moved to the ghetto in Vișeul de Sus (Oberwischau, q.v.) and subsequently deported to Auschwitz on three trains that left on 19 May, 21 May and 25 May.

Bredenbad (Romanian: Ocna Șugatag; Hungarian: Aknasugatag). Present-day Ocna Șugatag in northern Maramureș County, Romania, near the border with Ukraine.

The Romanian *ocnă* (Hungarian *akna*) means 'mine' but has come to refer specifically to a salt mine. The area around Ocna Șugatag has been mined for salt since Antiquity.

Brod (Yiddish:בראָד *Brod*; Polish; German: Brody; Ukrainian: Броди *Brody*). Present-day Brody in the Zolochiv Raion of the Lviv Oblast, western Ukraine.

As a very young man, around the year 1720, the Baal Shem Tov was a *melamed* (q.v. Terms) in a village outside Brod. Thanks to his growing reputation as a *tzaddik* (q.v. Terms), he soon became the leader of the city's Hassidim and married the sister of Gershon Kutover (q.v.), the Rabbi of Brod. In 1772, the Jewish community of Brod outlawed Hassidism and Hassidic practices as heretical, anathematising the Baal Shem Tov, who was unsuccessfully defended by his brother-in-law.

A town dating back at least as far as the eleventh century, Brod came under Austrian rule in 1772, after the First Partition of Poland. In 1779 Brod was granted the status of free city, and the resulting increase in trade made it one of the most important centres of commerce in the Austro-Hungarian Empire. By the nineteenth century, the Jewish share of the population of Brod was one of the highest in all Eastern Europe, at almost ninety per cent. Along with Lvov and Tarnapol (q.v.), Brod was one of the main centres of the Haskalah, or Jewish Enlightenment, in Galicia. From 1882 onward, Brod saw an influx of Jews fleeing Russia after the passing of a *gezerah* (q.v. Terms) by Tsar Alexander III—the anti-Semitic 'May Laws', a series of repressive and discriminatory measures that led to mass emigration of the Jews from Russia. By then the local Jewish population had reached a peak of fifteen thousand, but the city was already in economic decline, having lost its status as a free city in 1879. During the First World War, the Russian Army burned to the ground hundreds of Jewish homes and buildings in Brod. With the break-up of the Austro-Hungarian Empire, Brod became part of the Second Polish Republic. After the German invasion of Soviet-occupied Poland in 1941, the remaining Jewish population of Brod, which then numbered some nine thousand, perished in pogroms perpetrated by local Ukrainians and in massacres carried out by the Nazis in nearby forests, and those who remained were deported to the gas chambers.

Bukowina, a historical region that lies within the present-day Suceava County, Romania, and Chernivtsi Oblast, Ukraine. The region was annexed by the Habsburgs in 1775 and became part of Greater Romania after the disintegration of the Austro-Hungarian Empire.

Bushtino (Yiddish: בושטינא *Bishtina/Bushtina*; Romanian: Bustea; Hungarian: Bustyaháza; Slovak: Buštín; Ukrainian: *Буштино Bushtyno*) The present-day town of Bushtyno on the Tisza River, in the Tiachiv Raion of the Zakarpattia Oblast in western Ukraine.

There was a Jewish community in Bushtino by the second half of the eighteenth century, served by the rabbi of the nearby city of Teutschenau (q.v.). The majority of the town's Jews were Hassidic and Bushtino is famous throughout the Hassidic world as the last resting place of Mordechai Leifer (1824–1894), Rabbi of Nadvorna, whose tomb is now a site of pilgrimage.

Under Habsburg rule, Bushtino was part of Máramaros and in 1872 the Tschop-Marmarosch-Sighet railway was laid through the village. After the First World War, it was absorbed by the new state of Czechoslovakia and in 1940 became part of Hungary once more. In April 1944, the Jews of Bushtino were deported to the ghetto in Mátészalka, Hungary, and then to the gas chambers at Auschwitz.

Drohobycz (Yiddish: דראָהאָביטש *Drohobitsh*, *Drubitsh*; Ukrainian: *Дрогобич Drohobych*; Polish: Drohobycz). Present-day Drohobych in the Lviv Oblast, Ukraine.

By the time of the Baal Shem Tov (1698–1760), a Jewish community had been re-established in Drohobycz, after expulsion of the town's Jews in the sixteenth century. Hassidism spread to the town at the end of the eighteenth century. Drohobycz is famous as the home town of writer and artist Bruno Schulz (1892–1942). Confined to the Drohobycz Ghetto during German occupation, Schulz was shot dead in the street by a Gestapo officer.

From as early as the ninth century, there was a salt-mining settlement in the area where Drohobycz was later to develop. In the early fifteenth century, Jewish contractors from the salt mines settled in Drohobycz and formed a small community, but in 1578, the Jews were expelled from the town when the Polish-Lithuanian Commonwealth granted it the official privilege *de non tolerandis Judaeis*. After the 1772 partition of Poland, the town came under the rule of the Habsburg Monarchy. Oil was discovered in the area at the beginning of the nineteenth century, and by the 1860s, the town's Jews were prominent in the oil extraction, refining, and export industries. After the First World War, the town became part of the Second Polish Republic amid the collapse of the Austro-Hungarian Empire, and in 1939 it was annexed to the Soviet Union. After Nazi Germany's invasion of the Soviet Union in July 1941, Ukrainian nationalists went on a three-day rampage, murdering many of the town's Jews, who by then made up forty per cent of the populace. By October 1942, ten thousand Jews were concentrated in the town's ghetto, with less than a thousand surviving when the ghetto was liquidated in the summer of the following year.

Galil Takhton גליל תחתון (Hebrew), *Unterland* אונטערלאַנד (Yiddish) 'Lower Province'. Collective name for the Jews who lived in the north-east of the Kingdom of Hungary, or what is now eastern Slovakia, the Zakarpattia Oblast of Ukraine, and north-western Transylvania, roughly the region between the Tatra Mountains and Klausenburg (present-day Cluj, Romania). The term was neither official nor geographic, but rather it reflected the lower cultural, economic, religious, and linguistic status of the Unterlander Jews in the eyes of the rest of Hungarian, or Oyberland (אויבערלאַנד), Jewry. Among other differences in accent, the vowel ו, pronounced *u* in the Oyberlander dialect of Yiddish, was pronounced *i* in the Unterlander dialect, a pronunciation that was a particular object of derision among Oyberlander Jews (cf. Terms, *kigel*, q.v.).

Horodenke (Yiddish: האָראָדענקע *Horodenke*; Polish: Horodenka; Ukrainian: Horodenka) Present-day Horodenka in the Kolomiya Raion of the Ivano-Frankivsk Oblast, western Ukraine.

Nachman (c. 1700–1765), a *tzaddik* (q.v. Terms) and early follower of the Baal Shem Tov, was rabbi of Horodenke.

Part of the Polish-Lithuanian Commonwealth, after the 1772 partition of Poland the town came under the rule of the Habsburg Monarchy. By the late-nineteenth century, Jews made up around forty per cent of the town's population. In 1941 and 1942, the German Wehrmacht and Ukrainian Auxiliary Police murdered three thousand Jews from Horodenke in three separate 'Aktionen'.

Khust (Yiddish: חוסט *Khist/Khust*; Ukrainian: *Хуст*; Romanian: Hust; Hungarian: Csebreny, Huszt; German: Chust) Present-day Khust, Zakarpattia Oblast, western Ukraine.

There was an established Jewish community in Khust by the mid-eighteenth century and a century later it was one of the largest in northern Hungary. In the second half of the nineteenth century, the Khust yeshiva, one of the largest in the world at that time, trained most of Hungary's Orthodox rabbis. The rabbis of Khust were active in preventing Hassidism taking hold within the local community.

After the break-up of the Austro-Hungarian Empire, Khust became part of the newly formed Czechoslovakia. In 1939, the town was occupied by Hungarian troops and the Jews were forced into labour battalions. In the spring of 1944, ten thousand Jews were herded into the ghetto at Khust before deportation to Auschwitz.

Kitev (Yiddish: קוטעוו *Kitev/Kutev*; German: Kutten; Polish: Kuty, Romanian: Cuturi; Ukrainian: Kuty) Present-day Kuty, a town in the Kosiv Raion of the Ivano-Frankivsk Oblast, south-western Ukraine.

Kitev was the home town of Abraham Gershon (q.v. Persons), the brother-in-law of the Baal Shem Tov. According to Hassidic tradition, the Baal Shem Tov is supposed to have lived outside Kitev during his years of obscurity, and made a living by digging clay, which his wife sold in the town and in nearby Kossow (q.v.). Another legend has it that in the forests and mountains around Kitev the Baal Shem Tov met a famous local Ukrainian outlaw named Oleksa Dovbush, whom he dissuaded from visiting his depredations on the Jews.

Lying on the border of the historical Galicia and Bukowina (q.v.) regions, Kuty was the fiefdom of the famous Potocki family, one of Poland's wealthiest and most powerful noble houses. Kuty was granted a charter as a city in 1715, at which time the Jewish community received permission to build a synagogue and cemetery. After the 1772 partition of Poland, the town came under the rule of the Habsburg Monarchy. During the First World War, the town's Jews suffered greatly under first Russian and then Romanian occupation. In 1919, Kuty became part of the Second Polish Republic, during which period the town finally became linked to regional road and rail networks. Whereas previously a large number of the town's Jews had worked as carters (see Terms, *balegule*, q.v.), they now entered the mechanised transport industry, mainly as drivers. On 1 July 1941, Kitev was jointly occupied by Hungarian and Romanian forces, with the Romanian soldiers in particular committing abuses against the Jews, such as kidnapping community leaders for ransom. After Romanian withdrawal, the

Hungarians continued to deport Jews for forced labour in Nazi-held territories. Deportations of the Jews and looting of Jewish property increased after the Germans took control in September 1941. On 10 April 1942, trucks carrying S.S. and Gestapo troops arrived in Kitev and proceeded to shoot Jews in the streets and to set fire to Jewish homes, throwing those who tried to escape back into the flames. The massacre claimed around 950 lives. On 24 April, five hundred Jews were deported from Kuty to the Kolomyia ghetto. Finally, on 7 September 1942, the town's remaining eight hundred Jews were deported to Kolomyia and from there to the Bełżec extermination camp.

Kossow (Yiddish: קאָסעוו *Kosev*; Romanian: Cosău; German: Kossow; Polish: Kosów; Ukrainian: *Kociв Kosiv*) Present-day Kosiv in the Ivano-Frankivsk Oblast, western Ukraine.

There was a Jewish community in Kossow by the early eighteenth century and in the second half of the century it became an important centre of Hassidism. According to Hassidic legend, in the 1720s the Baal Shem Tov lived in a cave by the nearby lake, making charcoal which his wife sold in the town. Another legend has it that in the Carpathian Mountains near Kossow the Baal Shem Tov once helped Ukrainain outlaw Oleksa Dovbush escape capture by soldiers when he showed him a secret path through a gorge, in gratitude for which the bandit gave him a pipe which he smoked to the end of his days. Kossow was the birthplace of Menachem Mendel Hager (1830–1884), the founder of the Kosov and Vizhnitz (q.v.) Hassidic dynasties.

Having been part of the Polish-Lithuanian Common-wealth, Kosov came under Habsburg rule in 1772. After the First World War and with the breakup of the Austro-Hungarian Empire, the town became part of the Second

Polish Republic. By the turn of the twentieth century, the Jewish population of Kosov numbered just over 2,500, around eighty-two per cent of the total. It was occupied by the Soviet Union in September 1939 and then by Nazi Germany in July 1941. In October 1941, the Germans shot two thousand Jews in Kosov, burying them in a mass grave. By September the following year, the town's remaining Jews had either been shot or sent to the Bełżec extermination camp.

Lemberg (Yiddish: לעמבערג *Lemberg*; German: Lemberg; Polish: Lwów, Ukrainian: Lviv), the capital of the Habsburg Kingdom of Galicia and Lodomeria, the present-day city of Lviv, in western Ukraine.

Mezeritch (Yiddish: מעזריטש, מעזעריטש *Mezritsh/Mezeritsh*; Polish: Wielki Międzyrzecz; Ukrainian: *Великі Межирічі Veliki Mezhyrichi*). Present-day Veliki Mezhyrichi in the Korets Raion of the Rivine Oblast, western Ukraine.

Mezeritch, in the historic region of Volhynia (covering what is now south-eastern Poland, south-western Belarus, and western Ukraine), is famous thanks to Dov Ber ben Avraham (q.v. Persons), known as Der Mezritsher Maggid, the chosen successor of the Baal Shem Tov, who settled in the town in the early 1760s. At the time, Mezeritch was already home to a school of Jewish mysticism, which had gathered around kabbalist Yaakov Kopel Lifshits (d. 1740). Through his systematic exposition of the teachings of the Baal Shem Tov, Dov Ber can be said to be the founding father of organised Hassidic Judaism, which spread from Mezeritch to Poland, Galicia, and Russia.

Mezeritch received a charter from Polish King August II in 1726. In 1793, as part of the Second Partition of Poland, Mezeritch became part of the Volhynia province of the

Russian Empire. From 1919 the town was part of the Second Polish Republic. It was occupied by the Soviet Union in 1939. The Germans entered Mezeritch on 6 July 1941 and together with Ukrainian auxiliaries conducted a pogrom, looting Jewish property. Over the months that followed, there were frequent murders and deportations of Jews for slave labour. On 22 May 1942, there was a massacre, with Jews being buried in mass graves outside Mezeritch, and the town's remaining 950 Jews were herded into a ghetto. On 26 September 1942, nine hundred Jews from the ghetto were shot, and of the few dozen that escaped, some were later captured and murdered, others starved to death, and a handful were able to join Soviet partisan units.

Munkatsch (Yiddish: מונקאטש *Minkatsh/Munkatsh*; Romanian: Muncaciu; Hungarian: Munkács; Czech, Slovak: Mukačevo; Ukrainian: Mukachevo) Present-day Mukachevo in the Zakarpattia Oblast, in the westernmost corner of Ukraine, near the borders with Slovakia, Hungary, and Romania (Maramureş County).

Jews were recorded as living in Munkatsch as early as 1649. In the late nineteenth century, Hassidism began to take hold in Munkatsch, theretofore having been fiercely opposed by Rabbi Chaim Sofer, who was forced to retire by his followers in 1880. Munkatsch was the birthplace of Ludovic Bruckstein (1920–1988), the descendant of Hassidic rabbis and writers.

By the sixteenth century, Munkatsch was part of the Principality of Transylvania, but throughout the seventeenth century was subjected to increasing pressure from an expansionist Habsburg Empire. In 1726, the town came under Habsburg rule and was governed by the Schönborn family from the local Palanok Castle. In 1919, the town became part of the new Czechoslovakia. In the 1920s, there were more than ten thousand Jews in Munkatsch, making up more than half the population. A Jewish gymnasium school opened in 1924 and a Yiddish-language newspaper, *Yidishe Shtime*, was published in the town during this period. Munkatsch came under Hungarian control after the German invasion of Czechoslovakia in 1939, and the Jewish community was subjected to anti-Semitic persecution by the new authorities, with numerous men conscripted into forced-labour battalions. In April 1944, following German occupation, two ghettos were set up in Munkatsch, one for Jews from the town and the other for around fifteen thousand Jews rounded up from the surrounding area. From 15 to 24 May 1944, the Jews from the two ghettos were deported to the Auschwitz extermination camp.

Nadvorna (Yiddish: נאַדוואָרנאַ *Nadvorna*; Polish: Nadwórna; Ukrainian: *Надвірна Nadvirna*) Present-day Nadvirna in the Ivano-Frankivsk Oblast, western Ukraine.

There was a strong Hassidic presence in Nadvorna, and in the second half of the nineteenth century, Jews from all over the region flocked to the town to seek the blessing and counsel of Rabbi Mordechai Leifer (1824–1894), a famous *tzaddik* and founder of the Nadvorna Hassidic Dynasty, who is buried in Bushtino (q.v.).

After the 1772 partition of Poland, Nadvorna became part of the Kingdom of Galicia and Lodomeria, a crownland of the Habsburg Empire. An organised Jewish community was established in Nadvorna by the beginning of the eighteenth century. By 1880, Jews made up sixty-four per cent of Nadvorna's population, with wealthier members of the community owning oil wells, refineries, windmills, sawmills, and factories. In 1921, Nadvorna became part of the Second Polish Republic, when eastern Galicia was awarded to Poland by the Treaty of Riga, which ended the Polish-Soviet War. In 1941, when Nazi Germany invaded Soviet-occupied Poland, there were five thousand Jews living in Nadvorna, around half of whom, mostly women, children and the elderly, were killed in a massacre on 6 October. In the winter of 1941–2, a ghetto was established in Nadvorna, from which hundreds of Jews were transported to the Bełżec extermination camp. Those who managed to escape the ghetto were murdered by the local population and gangs of Stepan Bandera's Ukrainian nationalists.

Oberrohnen (Romanian: Rona de Sus; Hungarian: Felsőróna), present-day Rona de Sus, a majority ethnic Ukrainian village in Maramureş County, Romania.

Oberwischau (Yiddish: אויבער־ווישא *Oybervisha*; Romanian: Vişeu de Sus; Hungarian: Felsővisó) Present-day Vişeu de Sus, Maramureş County, Romania.

As elsewhere in Maramuresch, Hassidism had a particularly strong influence in Oberwischau.

The Jewish population of Oberwischau grew significantly in the last two decades of the nineteenth century. A *chevra kadisha* (q.v. Terms) was established there in 1895 and a Hebrew press in 1896. The same as in Borscha (q.v.), the Jews of Oberwischau were mainly occupied as manual labourers in the timber industry that thrived in the heavily forested Maramuresch region. In the spring of 1944, the Hungarian fascist authorities set up a ghetto in the town, into which around thirty-five thousand Jews were herded before being sent to Auschwitz. Around seven hundred Jews survived the extermination camp and returned to Vişeu de Sus in what was by then Soviet-occupied Romania, but by the beginning of the 1970s, the local Jewish community had dwindled to non-existence as a result of emigration.

Pistyn (Yiddish: פיסטין *Pistin*, Polish: Pistyń; Ukrainian: *Пістинь Pistyn'*) Present-day Pistyn', Kosiv Raion, western Ukraine.

There was a Jewish community in the town from the second half of the eighteenth century, which reached its peak near the end of the nineteenth century, before dwindling due to emigration and the ravages caused by Russian occupation during the First World War. Chaim Josef Bruckstein (d. 1865) and Israel Nathan Alter Bruckstein (d. 1868), the great-great-grandfather and great-grandfather of Ludovic Bruckstein, served as rabbis of Pistyn.

Orginally part of the Polish-Lithuanian Commonwealth, Pistyn became part of the Habsburg Empire in 1772. After the disintegration of the Austro-Hungarian Empire, it was part of the short-lived West-Ukrainian People's Republic and then the Second Polish Republic, until Soviet occupation in 1939. By the inter-war period, just over five hundred Jews remained in Pistyn. On 9 April 1942, Ukrainian auxiliaries under the command of the Gestapo went on a six-hour rampage through the town, shooting several hundred Jews in their homes and on the street, before ordering the survivors to bury the dead in a mass grave.

Podkamin (Polish: Podkamień; Russian: Podkamen; Ukrainian: *Підкамінь Pidkamin*) Present-day Pidkamin in the Brody Raion of the Lviv Oblast, Ukraine.

There was a Jewish community in Podkamin as early as the seventeenth century, initially dependent upon the community in Lemberg (q.v.).

After the 1772 partition of Poland, Podkamin came under Habsburg rule. During the First World War, Podkamin was largely destroyed, causing many Jews to leave the town. In August-September 1941, after the German invasion, most of the town's Jews were deported to the Bełżec extermination camp. By December 1942, most of the Jews who remained had been deported to the Brod (q.v.) ghetto, with the few who managed to escape being murdered by the local population and Ukrainian nationalists.

Premishlan (Yiddish: פרימישלאַן *Primishlan*; Polish: Przemyślany, Ukrainian: *Перемишляни Peremyshliany*) Present-day Peremyshliany, a town in the Lviv Oblast, Ukraine.

Premishlan is famous for the Hassidic dynasty founded by Rabbi Meir Hagadol of Premishlan (1703–1773), a follower of the Baal Shem Tov. His grandson, Rabbi Meir the Second of Premishlan (1783–1850), was a noted *baal-nes* (q.v. Terms).

Part of the Ruthenian Voivodeship, after the 1772 partition of Poland the town came under Habsburg rule. After the breakup of the Austro-Hungarian Empire it became part of the Second Polish Republic. In June 1941, the Germans occupied the town, burning down the synagogue and throwing ten Jews into the flames alive. In November, 450 Jewish men were shot in a forest near the town and over the following months many more were deported to labour camps. In December 1942, three thousand Jews were deported from the Premishlan ghetto to the Bełżec extermination camp. On 22 May 1943, the Germans and Ukrainian auxiliary police shot two thousand Jews from the ghetto in the forest near Premishlan.

Pressburg. The German name for Bratislava, Slovakia, during the time of the Austro-Hungarian Empire.

Prislop (Hungarian: Jóháza) Village at the south-western edge of what is now Maramureș County, Romania.

Rizhin (Yiddish: רוזשין *Rizhin/Ruzhin*; Russian: *Ружин Ruzhin*; Polish: Rużyn; Ukrainian: *Ружин Ruzhyn*). Present-day Ruzhyn, in the Zhytomyr Oblast, central Ukraine.

By the 1830s, Rizhin, part of the Russian Empire, was an important site of Hassidic pilgrimage, home to the court of Der Heiliger Rizhiner, Rabbi Israel Friedman (1796–1850), a direct descendant of Dov Ber, the Mezritcher Maggid (q.v. Persons). Der Heiliger Rizhiner was as famous for his regal opulence as he was for making Rizhin a centre of Jewish learning, and drawing the odium of Tsar Nicholas I, he was imprisoned in 1838. On his release, he fled to Bukowina (q.v.), in the Austro-Hungarian Empire, establishing a Hassidic court and beth midrash in Sadigura.

By the mid-nineteenth century, more than half the town's population was Jewish and local Jews owned a winery and sugar factory. In 1905, the Jews of Rizhin, as elsewhere in the Russian Empire, fell victim to pogroms and looting after the Tsar falsely blamed the failed Revolution on a Jewish plot. In 1919, amid the chaos of the Russian Civil War, another pogrom struck the Jewish community, which by then had dwindled to just over a thousand. In the 1930s, Rizhin suffered greatly during the Great Famine engineered by Stalin, and there were cases of cannibalism reported in the area. On 17 July 1941, the invading German Army entered the city and in September, local Ukrainian auxiliary police shot seven hundred and fifty Jews, burying the bodies in a mass grave in a forest at the edge of the town. The town was liberated by the Red Army at the end of 1943, but only a handful of the Ukrainian perpetrators of the mass killings were ever held to account by the Soviet authorities.

Rohnen (Romanian: Coştiui; Hungarian: Rónaszék; Ukrainian: *Кошпіль Koshtil'*)

Present-day Coştiui, Maramureş, Romania.

Sassow (Yiddish: סאַסאָוו *Sasov*; Polish: Sasów; Ukrainian: *Сасів Sasiv*)

Sassow became an important Hassidic centre in the late-eighteenth century thanks to Moses Leib Sassover (q.v. Persons), the founder of the Sassover Hassidic dynasty.

Founded in 1615, Sassow was part of Poland until 1772, when it came under Austrian rule. By 1764, the Jews of Sassow numbered 223 and by 1880, 1,906, just over half the total population. The local Jewish community manufactured candles and embroidered strips for tallises, which Sassow exported as far away as Berlin and New York, but after the First World War, the town went into economic decline, due in large part to the destruction of the local paper factory, which had supplied the whole of the Austro-Hungarian Empire. During Operation Barbarossa, Sassow was occupied on 2 July 1941, but the local Ukrainian population began murdering the Jews even before the Germans entered the town. After German occupation, local Ukrainians continued to conduct pogroms, looting Jewish property and burning down the town's synagogue. In 1942, a labour camp was set up and seven hundred Jews were forced to work in nearby quarries. The camp was liquidated the following summer and all the prisoners were shot.

Sighet (Yiddish: סיגעט *Siget*; Romanian: Sighetu Marmaţiei; Hungarian: Máramarossziget; German Marmaroschsiget, Siget; Ukrainian: *Сигіт Syhit*) Present-day Sighetu Marmaţiei, Maramureş, Romania.

There was a Jewish community in Sighet by the second half of the eighteenth century and the town was a strong centre of Hassidism. Sighet was the birthplace of writer and Nobel laureate Elie Wiesel (1928–2016), who was deported to Auschwitz from the town in May 1944. Ludovic Bruckstein (1920–1988), born in Munkatsch (q.v.), grew up in Sighet and was likewise deported to Auschwitz in May 1944, along with his family and all the town's Jews.

Part of the the Kingdom of Hungary from the eleventh century, by the mid-fourteenth century Sighet was a *libera regia civitas* (free royal city) and capital of the *comitatus* (county) of Máramaros, which became part of the newly founded Principality of Transylvania in 1570. In the aftermath of Prince Francis II Rákóczi's unsuccessful War of Independence (1703–1711) against the Habsburgs, Transylvania and Máramaros became dominions of the Habsburg monarchy until the disintegration of the Austro-Hungarian Empire in 1918. During the Hungarian-Romanian war of 1919, Romanian troops entered Sighet in January, and the following year, Maramureş and Transylvania were awarded to the Kingdom of Romania by the Treaty of Trianon. In 1940, Hungary annexed northern Transylvania as part of the Nazi-brokered Second Vienna Award. In August 1941, the fascist Hungarian authorities deported twenty thousand Jews from Sighet and the rest of the region, sending them on cattle trucks to Kamenets-Podolsk in German-occupied Ukraine, where, on 27–28 August, they were massacred by Einsatzgruppen. By April 1944, almost thirteen thousand Jews from the town and surrounding villages were concentrated in the Sighet ghetto. From 16 May to 22 May, the Jews were deported from the ghetto to the Auschwitz extermination camp on four trains of cattle trucks.

Shepetovka (Yiddish: Shepetivke; Polish: Szepetówka; Ukrainian: *Шепетівка Shepetivka*) Present-day Shepetivka, Khmelnytskyi Oblast, Ukraine.

By the late seventeenth century, there were around twenty thousand Jews in Shepetovka, a number that had risen to more than fifty thousand by a century later. Rabbi Pinchas Shapiro of Koretz (1726–1791), a famous scholar and disciple of the Baal Shem Tov, is buried in Shepetovka.

Part of the Polish-Lithuanian Commonwealth from the late sixteenth century, Shepetovka was absorbed by the Russian Empire in 1793. In the late nineteenth and early twentieth century, the town's Jewish population began to emigrate in large numbers. Briefly part of the Republic of Poland (1919–20) in the aftermath of the First World War, Shepetovka then became part of the Soviet Union. Thousands of Jews from Shepetovka were shot by the Germans and local Ukrainian auxiliaries during Nazi occupation in 1941 and 1942.

Slatina (Yiddish: סעלאָטפֿינע *Selotfine*; Romanian: Slatina; Hungarian: Aknaszlatina; Slovak: Slatinské Doly; Ukrainian: Solotvyno) Present-day Solotvyno, a town in the Tiachiv Raion of the Zakarpattia Oblast, south-western Ukraine, which lies on the opposite bank of the Tisza River from Sighet (q.v.), Romania.

There were Jews living in Slatina by the seventeenth entury. After the disintegration of the Austro-Hungarian Empire, the town became part of Czechoslovakia. It came under the control of Hungary after the German occupation of Czechoslovakia in 1939. In 1940s, the Hungarian authorities imposed anti-Semitic laws and forced many of the town's Jewish men into labour battalions. In 1941, Jews who could not prove Hungarian citizenship were deported to Kamenets-Podolsky, in German-occupied Ukraine, where they were massacred. By April 1944, five thousand Jews were concentrated in a ghetto, from where they were deported to Auschwitz on two trains that left Slatina on 20 and 23 May.

Soczowa (Romanian: Suceava; Yiddish: שאָץ *Shotz*; German: Sedschopff, Sotschen, Soczowa, Suczawa; Polish: Suczawa; Hungarian: Szucsáva). Present-day Suceava, Romania.

Jews first came to Suczawa in the early fifteenth century, when Alexander I of Moldavia invited Jewish merchants to settle in the town. The Jewish community grew in the eighteenth and nineteenth centuries with the arrival of Jews fleeing pogroms in Russia and Galicia. There was a large synagogue in Suczawa, built at the beginning of the nineteenth century, and numerous *battei midrash* and prayer houses. Rabbi Yoel Moskowicz (1810–1886), the son-in-law of Rabbi Meir of Premishlan (q.v.), and Rabbi Mosheh Hager (1863–1927) both founded Hassidic courts in Suceava.

The city was the capital of the Principality of Moldavia from 1388 to 1564, after which Alexander Lăpuşneanu moved the princely seat to Jassy (Iaşi). In 1775, the city came under the rule of the Habsburg Empire, as part of the Kingdom of Galicia and Lodmeria and later the Duchy of Bukowina. In 1918, Suceava, which under the Austro-Hungarian Empire had large German, Jewish, Polish, and Armenian communities, became part of the Kingdom of Romania. The same as Jews throughout Romania, Suceava's Jewish community fell victim to the harsh anti-Semitic laws passed by nationalist poetaster Octavian Goga when he became Prime Minister in December 1937. Persecution worsened under the Iron Guard régime between September 1940 and January 1941. Under Nazi-allied dictator Ion Antonescu, the Jews of Suceava and surrounding towns and villages were concentrated in a ghetto and subsequently deported to camps in Transnistria. Among the deportees was major Romanian Jewish writer Norman Manea (1936-), who was then aged five.

Tarnopol (Yiddish: טאַרנאָפּל *Tarnopl*; German: Tarnopol; Polish: Tarnopol; Ukrainian: *Тернопіль Ternopil*). Present-day Ternopil, a large city in western Ukraine.

There was a Jewish community in Tarnopol from its founding, and by the seventeenth century, Jews made up a majority of the city's population. The Great Synagogue of Tarnopol was built between 1622 and 1628, but was destroyed during the Second World War.

Tarnopol was founded by Hetman Jan Amor Tarnowski in 1540 after King Sigismund of Poland granted him a charter, and Tarnopol Castle was instrumental in defending against Tartar attacks. The city was occupied by a Muscovite and Cossack army in 1655, heavily damaged by the Turks during the Polish-Ottoman War of 1672–76, and sacked by the Tartars in 1694 and then the Russians in 1710 and 1733. Tarnopol came under Austrian rule in 1772 and then Russian rule in 1809 before returning to Austrian rule in 1815. In 1870, a railway linking Tarnopol with Lemberg (q.v.) was inaugurated. In 1918, amid the break-up of the Austro-Hungarian Empire, Tarnopol was the capital of the short-lived West Ukrainian Republic. In 1920, Tarnopol became part of the Second Polish Republic and was occupied by the Soviet Union in 1939 as a result of the Molotov-Ribbentrop Pact. In July 1941, during the German invasion, thousands of Jews were massacred in Tarnopol by the S.S. and Ukrainian auxiliary police and locals. In September, a ghetto was set up, concentrating around thirteen thousand Jews under appalling conditions that resulted in a high rate of mortality. In August-September 1942, more than six thousand Jews from Tarnapol and other nearby ghettos were confined inside cattle trucks at the railway station for two days before being transported to the Bełżec extermination camp northwest of Tarnopol, with many perishing of thirst and suffocation before they reached their destination. In September-October, more than a thousand Jews from the ghetto were rounded up and deported to the Bełżec extermination camp. In November, around 2,500 Jews from Tarnapol and the surrounding area were murdered in two 'Aktionen'. By March 1943, only some seven hundred Jews remained in the ghetto, which was liquidated on 20 June. Many of the Jews who had managed to escape the ghetto in the meantime were turned over to the Germans by locals or were murdered by Ukrainian peasants and nationalist militias right up to the re-establishment of Soviet control over the city.

Teutschenau (Yiddish: טעטש *Tetsh*; Romanian: Teceu Mare; Hungarian: Técső; Slovak: Ťačovo; Ukrainian: *Тячів Tiachiv*; German: Groß-Teutschenau). Present-day Tiachiv, a city on the Tisza River in the Zakarpattia Oblast, western Ukraine, on the border with Romania.

Although there was a small number of Jews living in Teutschenau in the early eighteenth century, an established community did not develop there until the early nineteenth century.

The town was part of the comitatus of Máramaros until the disintegration of the Austro-Hungarian Empire, when it became part of the new Czechoslovakia. By the Treaty of Trianon (1920), the small district of the town on the south side of the River Tisza was awarded to Romania, along with the other territories of northern Transylvania, and became known as Klein Tetsh (present-day Teceu Mic, Romania). In 1939, after the German invasion of Czechoslovakia, the town was absorbed by Hungary, which, the following year, annexed Klein Tetsh along with Northern Transylvania. By the time a ghetto was set up in 1944, after the German occupation of Hungary, many of the town's Jews had been deported to Nazi-occupied Ukraine or had perished in forced labour battalions. Eight thousand Jews from Teutschenau and the surrounding area were concentrated in the ghetto before being sent to the gas chambers at Auschwitz in May 1944.

Wischnitz (Yiddish: וויזשניץ *Vizhnitz*; Polish: Wyżnica; Romanian: Vijniţa; Ukrainian: *Вижниця Vyzhnytsia*). Present-day Vyzhnytsia in the Chernivtsi Oblast, western Ukraine.

The town was home to a Jewish community from as early as Moldavian rule, in the mid-eighteenth century. The Jewish community was persecuted under Austrian rule and in 1789 an order was given to expel all the town's Jews, although this was not fully implemented. By the turn of the twentieth century, there were 4,738 Jews living in Wischnitz, but the Jewish population decreased during the First World War, when the town was all but destroyed and large numbers of its inhabitants fled. Wischnitz lends its name to the dynasty of the Vizhnitzer Hassidim, founded by Rebbe Menachem Mendel Hager (1830–1884).

By the late sixteenth century, the town was part of the Principality of Moldavia. In 1774, it came under Habsburg rule, and from 1849 it was part of the crown land of Bukowina (q.v.) in the Austro-Hungarian Empire. Part of Greater Romania from 1918 to 1940, Wischnitz was subsequently absorbed by the Ukrainian Soviet Socialist Republic along with northern Bukowina. In August 1941, 2,800 Jews were deported from Wischnitz to the death camps and of the eight hundred survivors the majority emigrated to Israel after the war.

Aboab, Isaac. Early fourteenth-century Spanish Kabbalist and Talmudic scholar, born into a family of Spanish Jewish aristocrats who had been granted land, a tower, and a heraldic achievement by King James I of Aragon in 1263. Isaac Aboab was a merchant and man of affairs who in his old age settled in Toledo, where he founded a yeshivah. He is the author of *Menorat ha-Maor* (The Menorah of Light), a work on religious ethics structured in seven sections or 'lamps', which drew its materials from the *Aggadah* (q.v. Terms). The work enjoyed great popularity among the Jews of mediaeval Spain. Aboab was also the author of two works now lost: *Aron ha-'Edut* (The Ark of the Testimony), divided into ten sections, corresponding to the Decalogue, and *Shulchan ha-Panim* (Table of the Showbread), divided into twelve sections to symbolise the twelve loaves displayed in the Tabernacle.

Alashkar, Moshe ben Isaac (1466–1542). Prominent rabbi who lived in Egypt and later in Jerusalem.

Baal Shem Tov, Israel ben Eliezer (1698–1760). See Introduction.

Dov Ber, Der Mezritscher Maggid (c.1710–1773), Hassidic Kabbalist, the main disciple of the Baal Shem Tov. From 1760 to

1772 he was the head of the first Hassidic court, in Mezeritch (q.v. Places). After his death, his followers became charismatic spiritual leaders in their own right, founding Hassidic courts in towns throughout Galicia, which were to become the major Hassidic dynasties.

Gershon Kutover (1701–1761), Rabbi Abraham Gershon of Kitov (or Brody), the brother-in-law of the Baal Shem Tov. See Places, *Kitov* (q.v.).

Hillel (110 BCE–10 CE), rabbinic sage in Jerusalem. The House of Hillel, i.e., the school of thought he founded, was frequently in dispute with the House of Shammai (q.v.) on questions of religious ethics and ritual practice, with the former being for the most part more lenient than the latter in its interpretation of the Torah.

Kitzes, Ze'ev Volf (c.1685–c.1775). Hassidic rabbi. Kitzes was the leader of the Hassidim in Medschybisch (present-day Medzhybizh, western Ukraine). He initially opposed but later accepted the leadership of the Baal Shem Tov and became his disciple. Kitzes became legendary for his piety and strict observance of religious commandments, so much so that he became the subject of numerous, often humorous, tales and parables, in which he appears alongside the Baal Shem Tov, the master whose spiritual wisdom transcends the disciple's narrow adherence to the letter of the Law.

Maharil מהרי"ל (Hebrew), acronym (Ma.Ha.R.I.L.) for 'Our Teacher Rabbi Yaakov Levi'. Yaakov ben Moshe Levi Moellin (c. 1365–1427), Talmudic scholar and leader of the Jewish communities of Germany, Austria and Bohemia.

Moshe Leib of Sassov (c.1745–1807), Hassidic rebbe, student of the Maggid of Mezritch.

Nachman of Kosov (d. 1746), early Hassid and kabbalist. Nachman was a wealthy grain merchant, who built a *beth midrash* in Lodmer (present-day Volodymyr, north-western Ukraine) and later settled in Kitev (q.v. Places), where he became associated with a group of Hassidim. He was at first opposed to the authority of the Baal Shem Tov as religious leader of the Hassidim, but later accepted it, while preserving his own independence as a spiritual leader. Nachman taught *devekut*, the state of 'cleaving' (the literal meaning of the Hebrew word) to the higher Sefirot, or Divine Emanations, attained through ecstatic prayer and mystical contemplation, including kabbalistic techniques such as visualisation of the letters of the Tetragrammaton.

Rashi, acronym (Ra.Sh.I) of Rabbi Shlomo Yitzhaki (1040–1105). Commentator of the Talmud and Tanakh (q.v. Terms) in mediaeval Troyes.

Shmuel ibn Sid, or Sidilyo (c. 1530), rabbi in Egypt, son-in-law of Isaac Aboab (q.v.). A native of Toledo, he settled in Egypt after the Expulsion of the Jews from Spain in 1492. He was given the title *baal-nes* (q.v. Terms), or 'miracle worker', thanks to the part he played in preventing a massacre of the Jews in Egypt planned by Governor Ahmed Pasha in 1524. He was the author of *Kelalei Shemu'el*, an alphabetical handbook of rules for the study of the Talmud, which was first published in Venice a century later, in 1622.

Shammai (50 BCE–30 CE). First-century rabbinic sage, the older contemporary of Hillel (q.v.).

Yaakov Tam (1100–1171), Yaakov ben Meir, grandson of Rashi (q.v.) on his mother's side and foremost authority on the Halachah (q.v. Terms) in twelfth-century France.

Der Yetev Lev, Rabbi Yekusiel Yehuda Teitelbaum (1808–1883), Hassidic rebbe, grandson of Moshe Teitelbaum (1759–1841), the Rabbi of Ujhely (present-day Hungary), an influential Hassid. Der Yetev Lev was rabbi of Stropkov (present-day Slovakia), Ujhely, and Drohobycz (q.v. Places) the Jewish community of Sighet (q.v. Places) appointed him rabbi in 1858. He also served as the head of a yeshivah in the town. He was the author of *Yetev Lev*, a Hassidic commentary on the Torah, whence the name by which he came to be known.

THE AUTHOR

The writer Ludovic (Joseph-Leib, Arye) Bruckstein was born on the 27th of July 1920, in Munkacs, then in Czechoslovakia, now in Ukraine. He grew up in Sighet, a small town in the district of Maramureş, in the Northern region of Transylvania, a town well known for its flourishing pre-war Jewish community and Hassidic tradition. He wrote a number of successful plays including *The Night Shift* (*Nakht-Shikht*, 1947), based on the Sonderkommando revolt in Auschwitz. His other works include *The Confession* (a novel, 1973), *The Fate of Yaakov Maggid* (seven short stories, 1975), *Three Histories* (three short historical stories, 1977) – which have been amalgamated in this edition along with stories from *As in Heaven, so on Earth* (1981) – *The Tinfoil Halo* (short stories, 1979), *Maybe Even Happiness* (short stories, 1985), *The Murmur of Water* (short stories, 1987). *The Trap* (two novellas) appeared posthumously in 1989.

THE TRANSLATOR

Alistair Ian Blyth is one of the most active translators working from Romanian into English today. A native of Sunderland, England, Blyth has resided for many years in Bucharest. His many translations from Romanian include: *The Bulgarian Truck* (Dalkey Archive Press, 2016), *The Book of Whispers* (Yale University Press, 2017), and *Life Begins on Friday* by Ioana Pârvulescu (Istros Books, 2016). He is the author of the novel *Card Catalogue* (Dalkey Archive Press, 2020).